T0107539

I HEAR *your* HEARTBEAT

A Pilgrimage of Healing

L. Grant Hatch

Inspiring Voices books may be ordered through booksellers or by contacting:

Inspiring Voices
1663 Liberty Drive
Bloomington, IN 47403
www.inspiringvoices.com
1-(866) 697-5313

ISBN: 978-1-4624-0270-0 (sc)
ISBN: 978-1-4624-0269-4 (e)

Library of Congress Control Number: 2012945780

Printed in the United States of America

Inspiring Voices rev. date: 08/29/2012

Dedication

To all those who have loved and lost
and were afraid to love again.

Contents

Acknowledgements

I wish to thank my family at Saint Agnes parish, Mena Arkansas. Their love and encouragement is priceless. I want to give special thanx to my spiritual sister, Peggy, for her skill and knowledge in preparing the final manuscript. And most of all, hugs and kisses to my best friend and wife of forty-seven years, Sally, for her constant love, support, and encouragement.

++ *Preface* ++

The people, places and names in this story are all figments of my imagination. The emotions, yearnings and conflicts are real. They are real because they are, and have been, a part of the human condition since the dawn of human history. In a perfect world two young people meet, fall in love, marry and live happily ever after. Most of us do not live in a perfect world. Unrequited love and broken hearts are a common rite of passage in our teen age years. The resulting hurt to our heart and soul can leave scars that remain for life, haunting our existence. Sometimes even the smallest event can bring forth memories that may cascade into a journey of pain and remorse. If we are able to stay the course, we may find our way through the pain to healing and reconciliation. The end result of this journey is that those scars may be removed. This allows us to live in peace, joy and contentment with ourselves and others. To achieve those rewards, one must be willing to make that journey, no matter the risks, no matter the peril, no matter the hurt. We all have much to learn from Tallet Jinx's journey because we are all, to some degree, at some point in our life, Tallet and Gemima.

"In the end all these will pass away but
three will remain; faith, hope and love.
And the greatest of these is love."

– Paul of Tarsus

I

September Memories

The late afternoon sun painted the cloud tops crimson. The distant thunder promised relief from the early autumn heat. Tallet Jinx did not hear the thunder because he was lost in his novel of the old west. His imagination rode the deep arroyos and high ridges of the Big Bend of Texas with the cowboys who chased longhorns and Mexican bandits along the old Rio Grande. Tal was doing what he liked to do on any Sunday; relaxing on his patio and reading about the heroes and the villains of the old west.

The patio was a large area on the west end of his house, surrounded by a split rail fence. The only break in the fence was at the back corner which led to a small patio outside of his bedroom. Beyond the fence, a thick hedgerow of weeds and bushes provided a privacy barrier. A mesquite tree grew at each corner from seeds Tal had planted years earlier. A huge, ancient live oak grew in the middle of the patio. Its sprawling branches and thick canopy of leaves provided the comfort of deep shade. A glass of iced lemonade provided refreshment.

His face reflected every bit of the sixty some years of his life. Tal had worked most of his adult life trying to extract a profit from his Kayne County ranch in the Texas Panhandle. For the most part, he had succeeded. His labors had provided a difficult but comfortable living. The searing heat of summer and the bitter cold blizzards of winter made life anything but boring. Now, he could revel in the fruits of his labor.

Tallet was an old fashioned, twentieth-century man. He drove an old Ford pick-up truck that he had bought almost twenty years earlier. He liked it because it still looked good and ran good. The best part was, it had been paid for a long time ago. Oh, he liked indoor plumbing, electricity and air conditioning. The new technology? It was confusing and left him cold. Cell phones, computers and answering machines were strange, enigmatic inventions that were pointless. If someone wanted to talk to him, they should've called before he left home. If he wasn't home, well, then they should call back when he was home. His only surrender to the twenty-first century was allowing satellite television to be installed in the house and then, only at the insistence of his eldest son, Tad. Tad convinced him by assuring his father that if he didn't like satellite service, that he, Tad, would pay to have it removed. It took about three months before Tal begrudgingly thanked his son and had the billing address changed to himself.

His sister, Bekka, wanted high speed internet wireless service for her computer. Tal would have none of that. Finally, he agreed only if she would pay for it herself and keep it in her room. Bekka also brought an answering machine with her when she moved in. She didn't bother asking her brother's permission to plug it into the phone line. She knew his answer.

After several days of hearing its beeping and talking, Tal asked her, "What was that dang thing he kept hearing."

Bekka replied, "It's only a digital answering machine."

He grumped and groused about not wanting these new inventions in the house. She ignored her brother and, after a while, he said no more about them. She wasn't sure if he forgot about them or if he got used to them. No matter. They were no longer an issue and that was fine with her.

The thunder grew louder as the storm approached, bringing him back to the present. Thunderstorms in the Texas Panhandle could take on epic proportions. A sudden gust of wind told him it was time to go in. The ranch house was spacious and comfortable. His den walls were lined with memorabilia of his years breeding and herding Texas longhorns. An old set of longhorns spread almost seven feet across the wall above the mantle of the stone fireplace. They were his pride and joy, the biggest he had ever seen.

His cluttered desk in the corner belied the order he valued in life. The room was neat and clean, but the dust around the edges suggested the lack of the feminine touch. He did like things clean and neat. Sometimes, though, he found sentimental value in worthless items that anyone else would have quickly discarded. These items found their way onto shelves, into corners and windowsills adding to the bits of clutter around the edges of the room. One wall had Navy memorabilia, including a photo of the ship he had served on. The pictures of his family covered most of the wall opposite the fireplace.

The center photo was of his wife Lucy. Her death two years earlier had left a large hole in his life. They had been married 41 years at the time of her passing. He missed her blue eyes, auburn hair, her voice, the warmth of her touch but most of all, he missed the love he always saw in her smile. They began their ranch with not much more than a few bucks and an old pick-up. Together they fought bitter winters, sweltering summers, rattlesnakes, coyotes and bobcats to build a herd of long horns that were the envy of all the other ranches in the Panhandle. In the end, her heart wore out. She went to sleep one night and didn't wake up. The weeks and months of grief that followed were tough but he vowed it would not get him down. He knew he should, in the words of his father, 'just get over it'. It was hard for Tal to show emotion. He didn't like the vulnerability of appearing weak. Even so, there were more than a few nights he went to sleep with wet eyes.

Their sons, Tad, Ben and Will, were the loves of their life. Tad still helped around the ranch when he could. His brothers, though, had moved to the big city to pursue their own careers, create their own families.

Tallet heard Joey, his boarder collie, scratching at the door. The dog didn't like the rain and was afraid of the thunder. Tal opened the screen door to let him in, then sat down in his leather recliner and kicked up the foot rest. Joey sat beside him for an ear scratch. It was good therapy for both. It eased the loneliness in Tal and calmed the fear of his old friend.

The rain beat harder on the roof as the full brunt of the storm passed over. Tal liked the sound of the rain on the roof. The rain, even in its fury, was good news. His stock ponds almost always needed refilling. A gust of wind scattered the chairs on the patio. Just as he got up to slide the glass door closed, lightening flashed, the loud clap very close behind. Joey yelped and jumped into the recliner. He chuckled at his dog.

"You big coward! You can stare down a long horn bull an' chase off a rattler but a little flash, bang makes you jump!? Get down."

Joey let his boss have his chair back. Tal took the last sip of his now warm lemonade and went back to his book, preferring the distraction of the old west. He hadn't read long when his sister called from the kitchen.

"When do you want supper, Tal?"

Bekka had come to live with her brother to take up some of the burden left by the death of Lucy. Bekka, two years younger, wanted to be just like him when they were growing up. She loved to compete with him in whatever they did. And she liked to rub it in when she won. Her ability to out race him on horseback was especially infuriating to him.

Tal had always been protective of his kid sister, sometimes overly so. His protective nature had cost her more than a few boy friends, some she really liked. Bekka would complain loudly and angrily. In the end, though, she always knew it was because he loved her. She was a slight woman with the same brown eyes as her brother. She wore her hair long and braided. She was a retired nurse. Her modest income was enough to allow her to live in comfort as she cared for her brother.

Bekka had her own grief to bear. Her husband and only son were killed when a tornado ripped through their homestead on the west side of the ranch three years earlier. Tal had encouraged her to move on, to find someone else. No one else, though, could take the place of her lost loves. She didn't try to rebuild her home. She salvaged some family photos then burned the wreckage. It was her way of dealing with the grief that had cut her so deeply.

After Lucy died, Bekka asked Tal if she could move in with him, to help out. She reminded her brother that neither one of them had anyone else. They both needed someone to need and to be needed by. Tal said no. He assured her he could handle the house by himself. The truth was, he was used to taking care of her and didn't like the role reversal. Her cajoling and months of smothering loneliness finally changed his mind. It was good to have a woman's voice around the house again, even if it was his kid sister. In a real way, Tal, Bekka, and Joey were family. They gave each other what they needed; love, companionship and, occasionally, a bit of aggravation, just to keep life interesting.

"Hey, did you hear me?"

Tal put his book down. "Yeah, I heard you. Maybe later. I'm not hungry now."

That was a half truth. The smell from the kitchen had all ready gotten his attention but he wanted to finish the chapter.

The room grew dark even though the storm clouds had moved on. The frogs began croaking, signaling the end of the rain. He put Joey out, picked up his empty lemonade glass, and went to the kitchen. "What's on the stove?"

Bekka didn't turn away from the pot she was stirring. "You can't be too hungry if you have to ask," she said matter-of-factly.

"If you weren't my sister, a good cook and someone I like to talk to, I'd fire you."

"You can't fire slaves. You have to sell them. That's why I'm still here. That and the fact no one else would put up with you."

He laughed as he took his glass to the sink. He washed his hands as Bekka put the stew pot on the table. They sat down to their supper.

"Tal, I was looking for something in the desk and I found an old Valentine card signed, 'I don't like you very much! Love, Gemi'. Seems to be a very curious sentiment. And I don't remember that name. Do you remember what it means?"

Tal's spoon stopped halfway between bowl and mouth. Gemi. Of course he knew that name. He hadn't heard the name in quite a while. It was always there, though, in the back of his memory, gathering dust. It was a name he tried not to think about. It was a name that made him smile and hurt, all at the same time. He decided to be coy about it. "I'm not sure who it is. Are you sure it's not one of your friends?"

"It's an unusual name. I'm sure I would remember it." She paused to take a bite. "Wait, I remember. Wasn't she the girl you were sweet on when you were in high school?"

"Sweet on?", Tal thought. "I wished it was only that." Tal fought the moment, not really sure he wanted to talk about her memory? Finally he decided on a minimal response, just to satisfy her curiosity.

"Oh yeah, she was a girl I dated a few times when I was a senior. Could I see the card?"

"Sure."

Bekka went to the desk in the study to get the card. It was yellowed from age, creased and frayed around the edges from being shuffled around the inside of a desk drawer for so many years. The memories it evoked were great in their detail.

"What does 'I don't like you very much' mean?"

Tal lowered his head. He didn't want Bekka to see the wry smile the card generated. "It was a way we kidded each other. It was our silly way of saying 'I love you'. That's all I really remember."

"That's all?", he thought. "I wish it were so."

There was more, much more, buried in his past. Yet, they came swirling back. Memories from long ago and far away. Memories he hadn't thought about in years. Memories he didn't want to recall. Memories he needed to embrace. Memories of a teenage boy who wanted to love a teenage girl. Memories of a teenage girl who, for a brief moment in time, seemed to love him. Memories colored with happiness and pain all at the same time. Memories he thought had been erased by the love and life that he and Lucy had shared for so many years. But the memories were coming back. And he wasn't sure he was ready for them.

Bekka took a bite of her biscuit. "I don't remember you talking about her much."

"Well, it wasn't much. Just a few dates. Besides, you were living with Aunt Dori. That's all." That is, that's all he wanted to say about Gemi.

Tal finished his bowl of stew and another glass of lemonade. "That was the best squirrel slumgullion you ever made, Bekka."

She smiled. She knew a compliment when she heard one, even if it was backhanded. "Thanks, I made it just the way you like it. I left the tails in so it would have a crunch."

Tal smiled at her retort as he went to the fridge. He grabbed a six pack of beer, one for now, five for later. "I'm going to bed."

The comment drew a concerned look. "So early? You okay?"

"I'm fine. This change in weather got my bones to achin'. Besides, I want to finish my book."

With that, he was gone from the kitchen.

Tallet's room was at the other end of the house from his sister. It was a good arrangement because their restlessness wouldn't disturb each other. He went through his room, through the sliding door, to the open patio. The wind had come around out of the northwest behind the storm. He could see the lightening flashes in the clouds to the east, but they were too far away to hear the thunder. The sun was gone and the clear, moonless night was putting on quite a show. He leaned on the rail and popped a beer. He hoped to see a meteor or two. He didn't have to wait long. Joey came through the bushes and over the rail, wagging his tail. Tal smiled as he reached down and rubbed the dog's ears.

Gemi's memory was in the forefront of his thoughts. He tried to recall her face. Then he remembered the yearbook. He went to the bookcase in his bedroom to get it. He flipped through the pages looking for her photo and found what he wasn't expecting. Gemi was standing at a classroom table. She was wearing his favorite sweater . . . and the ring he had given her, wrapped in angora yarn to make it fit her finger. He looked at it for what seemed like an hour. In reality it was only a few minutes. He returned the book to the shelf and went back to his patio, to sit and look at the dark of night.

"Memories," he thought. "How curious they can be. The smell of fresh baked bread, the faint sweetness of sage in bloom floating on a spring zephyr, a song fragment heard in passing. All these things evoke memories, mostly pleasant." The memories brought on by that valentine card and yearbook picture were none of the above and all of the above. Gemi's memory was too hard to remember, too tender to let go. He wished Lucy was with him. Since her death loneliness seemed to be a way of life. Her presence soothed the ached of that memory. Without his wife, there alone in the dark, he had no choice but to remember the best, worst thing that ever happened to him. And his heart went back in time. It was September, 1961, Kayne county high school. He was seventeen, she was fifteen and . . . .

II

Meeting Her

"Hey Tal, wait up, will ya!"

"I can't Dusty. I'm late for class now."

"You're going the wrong way. Math class is this way!"

"I'm not going to math. I'm going to art."

"C'mon pal, don't tell me that. We have been in the same class since fourth grade. What am I going to do without your help?"

"Look, I know we've been friends forever and we've always helped each other. I found out I had enough tech credits to graduate. I don't want nothin' more to do with math or science. I want two easy credits so I can get out of school with a diploma and my sanity. Calculus became art."

"So what happened to physics?"

"I dropped it. I'm taking wood shop instead . . . another easy credit."

"Wood shop! Are you crazy?! They got sharp things in there. You won't come out with all your fingers." Dusty tried to emphasize his point with a deeper voice. "You're letting me down, old buddy!"

"We'll talk about it later. Gotta go."

Tal rushed off. He entered the art classroom and immediately looked for a desk in the back row. He wanted to be as far from the teacher as possible, preferably behind someone with broad shoulders or big hair that he could hide behind. He liked to perch his chin on his hands and take a nap. Big girls with big hair were the perfect thing. The room was arranged with tables, two chairs each. And the only chair left open was in the front row, dead center, next to a girl. "Great," he thought, "exactly what I don't want."

Quietly cursing Dusty for making him late, he sat down, leaned back, crossed his legs at the ankles, folded his arms across his chest and stared straight ahead.

The teacher called the classroom to order. "Good morning, class. I am Miss Margret, your teacher. You are arranged in pairs because the person next to you will be your partner in various projects this semester."

Tal groaned. "This is worse than I thought."

"Please take a few minutes and quietly introduce yourselves to each other."

The girl looked at her table mate. He was a tall and thin, with brown eyes and hair. She tapped him on the arm. "Hi."

He continued staring straight ahead.

"You gonna talk to me?"

"No," he said, without turning his head.

She offered a hand shake. "Since we are stuck with each other, can we at least be on a first name basis? I'm Gemi Renner."

Tal shook her hand then turned to look at her. He was struck by how beautiful she was. Her hand was soft and delicate with long slender fingers. Her smile revealed soft dimples that seemed to be a perfect part of an already perfect face. Her dark brown, almost black hair was cut short and curled around her ears, framing a round face with soft features that reflected a feminine gentleness he had never seen before. What struck him most were her eyes. They were a soft, sky blue with a deep tenderness that made him forget for a moment where he was.

Gemi reached up and playfully tapped his forehead. "Hellooo, anybody in there?"

"Gemi? That's a funny name."

"It's short for Gemima."

Tal glanced at her class folder. "Isn't Gemima spelled with a 'J'?"

"It's a long story. Who are you?"

"I'm Tallet Jinx."

"That's a funny name."

His eyes furrowed and flashed with anger. He found her sassiness both irritating and attractive. "When do you graduate?"

"I'm a sophomore. How 'bout you?"

Tal glanced at her body. She was full and round in all the right places, not like most other sophomore girls. "I'm a senior. Come June, I'm outta here."

Gemi smiled. The look in his eyes told her he was distracted. She didn't know why. "So, I suppose you don't like school?"

"You're pretty smart, for a girl."

Gemi wondered if that was a compliment or a slap. She knew of Tal from the previous year. She had seen him in the halls and thought he was the cutest boy in school. She wondered who he was. Now, she was glad for the opportunity that fate had afforded her. She thought about what new things the year would bring. Who knows, maybe they could at least be friends, hopefully more. The possibilities made her smile.

"What's your next class?"

"Lunch." Tal's tone was abrupt.

"Me too. Can we go together?"

"No."

Her smile began to fade. Tallet had to look away from those eyes. My gosh, those were beautiful eyes. If he looked much longer he might've said 'yes'.

Gemi tried again. "Can we talk about it?"

"We just did."

Gemi didn't understand his abrupt manner. She hoped it wasn't because of her teasing him about his name.

The teacher called the class back to order and called the roll. At the bell Tal rushed out without saying a word to anyone. Gemi wanted to talk to him outside of class. She quickly gathered her belongings and hurried out to the hallway in hopes of catching him. She strained on her tiptoes, looking in both directions, but he was gone, lost in the crowd of kids that filled the hallway.

It was late in the afternoon. Tal and Dusty were standing in the student parking lot talking about their first day as seniors. Gemi came up from behind and put her hand on his arm. "Hi, Tal. Why did you rush out so quickly? I was hoping we could talk more."

He didn't turn to look at her. "I had places to go, people to see and things to do."

"Could you take me home? Please?" Gemi hoped a ride would offer some time to get aquatinted.

Tal looked at her and smiled. He did not want any romantic entanglements. His approach to his senior year was to get in, get it done and get out without having to suffer through any complications, especially those that a girlfriend always brought. He feigned a grimace and spoke in a very serious tone of voice. "Ah, gee, Gemi, I would love to. The problem is my dad told me not to bring home anymore girls. If I did, he said he'd have to start shootin' 'em. He thinks I got too many now. I hope you understand. I like you and I don't want to hurt you. Besides, I'm running out of places to hide the bodies."

"Yeah," Dusty chimed in, "he had to give me a couple last week just to get his dad off his case. He didn't do me any favors. They were ugly ones."

Both boys struggled to stifle their laughter.

Gemi glared at them. She did not like being the butt of their joke. "Most villages only have one idiot. How'd Kayne manage to get two?"

Her sarcasm broke the dam. Both boys roared with laughter. She stood her ground, even as her anger flared at them. Meeting Tal in art class provided the opportunity to get to know him that she had hoped for. Gemi wasn't going to be this easily discouraged. Finally, Tal stopped laughing enough to speak.

"Dusty, this is Gemi. Gemi, this is Dusty Rhoades. We've been friends since first grade."

Gemi thought this was another joke at her expense and her patience was at an end. "When you get home, tell your father, Gravel Roads hello." With that, she turned and stomped away.

"Tal, I think she likes you."

Tal hesitated for a moment then remembered those eyes. "I'll talk to you tomorrow, Dusty." Then he rushed off after Gemi.

"Gemi, stop. Come back. I'm sorry. We didn't mean to make fun of you. Stop, wait a sec." Gemi slowed her pace just enough to allow him to catch up. "If you missed your bus I'll give you a ride."

Gemi stopped. She glanced across the school parking lot at her waiting bus then turned back to Tal. "Well, I would like a ride home."

Tal walked Gemi back to his car. It was an eight year old Ford that a customer had brought to his father's garage for repair then decided it wasn't worth the money. Tal was glad to claim it. There were a few rust spots and the seats had a few holes, but the car offered all the comforts Tal wanted and needed; a heater and a radio. Plus, it ran good and it was fast. They both got in. Tal tuned in a top forty station for her entertainment. Gemi slid to the center of the seat and put her hand on Tal's shoulder.

"I'm sorry I made you mad. Dusty and I have been good buddies since we were six. We know how each other thinks. We've made a career out of teasing girls. And his name really is Dustin Rhodes."

"Dubious achievements aren't something to be proud of."

He saw through Gemi's thinly veiled sarcasm, but he figured he deserved it. Gemi pointed the way home. "Why didn't you want me to go to lunch with you?"

Tal didn't want to tell her he wasn't interested in a girlfriend, casual or other wise. He brushed off the question. "I needed to get some stuff done and was in a hurry. Sorry."

She gave him a playful poke in the ribs. "Well, you could have been nicer about it."

The fifteen minute drive to her house passed quickly. Tal pulled into her drive and put the car in park. The house was a long, rambling ranch style with a wrap around porch. It had three dormers across the front roof and a three car garage at the far end. He saw the light of the family room coming through double, stained glass entry doors. "Impressive," he thought. He could feel the warmth of her hand on his shoulder and could smell the sweetness of her hair. He found her presence to be appealing and very distracting.

As she moved toward the door, he offered a handshake. "I suppose you're right. I could've been nicer. Am I forgiven?" He looked into her eyes again. They were easy to look at, far too easy. And even harder to look away from.

Gemi smiled as she shook his hand. "Just this once. See you in class tomorrow?"

Tal smiled back. "Maybe, maybe not. It depends on whether or not Dusty lets me out of my cage."

Tal headed home, amused by Gemi's wit and gentle nature. She was not on his radar for romance. He had learned the hard way that wearing your heart on your sleeve could be painful. He'd several girlfriends since grade school. What he saw as romance, the girls saw as friendship. As a result, he got his heart broke, usually about once a semester. He was determined to make his senior year the exception.

Gemi thought of Tal most of the evening. The idea of having Tal as a classmate and what all that might mean titillated her imagination. She hoped their proximity would provide her a chance to win his attention.

Tal didn't think about her very much at all. When he did, he thought of her as an irritation he would have to deal with, only because they shared a desk. More so, he thought about how easy his senior year would be without the heavy burden of math and science homework . . . and, oh yeah, no girls. That would make it even easier. Even so, there were those captivating eyes . . . .

* * *

The discomfort of the late evening chill brought Tal back to the present. He heard coyotes howling on the ridge to the west. Joey pricked up his ears and growled. "Easy, Joey. They mean no harm." Joey decided to go investigate anyway. He got down, jumped the rail and was gone in a second. Tal finished his last beer and went in. He undressed and got into bed. The alcohol was enough to make him sleepy. He closed his eyes and was gone. He dreamed dreams of his youth. Thankfully, none of them were about Gemi.

III

The Polar Bear Incident

Tallet Jinx awoke to broad daylight. It had been a while since he had slept past sun-up. He jumped out of bed towards the bathroom but had to stop after a few steps. He felt light headed, dizzy and short of breath. He stretched his left arm up and out trying to relieve the tightness and pain he felt in his chest. Maybe drinking a six-pack before bed wasn't such a good idea. Then he remembered why he did.

Gemi. Her memory was becoming an unwanted preoccupation.

He washed, dressed in his everyday work denims, pulled on his boots and headed for the kitchen. Bekka was at the table with her coffee.

"Morning, Tal. Need some breakfast?"

"No thanks. I need to get out on the range. I'll be back for lunch."

"Where're you goin'?"

"Huerfano."

Tal grabbed a bottle of cola from the fridge, then paused at the backdoor to pull on his hat. He went to the barn and quickly saddled Paint, his favorite quarter horse. He mounted up and headed out the door at a trot. He put his fingers to his mouth and blew a loud whistle.

"C'mon, Joey, lets go."

Joey came out from the dark recesses of the barn at a full run, tail wagging, eager to follow Tal wherever he was going.

They headed off to the west, bound for the high ridge where the coyotes sang their song the night before. As he rode along he felt the cold crispness of the morning air against his face. The crystal clear morning sun sparkling off the dew made for a spectacular day.

Tal's destination was a curious landmark. He had found this spot soon after buying the ranch. At the time, he was searching for some longhorns that had strayed during the winter. He had ridden over a gentle rise and into a low, broad valley. Towards the middle of the valley was a large mound about a hundred yards wide and maybe fifty feet high. Atop the mound was a lone, ancient mesquite tree. The mound seemed lonely and strangely out of place in that valley, like something nature had abandoned and forgot. The first time he rode up to that tree he knew he had found someplace special. He called the hill 'el Huerfano', Spanish for 'the orphan'. After some research he found that the Comanche who passed through during the nineteenth century believed it had supernatural healing powers. The Indians would come here to commune with their ancestors and prepare for a battle. They called it the 'Medicine Mound'. He knew the history was true because he found many potsherds and arrowheads on the hill. Whenever he had a hard decision to make, he would come to this spot to think.

Joey and Paint loved this spot as much as Tal.

There were many jackrabbits and prairie dogs for Joey to chase. Over the years, he had learned how to catch the prairie dogs. He would sneak up on them, keeping low to the ground, down wind of the burrow. When they popped up out of their hole, he'd grabbed them. Sometimes he would eat them, other times just play with them 'til they were dead. Tal didn't mind. There were thousands and the prairie wouldn't mind one less burrowing, miscreant rodent.

Paint liked the deep, succulent grass that seemed to go on forever, undulating in the wind like the waves on the open ocean. He'd let Paint wander and graze until he had his fill. Sometimes the horse would wander back to Huerfano. Sometimes he would lie down in the sun for a nap. If he didn't hear Tal's whistle, Tal would send Joey out to find him. It wouldn't be long 'til Joey emerged from the tall grass, reins in his mouth, Paint following close behind.

One day Lucy asked him where he went when he was gone all day. Tal told her about Huerfano and offered to take her along. That day, Tal found a seven foot western diamondback rattler occupying his spot under the mesquite. He dispatched the viper with a branch off the tree. It didn't help. The snake unnerved her to the point that she wouldn't go back, no matter what. Whenever Tal came in from being gone all day, she would ask where he had been. Tal would say, "Huerfano." She knew that the hill was where Tal went to think his way through a problem that was difficult to solve. Sometimes just to think. She never ask why he went there. She knew he wouldn't answer anyway.

It was a place of supreme quiet and peace, isolated and alone. He dismounted near the mesquite tree. He retrieved his soda from the saddle bag and turned Paint loose to graze. He sat down, cracked his cola, leaned back against the tree and listened. Intently. And he loved what he heard. Nothing. Nothing except the wind in the grass. That is why he loved this place so. Miles away from roads and houses, it afforded him the luxury of complete silence. It was a deep, penetrating, silence that left him alone with his thoughts. It was also a restorative silence that allowed him to blot out the noise and confusion of the world. He sat there, taking it all in. The northwest wind behind the last evening's storms had freshened the land. The brilliant blue sky and bright sun quickly warmed the chilly, fall air. He watched the grass stretch beyond the next rise, waving in the wind, as if it were beckoning him to follow. It reminded him of his days at sea, sitting on deck watching the waves in their eternal motion. He pulled his hat down, closed his eyes and just listened.

Tal found himself on the horns of an interesting dilemma. He wished the memories of Gemi would go away. At the same time he wished he could remember more. He searched his memory for even the smallest relics of Gemi and what she had meant to him. He remembered how much he loved her and wanted her for a lifetime. He also remembered the betrayal, the reason for all the pain. He needed to remember more yet he wanted to forget it all. When was her birthday? He wished he could remember the sound of her voice, the sweet smell of her hair. In a moment of introspection, he found himself amused by the seeming contradiction. At Huerfano, a place so full of silence and beauty, the bits and pieces of her memory, the traces of love seemed so much more valuable to him than the forgetfulness he wished for. At this moment, her memory didn't seem so bittersweet.

Tal was so wrapped up in his thoughts that he didn't hear Joey drop a stick at his side. Joey wanted to play, but Tal was ignoring him. So Joey did what he usually did to get Tal's attention. He stuck his cold, wet nose in Tal's ear. He jumped and gave the dog a gentle slap to push him away, but Joey kept coming back to his face. The collie wanted to play and was not going to be denied. One last effort, Joey stuck his big, black nose in Tal's face. And he was reminded of Gemi once again. He laughed out loud because it was a funny, funny memory. He threw the stick for Joey and allowed his thoughts to go back in time.

* * *

Miss Margret called the class to order. "Today we will begin our first co-project. Before each of you there is a sheet of construction paper. During the first half of class, each of you will begin to draw whatever you like. Our medium will be crayon. The second half of class, each of you will trade pictures with your table mate and you will finish each other's drawing. The purpose of this exercise is to encourage creativity and cooperation. You may begin."

Tal thought for a moment, then he picked up a black crayon. In the middle of the sheet he drew a black spot about an inch in diameter and right above, two smaller black dots. Then he put down the crayon, put his elbow on the desk, leaned on his hand and turned his gaze toward Gemi. For her part, she didn't notice at first. She was too busy drawing trees, clouds and hills. Finally, Gemi feeling the weight of Tal's stare, turned to see his goofy grin.

"What are you doing? You need to be working on your drawing."

"I'm done," Tal replied.

"You can't be!"

"Well, I am."

"Let me see."

He showed Gemi his paper with three black dots.

"What on earth is that?"

"That is my master piece. It is a polar bear in a blizzard," Tal said proudly.

"All I see is three black dots!"

"Yeah, that's his nose and eyes."

"Where is the rest of him?"

"It's a blizzard . . . polar bears are white. Everybody knows you can't see a polar bear in a blizzard. All you can see are his eyes and nose."

Gemi's voice was reaching a high pitch. "Did your mother drop you on your head when you were a baby!? That is the stupidest thing I have ever heard of! How on earth can I finish that?"

Tal just smiled. "I don't know. One thing for sure, whatever you do, you'll probably ruin it. You could try to be creative, like Miss Margret said."

Gemi stood up, threw down her crayon and shook her finger in his face. "If I get a bad grade because of your lunacy, I'll, I'll . . ."

Miss Margret interrupted. "Tallet and Gemima, is there a problem?"

"Yes, Miss Margret, I am partnered with a nut case. He expects me to finish his three black dots."

"Tallet, what do you have to show for the past twenty minutes of class time?"

Tal showed the teacher his 'masterful creation'.

"Tallet, would you please explain yourself."

"I told Gemi. It's a polar bear in a blizzard."

Gemi let out a grunt of total exasperation as she threw her hands in the air. "Miss Margret, you see what I have to deal with. Can I have another table mate?"

"Yeah," Tal chimed in, "I want a divorce. We are having uh, irreconcilable, creative differences. Yeah, that's it, differences. She don't appreciate my genius."

By this time the class was laughing at all three of them. In a effort to regain control, the teacher sent Tal and Gemi to the principal's office. This was not the first trip for Tal, but it had never happened to Gemi before . . . . and she was fit to be tied. At the principal's office, Gemi took a seat near the door at the end of the row, crossing her legs and folding her arms. Tallet sat down next to her. She immediately jumped up and stomped to the other end of the row.

"Stay away from me . . . , or else!!!"

Her tone of voice told Tal she meant it. For a moment he thought he saw smoke rising from her ears.

Finally, the principal called them into his office. "Okay, children, what is going on?"

Gemi began to cry. Tallet looked at the principal. "She's discouraging my creativity."

Gemi shot back. "He's an idiot!!"

Tal told the principal what had happened in class. The principal bowed his head to stifled a smile. He knew Tal and wasn't surprised by his little prank. He put on his best serious face and looked at the two.

"Okay, kids, back to class. Tal, you apologize to Miss Margret. I think a two-day detention will help you take your assigned work a little more seriously. I think you should apologize to Gemima, also."

As Gemi got up to leave, Tal saw a smile creep across her face. She saw the principle's assigned punishment as divine retribution. Tal sensed she was glad.

Gemi left the office quickly. Tal called after her. "Gemi, wait."

She didn't turn around. "Shut up," she hissed, "leave me alone." Then she rushed off.

Tal stood there for a moment, feeling a smattering of remorse. He wondered if he pushed her too far. Then he remembered. That's what he wanted to do. The next day, he was in his usual, last minute mode, and Gemi was not at their desk.

"Miss Margret, where's Gemi?"

"She left a note on my desk that she would be absent for personal reasons."

Tal went to his seat. On his side of their table he found a small, plastic polar bear standing on a note. "Why are you being so mean to me? Can't we be friends? Love, Gemi."

He smiled to himself. Friends? It wasn't the 'friends' part he was afraid of. It was the 'Love, Gemi'. The possibilities of what that meant violated the 'no romantic entanglements' priority of his senior year. Still he was intrigued. She was a cutie. And when she looked at him, he saw a glisten in those eyes, those beautiful sky blue, deep, hypnotic eyes. He smiled as he put the bear and the note in his pocket. And he wondered what it might mean.

* * *

The sun was high when he felt the first pang of hunger. His thoughts turned back to Joey and the game they were playing. Getting up, he tossed the stick once more and went looking for Paint. He saw the horse had wandered about a mile, browsing the high grass. He whistled and Paint came back to him at a trot. Tallet mounted up and headed in for lunch.

At the barn, he unsaddled Paint and turned him loose in the corral. The horse went directly to the hay trough, like he hadn't eaten all day. Tal hung his saddle in the barn and headed for the kitchen. Bekka heard him pulling off his boots.

"'Bout time you dragged your carcass back to civilization. You got company in the den. Go sit. I'll bring lunch."

Tal went to the den to find his old pal. "Hey, Dusty, you old horse thief, how the heck are you?"

"Hey, Tal, you old bandit, when did you get out of jail?"

They both laughed and gave each other a big, bear hug.

They ate their lunch as the talked about horses, steers, longhorns and, as always, the weather. They hadn't seen each other for several months so they had a lot to catch up on. Finally, the afternoon grew long and it was time for Dusty to leave.

"Tal, it's been great, but I gotta go. Let's touch base more often. Too many months is too long."

"I'm all for that. Before you go, let me ask you something. Do you remember Gemi Renner?"

Dusty didn't have to think long. "I sure do. She was only the prettiest girl to ever wrap her arm around yours."

Tal grinned. "Do you remember what happened to her?"

Dusty was surprised. "You mean you don't? She was your girl, wasn't she?"

"Yeah, she was. It was so long ago, though."

"I have a vague memory of her family moving away while you were in the Navy. Beyond that, no. I do remember the time you took her out to meet Ole Jim. She was getting to you and you wanted to scare her away. As I remember, it didn't work?"

Tal remembered. "No, it sure didn't. She did get to me. That was a fateful night. She has been on my mind a lot lately. Believe it or not, I've been missing her, wondering what happened to her. I would like to talk to her one more time. I don't know, though. It's been so many years, so many miles. Maybe it's old age, maybe its loneliness. I don't know. If you remember something about her, let me know, will you?"

Dusty gave his old bud another brotherly, farewell, bear hug. Tal returned the affection.

"Will do, Tal. Stay well."

With that Dusty was gone and Tal was alone with his thoughts.

Ole Jim. That was a name he hadn't heard in a long time. The name was pivotal because it was Ole Jim that brought Tallet Jinx and Gemima Renner together for their first kiss, and for forever, at least in memories.

Tal went to the kitchen looking for his sister. He found her emptying the dish washer. "Hey, Bekka, I'm going to skip supper. The late lunch didn't leave much of an appetite. I'm going to my room for the evening."

"Are you okay?"

"Oh yeah, I'm fine. I just need to stretch out for a while. The ride out to Huerfano left me weary."

Tal grabbed a six-pack from the fridge and went to his room. He closed the door hoping that privacy and beer would give him comfort. It wasn't to be.

IV

Scaring Her

Tal sat back in his recliner then reached for the remote and the light. He paused to think about what he really wanted. He chose the dark and the silence of the room. He opened a can of beer and took a long drink. Putting his head back, he found himself wrestling with his emotions. He again felt himself irresistibly drawn to her memory. He remembered the fear he felt when he looked into her eyes. He remembered how he hoped their first date would also be the last.

* * *

Tallet sat down at their table for art class. He hoped that the Friday assignment would be simple. He wasn't in the mood to think let alone be creative. Gemi seemed more at ease today. Perhaps the polar bear incident was forgotten. She greeted Tal with a warm smile and a touch of her hand on his arm. He welcomed the overture. At the same time, he didn't like it.

"You want to go out for a burger with me tonight?"

Gemi flashed a broad smile. Her dimples charmed Tal and warmed his heart. Her eyes sparkled with agreement. "Yes, I would. What did you have in mind?"

"I'll pick you up at six. I need a reminder of where your house is."

"I'll be in town anyway. I'll meet you and you can give me a ride home later."

Tal thought for a moment. "That'll work. Meet me at Jim Bob's Burgers on the square."

Gemi was thrilled. Maybe he was finally warming to her friendliness.

Gemi was early and Tal was late. She was beginning to fear he wasn't coming. She was relieved when he finally showed up. Tal offered his arm as they entered Jim Bob's. The café was the local hang-out for Kayne High. Football jerseys, photos, pom-poms and other assorted trivia covered almost every inch of the walls. Just about everything was painted blue and gray. The juke box had all the latest songs and was played constantly. Tal chose a booth in the corner, away from the usual Friday night noise. They waitress took their order and the menus. Tal looked across the table at Gemi . . . and those eyes. "My gosh", he thought, "those eyes were beautiful!"

"I'm so glad you asked me out, Tal. I've been hoping you would."

Tal ignored the comment. "When we met in class, you told me your unusual name was a long story. I'd like to hear it."

Gemi laughed. "Oh, you mean the 'G'? Everybody asks me about that. When mom was carrying me, she craved pancakes. She ate pancakes at least once, sometimes three times a day. So when I finally arrived, she wanted to name me Jemima, after the food she believed kept us alive. Dad wanted a son so he could have a George junior. He wanted to name me 'Georgia'. Well, Mom refused. Dad wouldn't give in either. Finally, the hospital called and said they needed a name for the birth certificate. Dad said Mom could have her way, only if he could have a child with the same initials. Mom agreed, so I am Gemima . . . with a 'G'.

Tal smiled. "So what's your middle name?"

"Brianna. Gemima Brianna Renner. My Dad is George Brian. So Mom got her way and Dad got his. What about you? Tallet isn't the most common name."

The waitress brought their order then hurried off to the next customer. They both dug in, talking while they ate.

"You don't want to hear about me."

Tal was still hesitant, very wary about opening himself to anyone, especially a girl. He liked the hurt-proof shell he had built around his heart. He had already broken his 'no girls' rule for his senior year by asking her out. He wanted to keep some distance. If Gemi got too close, he could pull the plug with minimal pain.

Gemi gave him a playful slap on the arm. "Sure I do. I want to know everything about you."

"Like that's gonna happen," Tal thought. He decided to answer her question, in the spirit of friendly conversation.

"My father is a trucker. He liked to read novels about the old west when he was alone on the road. His favorite novel had a hero named Tallet Ethan. So that's my name. Tallet Ethan Jinx."

"Were you were born and raised in Kayne?"

"Yep. What about you? Where are you from? I thought I knew every girl around. I was surprised to see your smilin' face in class."

"My father works in road construction. We moved here a year ago from Illinois. He knew there was good money to be made building roads for the oil drillers."

Tal made the connection. "Oh yeah, Renner Road Construction, Inc. I've seen the signs around the county."

By this time they had finished their meal.

"Hey, would you like to see one of your Dad's roads?"

Gemi jumped at the chance to spend more time with Tal, even though she couldn't care less about a gravel road.

They got into the car and Tal headed out of town. The road he had in mind led to an isolated corner of the Boy Scout ranch, northwest of town. He knew it would be a great spot to scare Gemi away from him, maybe for good. He turned off the main road, pointing to the 'Renner Road Const. Inc.' sign to reassure Gemi he was on the level. He drove about three miles into the rolling hills of the panhandle then turned off the gravel road onto a narrow, rutted trail that wound through the mesquite trees and up a gentle rise. The trail ended on the crest of the rise, in a small clearing, surrounded by fallen logs and campfire remnants. They got out of the car and walked around the clearing. It was an hour past sundown. The glow of a half moon provided enough light so that Gemi could see where Tal was leading her. Tal picked a log facing the moon. He asked Gemi to sit down first so that he could sit also, just not too close. She was a city girl so the dark and the noises of the night were frightening. She felt safe with Tal, though. That was about to change.

"This is very nice. Don't you think it's a little spooky?"

"Nah, this is a really cool place. Thought maybe you'd like it too."

"How did you find this place?"

"Me an' Dusty spent a lot of summers on this ranch. Boy Scouts like to hike. That's why we know just about every inch of the place."

Tal reached down and picked up a small rock. When Gemi wasn't looking, he tossed it over his shoulder into the brush.

Gemi jumped. "What was that?"

"Don't know."

Just then a coyote bayed at the moon. Gemi jumped again. She pulled her jacket hood up over her head. It wasn't only the chill of the night that made her shiver.

"Tal, I don't like it here. Can we go?"

Tal was used to nights on the prairie. He knew the sights and sounds and was not afraid. This was the moment he wanted. He decided to exploit it. He waited until Gemi looked away, picked up another rock and tossed it over his other shoulder. He got the result he wanted. The rock scared a large armadillo. It came running out of the brush within a few feet of Gemi. She screamed, ran and jumped up on the roof of the car.

"Take me home!"

Tal laughed. "Are you afraid of Ole Jim? He's only a killer armadiller. They don't bite . . . . hard. Besides, if he bites you, you won't feel a thing. The poison numbs your whole arm before he can pull his fangs out."

Gemi was terrified, on the verge of panic. "Take me home. Now!! I want to go home. Now!!" Her voice was half pleading, half screaming.

"Okay, but you have to come down off the car. I can't drive with a girl on my roof. I'd get arrested for sure." His nonchalance only deepened her fear.

The armadillo wandered across the clearing, near to where the car was. Gemi screamed again as she saw the animal come closer. She was not only scared. She also very angry because Tal didn't seem to care about her or the danger she felt. He stood near to where they had been sitting, laughing at her. Finally, Tal snuck up behind the armadillo, grabbed it by the tail and picked it up. Gemi screamed again. She thought she was finished for sure. She was out in the country, did not know where, did not know the way back and the only person who did was about to be killed by Ole Jim, the venomous armadillo . . . . and Tal could not contain his glee.

"Oh, c'mon down. He won't hurt you. They're harmless. He's just rootin' for grubs."

Gemi realized he had been teasing her all along. Her fear and anger exploded into full blown fury. She slid down off the car, stomped over and stood in front of him. She glared at him then slapped his face. Her slap stunned him. He dropped the wriggling armadillo and it made its escape into the brush behind the car. She reloaded and slapped him again, this time as hard as she could. Tal's laughing face went blank and silent. This is not how his little prank was suppose to go. He thought he was in control of the situation. Now he found himself spiraling out of control, down into a triple threat of negative emotions. The pain of yesterday's rejections, the burden of today's insecurities, and the fear of tomorrow's loss coalesced into a paralyzing fog. He wanted to scare her into leaving him alone. Now he didn't know what to do. He could handle an armadillo. He didn't know what to do with a furious female.

"Why did you scare me like that? I thought we were going to have a fun evening together. I don't understand you." She let all of the anger pour out. "Why did you make me so afraid?"

Tal stood there at a loss for words. Gemi turned and started to open the car door. He grabbed her arm and she tried to yanked it away.

"Gemi, wait."

He didn't know if it was the shock of her slaps or the height of her rage. He blurted out the first thing that came to mind. The truth. "I wanted you to be afraid of me because I'm afraid of you. You scare me!"

Gemi stopped struggling to get away as her anger began to fade. "That's stupid. How can I scare you? You were practically raised out here on the prairie by coyotes an' those arma . . . thingies."

"Armadillo."

She waved her hand in his face. "Whatever!! I'm from the city. I believed you about the armadillo." She paused to take a breath. "Why would I scare you?"

"Why do you scare me? Well, I'll tell you why."

Tal searched for the words as he stepped close to her. "The first time I saw you, that first day in art class, I thought you were the prettiest thing I had ever seen. Then I saw your eyes . . . for the first time. Geez, Gemi, have you ever seen your eyes?" Tal didn't give her time to answer. He had found the words and now he was on a roll. "An' when I sit next to you, you smell like baby powder, an' vanilla, an' cinnamon, an' you smell all over like a girl, an' I want to bury my nose in your hair and take a deep breath, an' never exhale, an' your hands are warm when you touch me, an,' an' hour later I can still feel the warmth where you touched me an', an' your hair, an' your face, an' those dimples, an' those eyes, an' when I go to sleep at night, the last thing I see are your eyes!!! Geez, Gemi have you ever seen your eyes?!!, an', an', an' . . ." Tal's voice trailed off. There was more to say, a lot more, but he had run out of words . . . . for now.

Gemi's rage had dwindled down to a remnant. She smiled at him and batted her baby blues. She reached up and began to finger the pearl snap buttons of his shirt. "So, does this mean you like me?" Her tone of voice was coy and flirty.

His answer came quick. He turned and took a few steps away. "No, I don't like you."

His inner conflict of wanting Gemi and the fear of giving his heart to another girl was driving his emotions.

"Now I am confused. You don't like me, but you like everything about me?"

Tal turned back to face her. He stepped close to her and put an arm around her waist. "What I mean is, I don't like you, I mean, I can't, I mean how can you like someone when you think you love . . . ?"

Tal couldn't finish the sentence. He was trapped by his own contradiction. The shock of hearing himself vocalize what was in his heart, yet so frightening to put into words, left him at a loss. He put his other arm around her waist. He moved his lips to hers, stopping just before they touched. He did not know how, or even if, the gesture would be accepted.

All the anger Gemi had felt was gone. She wrapped her arms around him and pressed her body against his. They stood in the middle of the clearing, in the moonlight, embracing one another. She kissed him tenderly, passionately. He pulled her even closer, closer than before. The kiss lasted for what seemed to be forever. Finally, Gemi pulled her head back just enough to speak. Her voice was soft and warm, her breath sweet. Their lips still touching she said, "I don't like you either, very much . . . since the first time I ever saw you." Then she kissed him again.

He buried his face in the collar of her coat, kissing her neck and whispering the words. As gently as he could, he said the words he hadn't said to anyone in a long time, words he was afraid of because of what they meant, words he thought he shouldn't say because they made him vulnerable, open to hurt. "I love you, Gemi. I'm sorry I scared you."

"I love you too, Tal."

They got in and Tal started the car. She moved to the center of the seat, leaned against him and curled up, her feet against the passenger door. He drove home slowly, not wanting the evening to end. The emotional outburst of the evening left her weary. Now, at peace and wrapped up in the moment, she drifted off to sleep, her head against his chest.

Tal's thoughts were in a spin. He was still afraid as he glanced down at her. "What did I do?", he thought. In his heart, he was lost in the warmth of the body that snuggled beside him. In his head he was bewildered, wondering how he could let this happen. He went with his heart. She was with him and, for now, nothing else mattered.

Tal pulled into her drive and gave her a gentle nudge with his shoulder. "Wake up, you're home."

Gemi awoke and moved ever so slightly, not toward the door. She snuggled closer to him.

"Gemi, wake up, you're home."

She stirred and pulled herself up to Tal's chest and looked up at him. Even in the dark, Tal could see those eyes. She put her arm around his neck and without saying a word, kissed him long and deep. He held her as close as he could, savoring every moment, every breath, all the warmth of her presence. Finally Gemi pulled away and reached for the door handle. "Good night, Tal. Pick me up for school Monday?"

He knew that meant getting up and leaving a half hour earlier than he wanted. Seeing her, being with her, was worth it. "Good night, Gemi. And yes, I'll be here. By the way, I don't like you. Very much."

Gemi smiled broadly. "Oh, wait." She dug a scrap of paper and a pen from the depths of her purse and quickly scribbled her phone number. "Here. In case you can't wait 'til Monday to talk to me. And, oh, I don't like you too. Very much."

Tal called her. Three times on Saturday and four times on Sunday.

Monday morning Tal had no problem arising early. Gemi entered his first conscience thought. On the way to her house he thought about the dance. Half way through art class, he slid a note across the table when the teacher wasn't looking. Gemi discreetly unfolded the paper and read it. "Would you go to the Homecoming Dance with someone who didn't like you very much?"

Her heart leapt within her chest. It was the question she had been hoping, wanting, to hear from the moment he told her he loved her. She quickly scribbled beneath his name. "Only if that someone would let me not like him back as much as he not likes me." Then she drew a heart with their initials in the center and passed it back.

Homecoming would be a dance for the ages. It was only two weeks away. For Tal and Gemi it would be an agonizingly long two weeks.

* * *

The pain in his chest sharpened, bringing him back to the present. He rose from his chair and undressed. He went to the bathroom to relieve himself and get a drink of water to wash the warm beer taste from his throat. He had finished the six-pack. The alcohol left him sleepy. He took some aspirin and went to bed. The pain in his chest and in his memories eased. The tiredness and the alcohol swiftly overwhelmed him. He fell into a deep, dreamless sleep.

V

Meeting the Parents

He awoke slowly to a grey morning. A blue norther blew in sometime after midnight bringing with it a cold, steady rain. He was slow to get out of bed. His head hurt and his chest felt heavy with congestion. A wave of dizziness made him pause in the doorway of the bathroom to steady himself. He went to the sink and looked at himself in the mirror. "I look terrible. Must be coming down with something," he muttered to himself. He washed his face, took some aspirin and went to the kitchen. Bekka was at the table drinking coffee and reading the paper.

"Well, look what the cat dragged in. 'Bout time you got your carcass out of bed." She got a look at his face. It was drawn and haggard, suddenly looking much older, older than even yesterday. "You look terrible!"

"Thanks, Sis, I love you too." The absence of his morning smile told her that he really wasn't well.

"Are you okay?"

His response was terse, dripping with thinly veiled irritation.

"Been better, been worse."

"Do you want me to call the doctor for you?"

"No, I don't. Besides, I don't feel like going out in the rain. I'll just spend the day in bed. Maybe tomorrow I'll feel better."

Tal went to the fridge for a cold bottle of cola then grabbed a bag of potato chips from the counter and headed for his room. As he shuffled down the hall, Bekka called after him.

"You gonna want lunch? That's not much of a breakfast."

"Don't know . . . check with me later."

Before Bekka could respond, Tal was in his room. He closed the door, got into bed. He pointed the remote at the TV and pushed the button. He found a football game to occupy his mind while he munched the chips. His mind wasn't occupied long. "Football," he thought. He remembered Gemi's dad was a big football fan. He remembered the first time he met her father. It also came close to being the last time he ever talked to George . . . or Gemi.

* * *

Tallet Jinx pulled into Gemi's drive way. He didn't have to blow the horn. Gemi came running out of the front door before he could stop the car. She got in and slid close, saying nothing. He wondered why she seemed subdued.

"Why so grim, Girl?"

"I told my parents all about you. They won't let me go to the dance until they meet you. Can you come for supper tomorrow?"

Tal hesitated. The frown she saw on his face betrayed his feelings.

"I assume you don't like the idea."

"I don't like meeting parents. Well, maybe mothers . . . . not fathers. They usually don't like me very much."

"Oh, I'm sure they will like you. I think you're great." She lowered her voice and drew close to his ear. "I've been bragging 'bout you."

Her reassurance didn't ease his hesitance. He knew how intractable parents could be. He also knew it was either meet the parents or no dance. He sighed a deep sigh of surrender. "Okay, okay. What time?"

Gemi smiled broadly, her dimples in full display, eyes sparkling. "We eat at six. Why don't you come 'bout 5:30?"

Tal's heart melted. He thought to himself, how can I say 'no' to that? "I'll be there."

Gemima answered Tal's knock at the door. She laced her arm through his and ushered him into the kitchen to meet her mother. Martha Renner was a heavyset women with a broad face and a welcoming smile. "Mom, this is Tallet Jinx, the boy I have been telling you about."

Tal offered a hand shake. "I'm pleased to meet you, Mrs. Renner."

She brushed his hand aside and gave him a generous hug. "Oh, call me 'Mom'. Everybody else does." Tal stiffened for a moment. Her kind, welcoming gesture was much more than he expected and something he was not used to. She smiled warmly and motioned toward the table. "Sit down. Here, have a glass of lemonade and tell me all about yourself. Gemima is excited that you asked her to the dance. She hasn't talked about much else."

Tal took a sip of lemonade. Before he could sit down, George Renner came stomping in through the back entrance. He quickly shed his coat, hat and boots then poured himself a cup of hot coffee to warm his bones.

Gemi gave her father a hug and a kiss. "Hi, Daddy. This is Tallet Jinx, the boy I've been telling you about."

Tal stepped up to offer a hand shake which was promptly ignored. George leaned back against the counter, crossed his legs at the ankles, folded one arm across his chest and lifted his cup to his lips. Pausing before he took a sip he stared over his cup at Tal.

"So, kid, what do you do when you aren't chasing my daughter around school?" He sipped his coffee and continued his stare, waiting to for Tal's reaction.

He could sense Mr. Renner's thinly veiled contempt and was not in the mood to be intimidated. Tal glanced over George's shoulder at Gemi. She was mouthing the words, 'please, please, please,' hoping and praying Tal wouldn't say anything to anger her father. Tal's resentment of George's intimidation trumped his feelings for Gemi. Tal set his glass down, hooked his thumbs in his levis. He stared back at Mr. Renner and replied in a matter-of-fact, monotone voice.

"It is nice of you to ask, sir. On week days I sell drugs. On weekends, I'm a horse thief."

Gemi's mouth fell open in shock, her face paled.

"Kid, I asked you a serious question. I expect a serious answer."

"My apologies, sir, I was only kidding about being a horse thief."

"And the weekdays?"

"What about 'em?" Tal stood his ground.

Anger flashed in Mr. Renner's eyes. "Now look, kid, I don't like a smart mouth!"

Mrs. Renner jumped in. "Now, now dear, let's eat. We can talk later."

Gemi could see the one thing she wanted most of all rapidly slipping away. Any chance of going to the homecoming dance with the boy she loved was quickly becoming an impossible illusion. In a last ditch effort to salvage any hope, she blurted out, "Daddy, he's the evening clerk at Corley's drug store!"

What happened next surprised Martha and absolutely shocked Gemi.

George Renner laughed . . . . out loud . . . . and not just a gentle chuckle. It was a roar from deep in the gut, a laugh that Gemi had never heard before. George walked to Tal and slapped him on the back. "You're all right, kid. I like your sense of humor." Then he laughed some more.

"Thank you, sir, I try to amuse. One more thing, please. My name is Tallet Ethan Jinx. Mrs. Renner has asked me to call her Mom. I will respect her request and do that. Out of respect for you and your family, I shall call you Mr. Renner. You may address me how ever you wish but please, do not call me 'kid'. I have been mostly on my own since I was twelve and working to find my way since I was fourteen. I may be young in your eyes but I am not a 'kid'." Tal again offered a handshake.

"You seem awfully sure of yourself."

"Sir, we have a saying in Texas. It ain't bragging if you can do it."

Perhaps for the sake of brevity or maybe to save face Mr. Renner laughed again. He shook Tal's hand and replied, "T.J., you may call me G.B., . . . and I would appreciate it if you would join our table for dinner."

Tal wanted to take Gemi to the dance. She was slowly creeping into every part of his heart, his soul, his every thought. Not being able to see her anymore was a most unpleasant thought. He could not, would not, compromise who he was just to please her father. Tal always believe in truth and honesty. He wanted George Renner's respect as well as his permission to date Gemi. Truth had worked before. And it worked this time. He stood up for himself and gained G.B.'s respect. Tal looked at Gemi and winked.

The look on her face was priceless. Tal wasn't sure if it was amazement or disbelief. Maybe going to the dance with him was going to happen. At least, for the moment, it wasn't out of the question. The one boy she wanted in her life more than anything else had impressed her father. That was a major accomplishment.

The rest of the evening went very smoothly. Everyone enjoyed getting to know Tal and he felt comfortable enough to tell most of his life story. When asked about being on his own since he was twelve, he demurred. He explained that it was a long story and would tell them another time.

It grew late and it was time for Tal to head home. Mom gave him a good-bye hug. He tried to respond in kind. The gesture was still strange and it made him uneasy. It had been a while since he had felt a mother's touch. G.B. offered a firm handshake and an open invitation to come back any time. With that, Tal headed out the door, Gemi close behind. The cold wind blowing around the corner of the porch penetrated her thin sweater. Eager for the warmth of his body, she slipped her arms under Tal's coat and laid her head on his shoulder. Tal closed his coat around her, holding her close.

"You were great tonight. My father likes you. That's not easy to come by."

"Told you I'd charm his socks off."

He pulled her closer and looked deep into her beautiful, blue, hypnotic eyes. He kissed her slowly and gently. Gemi hoped this moment would last. Finally, he pulled away. Reluctantly, Gemi let him go.

"Pick you up for school tomorrow?"

She smiled. "I'll be counting the minutes. Remember, I don't like you very much."

He smiled back and waved as he got in his car. "I don't like you more!"

He looked in his rear view mirror as he pulled away. She was waving with both hands. "She really does love me," he thought. "I hope it's for real," he whispered to himself.

* * *

Tallet Jinx did not hear the knock at his door. He was half asleep, lost in memories of his first love. Somehow the reality of his dreams and memories were less painful when his mind was back there with them. It was his sister's voice that brought him back to the present. He looked at the time. It was well past supper. He had spent the whole day in bed, something very uncharacteristic for him. Bekka opened the door a bit and called again.

"You okay?" Bekka knocked again. "Can I come in?"

He pulled himself up in bed, leaning back against the headboard. "Yeah, come on." His voice was hoarse, sounding as groggy as he felt.

"I'm worried about you brother. Something is going on with you."

Tal, ever the stoic tried to insist he was okay. He was fooling himself. The symptoms he was experiencing made it obvious he was not well.

Bekka asked again. "You okay? I'm calling the doctor."

"Yeah, maybe you should. See if you can get me a morning appointment."

His response gladdened her. "Do you want some supper? All you've had is some potato chips."

Tal groaned as he tried to lift his weight up on his elbow. "Not hungry. How 'bout some aspirin and a beer."

"That don't sound like a good combination."

"Maybe not, but it'll help me sleep. That's what I need the most."

Bekka did his bidding. He took his 'medicine'.

Bekka kissed him on the forehead and switched off the lights as she left the room. The heavy overcast brought an early darkness to his room. In the dark, he was alone with his thoughts, memories, wishes and the pain of lost love. Not for long, though. The alcohol worked fast. In minutes Tal was asleep. There was no pain when floating on the gentle waves of a deep sleep.

VI

October Memories

It was broad daylight when Tal awoke. Joey, barking at his door, brought him to full consciousness. He arose slowly, scratching and stretching as he shuffled to the door. He opened the door just wide enough to let the dog in. He reached down to scratch his ears. "Sorry. I know I've been neglecting you, old buddy."

Joey curled up in Tal's recliner. Tal showered, shaved and put on his work denims. He took a deep breath and another stretch as he shuffled down the hall to the kitchen. Joey followed close behind. He felt better than he had in week, even though the chest pain and heaviness in his arms remained. Bekka had the coffee hot as he came in.

Bekka pointed at Tal. "Well, would you look at this, Joey. Just this morning I was beginning to doubt there was life after death!"

Tal laughed as he sat down at the table, grateful for the tease. "Shut up and give me some of that mud you call coffee."

Bekka was also grateful for the tease. It told her that her brother was feeling better. "I got you a doctor's appointment for next Monday."

"Thanks. Don't think I'll need it. I'm feeling better."

Her reply was terse. She didn't agree with him. "Will see." She left it at that.

Tal finished his coffee and the breakfast. He went to the door, pulled on his boots, hat and jacket. "I'm headed for the barn for a while. C'mon Joey."

Tal was eager to get out of the house and do something, anything. He had felt like a slug for too long. The memories of Gemi had pulled him away from the days of autumn and his enjoyment of watching the south bound sun as it took with it the scorching heat of the Texas summer. The first blue-norther of last month brought with it the cooler temperatures he had waited for. The desire to be outside working in the fresh air stirred his ambition. Joey was an eager assistant. The border collie was bred to run and his instincts didn't like it when his master stayed inside.

Tal busied himself by cleaning the barn, starting with Paint's stall. He gave his faithful steed an extra ration of oats then curried his mane and flanks. He then turned his attention to the odd chores of keeping up a barn, oiling the saddles and the other tack. He got down bales of hay for the horses and reset the rat traps for the critters that were stealing his grain supply. He suddenly hesitated. Something was wrong. His stamina quickly left him. Tired and out of breath, he needed to sit down. He didn't understand. Even though the chill of the morning still filled the barn, he felt sweaty and short of breath. He didn't want Bekka to know what was happening. She worried too easily. He went out of the back of the barn and around the side, out of sight of the house, to his private patio. He slumped down in his chaise lounge, leaned back and pulled his hat down low over his eyes to block out the sun. Taking a deep breath, he tried to relax but the pain in his chest and arm grew worse. Gemi? How could it be? She was so long ago and so far away. Surely it wasn't that hurt he was feeling. It had many so years, so many dances since he had held her in his arms. The dance. Ah, yes. The memories from the night before came forward. The homecoming dance of 1961 was a moment from his youth that he remembered with great nostalgia. It was a magical night, the night he revealed the depth of his love and gave Gemi his heart and soul.

* * *

His phone rang right at six. He knew it was Gemi. "Hi, Gemi. What's up?"

It caught her by surprise. "How'd you know it was me?"

"I could tell by the ring."

"No, you can't. The phone has the same ring for everybody."

"Hey, have I ever lied to you that you know of?"

Gemi still hadn't quite figured out when he was or wasn't teasing. She greeted his strange question with silence, not sure what he meant. Finally Tal revealed his trick. "You always call at six. Right?"

Gemi looked at her clock. "Well, okay, you got me. Am I really that . . ."

Tal interrupted. "Really that predictable? Yes, you are."

Again Gemi was silent, not sure what to make of this guy. How could he be so lovable and so infuriating at the same time?

"I'm sorry Gem, what cha' got on your mind?"

She gave him a few more moments of silence so as to appear miffed. "I'm calling you to ask about the dance. What are you wearing and what time are you picking me up?"

"None of your business and six o'clock."

"C'mon, Tal, I want to know!"

"Tell you what, why don't we surprise each other. Just tell me what color you are wearing."

"If you do the same."

"Okay. I'm wearing a black suit with a white shirt. And you?"

This was her chance to get even. "It's a surprise. See you tomorrow. Bye."

With that, she was gone and Tal was left holding the phone. Literally. He smiled to himself. "She is sassy," he thought. He waited an hour or so and called Gemi back, hoping Mom would answer. He was in luck. "Hello, Mom? It's Tal."

"Oh, hi. I'll get Gemi for you."

"No, no, I'm calling you. Tell me, what color dress is she wearing to the dance?"

"Blue skirt and blouse."

Wonderful, he thought, my favorite color. "Thanks, and please don't tell her I called. Please? Bye."

The stage was set. The homecoming dance would be a most memorable evening.

Tal awoke early in the morning. He arose and quickly put on his Saturday denims. He had a lot to do, starting with making sure his car was clean, inside and out. He went to the florist shop to get a special corsage, a white carnation, the petal tips tinted blue. He ordered a red boutonnière for himself. He cleaned and pressed his best black suit and white shirt. He polished his best boots and, after double checking everything again, he showered, shaved and laid down for a nap. Sleep was not possible. The excitement, the anticipation, kept his mind going at top speed. He was glad to see the afternoon sun go low because it meant it was time. He quickly, carefully dressed, looking to every detail. Was his shirt straight? Was it tucked in evenly? Was his tie even, his belt buckle centered, the boutonnière straight? The care he took betrayed the deepening feelings he had for Gemi. He wanted every detail perfect so as to please and impress this girl. As he was leaving his room, he stopped at the door. He had one more thought. The ring. He went back to his dresser drawer and fumbled underneath the socks. He found it in the back corner. It was a gold ring with a red stone his mother had bought for his father many years ago. Maybe tonight was the night that this symbol of his parents love would come to mean something once again. Slipping the ring into his pocket, he left quickly and headed for Gemi's house.

It was unusual for Tal to be early for anything. For him, procrastination was an art form. Yet, there he was, pulling into Gemi's driveway, twenty minutes to six. Her mother answered the door.

"Come in Tallet. You look handsome tonight."

Tal felt his ears turning a bit red. It had been a while since he had heard a mother's compliment.

"Thanks, Mom."

"Gemima isn't ready quite yet. Please come in and join us."

She motioned toward the den. Tal entered the den and Gemi's father rose to greet him.

"Good evening, T.J. You're looking good. Hoping for some fun tonight?"

"Yes, sir, I am. I will take good care of your daughter."

Mom touched Tal's arm.

"Can I get you something to drink, dear?"

"Thanks, Mom, some ice water would be great."

His nervous anticipation had given him a serious case of cotton mouth. Mom brought the water.

"I'll let Gemima know you are here."

Tal sat down on the edge of a chair and took a long drink, trying to look patient. The ten minutes he waited seemed like an hour. He was soon to discovered it was well worth the wait. Gemi came to the door of the den.

"Hi, Tal, I'm ready to go."

Tal stood up and turned toward her. She was standing just inside of the door of the den, her figure back lit by the kitchen. She was an absolute dream. What he saw far exceeded his expectations. She was wearing a navy blue fitted skirt, a baby blue cardigan sweater, a sky blue satin handkerchief tied around her neck, the ends hanging loosely over her shoulder. Her pixie haircut curled around her ears, framing her face. Even in the subdued light of the den he could see the sparkle in those blue eyes that continued to captured his imagination. Tal found himself tongue tied. After all, what do you say to an angel.

"Ah, hi, er, ah . . ."

"Gemima", G.B. interjected with an amused tone, "her name is Gemima."

Tal blushed. "Of course it is!" He stepped forward to present the corsage to Gemi. "This is for you."

He paused and took a deep breath, hoping to recover his composure as he fumbled with the corsage, trying to pin it to her sweater. Mom came to his rescue.

"Here, let me help you, Tal."

Gemi was equally entranced. Before her stood the boy she had watched come and go at school for a year yet never had the opportunity to meet. Now here he was, eager to be her special escort for a special night. Tal was wearing his best black denim suit with a white pearl snap shirt and a black bolo tie with a silver slide at the neck. His thick, brown hair was neatly parted and combed back, his side burns framing his face. Tall, thin and handsome, he was hers for the evening, hopefully forever. She was sure she would be the envy of all the girls at the dance.

Mom retrieved a camera from a kitchen drawer.

"Okay, you two, stand together so I can get a picture."

Photos taken and good byes said, Gemi wrapped a white shawl around her shoulders. George and his wife stood in the doorway watching as Tal opened the car door and helped Gemi in. Carefully closing the door, he hurried around to the drivers side, got in, and they were off to the dance.

George spoke up first. "I didn't like the way they looked at each other."

"Why, dear?"

"Because they looked like they're in love. They're too young to be in love. Besides, we don't know anything about him . . . or his family . . . or what his plans are after graduation, if he graduates."

"You worry too much. Besides, we were the same age when we met. I remember my father having the same concerns about you. We made it okay, didn't we?"

George knew his wife was right. Sometimes he hated it when she was right. This was one of those times. He grunted and went back to his recliner and his newspaper, muttering under his breath. "I guess so. We'll see. Time will tell."

Tallet and Gemima walked arm in arm to the doorway of the school cafetorium. They stopped dead in their tracks, amazed at the sight. The homecoming committee had transformed the room into a temple, a shrine, a veritable altar at which the Kayne High School faithful could come and worship at the feet of their beloved Falcons. There was blue and grey everywhere. Crepe paper streamers covered the ceiling and the tables. Each table had a blue and grey candle/flower centerpiece. The stage had a large, blue and grey backdrop welcoming the alumni and urging everyone to 'cheer on their team'. Tal and Gemi looked at each other, then back to the room and said in unison, "Wow!!"

Just then Tal felt a tap on his shoulder. It was Dusty and his date, Anni. "Hi, old buddy, what do you think? Anni and me helped put it together."

Tal was thinking 'over kill' but he didn't want to throw cold water on Dusty's obvious pride of accomplishment.

"The faithful will be thrilled. Anni, meet Gemima Renner, my best girl."

Gemi blushed with pride at his introduction. The four walked into the party and found a table by the dance floor, near the stage. The deejay picked up the microphone.

"Welcome, everyone to the 1961 Kayne High School homecoming bash. Let's get the fun started."

The deejay put a fast tempo record on the turntable and turned up the amp.

"C'mon, Tal, let's dance!"

Gemi was feeling the beat and wanted to move her feet.

"Naw, let's wait for a slow song."

Tal was afraid to admit to Gemi that he had a birth defect. His sister, Bekka, was blessed with natural rhythm. She could make moving to any music appear as a great art form. He, on the other hand, was born with two left feet and when the music started, one of them went lame. Any attempt to dance to a fast tempo song would create a risk of serious injury to himself or anyone else who may happen to be in close proximity. Tal took a discreet step toward Dusty, hoping not to be noticed by Gemi.

"Hey, Dusty," he whispered, "the next fast dance, do the cut-in."

Dusty gave him a thumbs up. This was a trick they had used since grade school to confound the girls so they wouldn't have to dance to fast songs. The next dance met the criteria.

"C'mon Tal, let's dance!" Tal let Gemi pull him to the dance floor. Just as the music started, Gemi felt a tap on her shoulder. "May I have this dance?"

It was Dusty.

Gemi hesitated. Tal took a step beck and said, "Sure."

As Gemi raised her arms to dance with Dusty, Tal stepped in. He and Dusty locked arms and off they went across the floor, arms flying, legs kicking, feet stomping, both of them twirling to the music. Gemi, at first a bit indignant, began to smile.

Anni came up and stood beside her. "Betcha didn't know our escorts were the town clowns."

Gemi was getting to know Tal a little more everyday. She did know her date was the town clown. Now, he was her town clown, and his off-beat view of life was growing ever more charming.

"Maybe they will wear themselves out and behave the rest of the night."

The two boys came circling back around, huffing an puffing, all out of breath.

Dusty spoke first. "What do you think?"

Tal chimed in. "Are we good or what?"

Both girls stood with their arms crossed.

"Brings new meaning to 'dance like there's ants in your pants'," said Gemi.

"Fred Astaire just called. If you do that again, he will have both of you killed," said Anni.

The boys laughed at the girls and themselves. At intermission, they took their seats at table. It was then that Tal heard a familiar voice behind him.

"Hey, runt, whose your date?"

Tal didn't have to turn his head. He knew the voice. "Go away, Seven! She's with me."

Gemi turned to see who Tal was talking to.

The interloper punched Tal's arm. "C'mon, at least you could introduce us."

"Gemi, meet Eugene Henry Stevens. Eugene Henry, this is Gemima Renner. Now go. Beat it. Get lost." Tal's tone of voice dripped with contempt.

Eugene Stevens was big for his age. Broad shouldered, barrel-chested, tall with blond, curly hair, blue eyes and chiseled features. All the boys wanted to be like him. All the girls wanted to date him. He was ingratiatingly self confident, sometimes to the point of arrogance. Stevens had a way of reminding most people of their insecurities without saying a word. Tal was no exception. He was the quarterback for the school football team. He wore number seven on the field, hence the nickname. He preferred the nickname. Tal believed he couldn't compete with Stevens, at any level, and win. Deep down, his negative self-image and insecurities made him afraid of Stevens.

Seven ignored Tal and reached for Gemi's hand. "Please, call me Seven. How 'bout a dance?"

Tal pushed the hand away. "You know the law. I introduced you. Now beat it, Eugene."

Stevens knew Tal called him by his real name just to irritate him. The snarl in Tal's voice deepened the irritation. He glared at Tal then smiled at Gemi. "Sure, maybe next time." Then he walked away.

Gemi, wanting to be polite, called after him. "Nice to meet you."

Tal pulled his chair closer to Gemi. He put his arm around her, as if to protect her from the threat posed by Stevens. "It's never nice to meet that jerk!"

"You mentioned a law. What law?"

"In Texas we have an unwritten law. Ya dance with the one that brung ya."

Tal quickly pushed Seven out of his thoughts. He wanted to think only about the evening, his date, and what he hoped was to come. He thought about the ring in his pocket. He could feel the insecurities that were stirred by Seven's untimely intrusion. He was made uncomfortable by the conflict of fear and hope tugging at his heart. It was fear of making his heart vulnerable again. The hope was that maybe this girl was the one who would love him. His vow of a senior year without the entanglements of a girlfriend was gone. This girl was all he could think about. He wondered, hoped, she felt the same. He wanted someone to love and someone to love him. He loved Gemi. He believed she loved him. The question was, how much? Would it be enough? The moment came with the first song after the second intermission.

The deejay clicked on the microphone. "Okay, kids, let's get this party back on track. I have a love song just for the young lovers, so all you guys, grab your dolls 'cause this one's for you."

Tal took Gemi's hand and led her to the dance floor. The magic moment began with the first note. The music stirred their souls. The words spoke to their hearts. The intensity of their emotions swept them up. Yes, they were dancing . . . , two feet off the floor.

Wise men say only fools rush in,
But I can't help falling in love with you.

Tal pulled Gemi close to him, holding her hand against his shoulder. He kissed her neck, her ear and began whispering the lyrics. Suddenly they were alone in a room full of people. The blue and gray decorations were clouds floating in the air, carrying them along to their destiny. There was not the slightest hint of hesitation in her response as she pressed the fullness of her body into his. She turned her head to kiss him on the cheek and whisper the words into his ear.

By the time the song ended, neither had any doubt. They were of one heart, two teens in love with love and each other. They were cheek to cheek, heart to heart, one soul sharing the warmth of one body. They closed their eyes and visualized a dream land all their own. They didn't move, wanting the music would go on forever. Finally, Tal opened his eyes and looked deep into Gemi's eyes. He knew. This was the moment.

"Let's go outside," he whispered. "I want to ask you something."

Tal led her out the door and around the corner, into the shadows. Even in the shadows he could see those eyes, feel them penetrating his soul. He pulled her close and kissed her deeply, passionately. He broke the kiss and reached into his pocket for the ring.

"I know we met only a month or so ago, and I wasn't very nice to you at first. I hope you know me better now, and I was wondering if you could see it in your heart, I mean . . . would you be willing to . . . , you know, to wear this . . . ah . . ."

Gemi looked at the ring, then at Tal several times. He could see her eyes glistening in the half light. He stumbled to find the right words, glad for the dark that masked his embarrassment. He was sure the answer was 'yes'. He felt it in his soul as she pressed her body to his during the song. He waited for her to say it. However she said nothing. She put the ring on and made a fist to keep it from falling off because it was way too big for her delicate fingers. Finally Tal asked her again. "Gemi, would you, you know, I mean, wear, that is . . . well . . . go steady with me?"

Gemi smiled in joy for what was happening. She also smiled in amusement. This tall, handsome boy that she wanted in her life was so articulate with her father, with Seven, and, in fact, with most anyone else. With her, though, he couldn't string a complete sentence together. Tal was sure his offer would find immediate acceptance. He thought her silence was reticence on her part. Just as he began to wonder if he had enough courage to ask again, they heard Dusty calling for them.

"Tal? Gemi? You out here?"

Gemi cupped her hand over Tal's mouth.

"Don't answer," she whispered.

They stood in silence, waiting for Dusty to go back inside. It was a few seconds before they were alone again. Then Gemi kissed Tal's cheek.

"Let's go someplace and talk. Someplace where it's quiet. Someplace where we won't be interrupted? I know just the place."

Tal hesitated. "Sure, let's go in and say 'good bye' to . . ."

"No, let's just go. Take me home."

It wasn't the reaction he had hoped for but he was ready to follow her lead.

As they neared her driveway, Gemi pointed ahead. "Go to the next drive and turn there. Go around the barn and stop."

The headlights fell on her father's equipment storage barn as Tal made the turn. He parked and switched off the ignition. It was a perfect spot for young lovers. It was out of sight of her house and the road, and it was very dark. The only light was the faint glow of the radio dial. Tal pushed his seat back to make room for Gemi as she laid across his lap, feet curled up under her, her head resting on his left arm.

Gemi held her hand up to look at the ring. She took Tal's hand in hers, then she began to speak, haltingly at first.

"I remember you from last year. I had seen you in the halls and in the cafetorium. I thought you were the cutest guy and I wanted to meet you. The problem was, I didn't know you or any of your friends. I was afraid to just walk up and introduce myself. When you walked into art class and sat next to me, I was sure it was fate. I couldn't believe it. I just couldn't believe that someone I dreamed about would walk in and sit down beside me. Then you were mean to me. I didn't understand why because all I wanted to do was to love you, or at least be your friend. My parents and I have asked about you and your family. You won't tell. You seem afraid to say the word 'love'. I want to wear this ring, and I want to be with only you. This ring is not enough, though. I need to know more about you. You're really good at being the town clown. It allows you to hide from questions you don't like. I need to know. Tallet Jinx, who are you?"

Her words took him by surprise. She was right, of course. He still feared the vulnerability that could lead to another broken heart. Her disarming honesty and the warmth of her body in his lap were melting that fear away. He lifted her hands to his lips and kissed them. He knew he needed to trust her if he wanted her to love him. He began slowly as the last of his fears faded.

"I told you I had been on my own since I was twelve. That's when my mother died. My Dad took it pretty hard. He's an over-the-road trucker and is gone most of the week, sometimes most of the month. When he's home on weekends, he works in our garage, fixing cars. If I don't work with him, I don't see him much. I tried to keep the house going but it was hard. My sister, Bekka, needed the guidance that only a mother could give so my Dad sent her to live with Aunt Dori in Amarillo. That was good for her but it left me even more alone. I learned how to drive helping my dad in the garage. I needed to get around when he was gone. By the time I was thirteen I could drive just about anything on wheels. When I got into high school, I lied about my age to get a job. Sometimes the money Dad left didn't last long and I'd get hungry. I am afraid to say 'I love you' to anyone because when I do, I lose them. First my mom, then the girl I went out with last year and the year before. I tried to say 'I love you' to my Dad once as he was on his way out the door. He just said 'thanks' and kept on walking . . . didn't even look back. So the words come hard for me. If I say 'I love you' to you, I'm afraid I will lose you too. That is why I say 'I don't like you very much'." He paused to look for her reaction. Even in the faint glow of the radio, he could see her eyes glistening. She pulled herself up to put her head on his shoulder. "I'm afraid . . . I'm afraid that . . . if I love you, I will get my heart broke . . . again."

Her thoughts went back to the night with Ole Jim. She chose his own words to put his fears to rest. "I don't like you very much, Tal. I can't like you . . . because I love you."

Her words erased the last remnant of defense he had around his heart. There was no hesitation, no fear in his response.

"I love you. Very much. Will you wear my ring?"

Gemima smiled and wiped her eyes. "It's not very often a girl gets an offer like this from the town clown. Tallet, I do love you and would be proud to wear your ring."

The mutual pledge was sealed with a kiss. A long, deep passionate kiss. He kissed her ear, her cheek, her neck. He lowered his head and pressed his ear against her breast. The warmth of her skin on his face made him linger. He didn't move for the longest time.

"What are you doing?"

"I'm listening to your heartbeat. I can hear your heartbeat. I love your heartbeat."

She wrapped her arms around his head and held it closer to her, kissing the top of it. "It's not my heart. It's yours. I gave it to you five minutes ago."

"I don't need two. You can have mine."

Lost in each other's warmth, they became one. And neither wanted the evening to end.

* * *

Bekka knocked at Tal's bedroom door. Getting no response, she opened the door and stepped in. She could see Tal in the chaise lounge on the patio. She slid the door open.

"Tal, you okay? I went to the barn to talk to you and you weren't there."

He rose from his chair slowly, with effort, keeping his back towards her. He knew something was wrong and didn't want her to see him this way.

"Yeah, I'm okay. I guess."

"I'm worried about . . . ."

He cut her off and pushed past her. He went to the bathroom to wash his face and run wet fingers through his hair. Then he looked in the mirror. He was shocked by what he saw. It wasn't him. It was someone much older. His face was ashen and swollen. Could he have aged that much in a few weeks? Surely, it couldn't be the memories that made him look this way. He asked himself the more immediate question. "How do I hide this from Bekka?" He combed his hair, straightened his shirt and tucked it in. He pinched his cheeks to add some color. He pulled his frame up as straight as possible then went out to fool his sister.

It didn't work.

"You are not okay. I'm calling the doctor."

"No, don't. Not right now. Maybe something is wrong. It's probably from not sleeping well. Maybe the cold weather's gotten to me." At that moment, he coughed. She had never heard him so congested. And it scared her.

"Sit in your chair and relax for a while. Keep your head up. I will make you some lunch."

Her experience as a nurse told her it was more than the common cold. She went to the kitchen and called for a doctor's appointment. She would rather risk her brother's wrath than his health. She quickly made him a sandwich and a glass of soda. She brought it to his room and found him in his recliner, his head back, eyes closed. She could hear the rattle of congestion in his lungs as he breathed.

"Here's your lunch. Want the TV on? And we're going to the doctor tomorrow."

He wanted to protest her disobedience. He was simply too tired to care. "I'm fine. Yeah, hand me the remote. I'll sit, watch the tube, and rest. Would you close the barn for me? I would appreciate it. And bring me some beer from the fridge."

"No beer, pal, the alcohol will make your congestion worse."

He found an old movie just for noise but couldn't eat. He put down his unfinished sandwich, put his head back and stared at the ceiling as the TV entertained itself. His memories went back to her, and that Saturday night he and Gemi pledged their love after the dance. And he remembered the next day, how she got even with him.

VII

Turn About is Fair Play

Tal's phone rang late Sunday morning as he was heading for the door. He was delighted to hear her voice.

"Good morning, Tal. It's been twelve hours. Still love me?"

"You bet. Can't wait to see you again."

"Well, come on over. I got a kiss and a hug for you."

Tal laughed. "Can't. Gotta work this afternoon."

"C'mon, it's Sunday. Why do you have to work on Sunday?"

"I need the money. Besides, I can come over tonight."

"That's not soon enough! I thought maybe you could take me to meet your Dad this afternoon."

"Can't. I'm sorry. Gotta go. I'm late."

Her Mom could tell she was disappointed when she came into the kitchen. "What's wrong, Gemima?"

"It's Tal. I wanted him to come over but he has to work."

Mom thought for a moment. "I need to go to the store. Why don't I drop you in town and Tal can bring you home later?"

The idea came in a flash. Gemi knew exactly what she was going to do to spend the afternoon with Tal and maybe meet Dad. Plus, it would be getting even in a big way. She smiled broadly. "Thanks, Mom, great idea. I'll go get dressed." She went to her closet and changed into her denim jeans.

Tallet was finishing with a customer when he heard the door chime. He looked up as Gemi entered the store. He was surprised and delighted. Surprised to see her and delighted because she was wearing the same blue sweater and scarf from the dance. She also wore a waist jacket that matched her jeans. He smiled broadly when he noticed the fit of her blue jeans.

Now, Tal and Dusty had made watching girls in blue jeans a hobby and, in the process, had become experts. Some girls had to be taught how to wear jeans. Some girls learned it on their own. Occasionally a girl would walk by who was born with the gift . . . a girl who knew instinctively how to wear blue jeans. For these girls, wearing jeans was an art form. He looked at her and saw a Mona Lisa in denim. This girl had a natural born instinct for wearing blue jeans. He wondered if she looked as good walking away as she did coming. Gemi walked up to the counter and waited for the customer to leave.

"Good afternoon, sir," she said in a very business like tone, "I would like to see some shampoo, please."

Tal played along. "Why sure, Miss. This way please."

She followed him to the back corner of the store, out of sight of Mr. Corley. He stopped at the shampoo display then turned to face her.

"These are your choices of shampoo. We have a wide variety to . . ."

She interrupted his sales pitch. She pulled the lapels of his clerk's coat, drawing him closer and spoke softly. "Hey, Cowboy, kiss me."

Tal fulfilled her demand. Her warmth and passion made him forget for a moment where they were. He pushed her away and whispered impatiently. "What are you doing here? I told you I'd come get you later."

She smiled and replied in a whisper, "I think we should go now." With that she stepped back, slapped him and spoke loudly. "Please sir, that is not proper."

Mr. Corley heard the outburst and came to investigate. He found Tal trying to rub the sting from his cheek. Gemi had her arms folded across her chest, tapping her foot, feigning great indignation.

"Tal, what is going on here?"

Gemi looked at Mr. Corley with mock outrage. "Are you the manager, sir?"

"I am the owner, young lady. May I help you?"

Gemi raised her voiced, pushing her ruse to new heights.

"Sir, I came in here to buy shampoo. Your helper tried to kiss me. Just because I let him dance with me last night, he thinks he can kiss me." She feigned embarrassment and tears, burying her face in her hands as she turned her back to Tal. "I am so humiliated!"

Tal mounted a vigorous protest. "Mr. Corley, I did no such thing. You know me better than that. You taught me to respect all your customers and you know I do!"

By this time Gemi had some real tears going. She was on a roll and there was no stopping her now. She turned, glared at the owner and pointed at Tal. "He's lying! He kissed me." She pointed to his mouth. "See my lipstick? I think you should discipline him. Severely. If you don't, I will tell my parents what kind of people you hire!"

With that, Gemi put her hands to her face again, pretending to cry louder. In reality, she was to hiding a grin she couldn't suppress.

Mr. Corley saw the ring on her finger and guessed it was Tal's. Suddenly he realized what was happening. He looked down to hide his amusement, thought for a moment and decided to play along. He looked up at Tal. "Young man, you owe this young lady an apology."

"No, I don't and I'm not going to!" Now Tal's outrage was growing. Unlike Gemi's, his was for real. "She wanted me to kiss her so I did!"

"I'm not going to stand here and be insulted! I don't see how you can allow this kind of a person work for you. If you don't fire him, I will take my business elsewhere."

With that, Gemi turned on her heels and walked briskly out of the store. Tal couldn't help but notice. She did look as good walking away. He was at a loss for words. How could she do this to him?

"Mr. Corley, I'm sorry I . . . I . . ."

Mr. Corley put his hand up. Trying hard not to seem amused, he spoke to Tal quietly and firmly. "I think you should take the rest of the afternoon off and think about how you treat our customers."

"Mr. Corley, I didn't do anything. I swear. You know me better than that. I need this job. I need the money. She's playing some kind of game and I . . ."

Again, Mr. Corley stopped him. "Just go on, son. Business is slow. Go be with your girl. I'll see you tomorrow after school . . . and I'll pay you for today. Consider it a homecoming gift for you and your girl."

Tallet thanked Mr. Corley for his gift. He took off his clerk's jacket, handed it to his boss and left the store. He went to his car in the side parking lot and found Gemi leaning against the driver's door. He was still fuming. "Nice trick. Where did you learn that? You almost got me fired!"

Gemi opened the car door. She slid in and motioned for Tal to join her. She put an arm around his shoulder and spoke softly as she kissed him on the ear. "I learned it from a 'killer armadiller' named 'Ole Jim'. Besides, now we can spend the afternoon together. You can take me to meet your Father." Then she smiled, showing off her dimples and the sparkle in those incredible eyes.

Tal knew he'd been had. A moment of anger quickly turned to amusement. This was a smart, sassy girl and he knew he had better not play anymore tricks on her. "Okay, okay, I guess I deserved that. He didn't fire me, though. Hope you're not disappointed."

Gemi kissed him on the cheek and laid her head on his shoulder. With a tone of feigned resignation she said, "I guess I'll just have to try harder, next time."

Tal started the car and headed for home.

Gemi got her first glimpse of the Jinx homestead as he pulled into his drive. Home was a small, low ranch house in the middle of an overgrown yard. The grass was cut, but every bush and tree looked like it hadn't been trimmed in years. Tal drove around to the garage behind the house. It was a large, metal building with two overhead doors at the far end of the front side. It also showed years of neglect. It hadn't been painted and there were spots of rust everywhere. The roof was dented from many hail storms. An old wind turbine spun in the wind. Its rusty bearings made a loud, irritating, squealing noise. Tal took her inside through the entry door at the near end of the garage. It was dimly lit and dirty. What hadn't been used recently was covered with a layer of dust. What had been used glistened with a thin coat of oil and grease. It smelled of old grease, gasoline, coffee and stale cigarette smoke. Gemi was afraid to step anywhere, afraid her shoe might stick to the floor and she would end up with a bare foot. A buzzing radio in the corner was tuned to a country song. From some place in the gloom, she heard someone whistling, off key, to the song being played. Tal called to his father.

"Hey, Sparky, where are you?"

Gemi gave Tal a puzzled look. "Sparky? You call your Father Sparky?"

"Yeah. He always carries an old spark plug, from his first car, in his pocket. Says it brings him luck."

Just then they heard a loud bang, a dull thud and a string of obscenities that would make a sailor blush.

Tal looked at Gemi with embarrassment. "Colorful, isn't he?"

Gemi saw Sparky come from up from behind an old pick-up. He was wiping his greasy hands with an old rag. He was a tall, thin man with tousled, grey hair and sharp features. She noticed that Tal resembled him only vaguely. She was very glad because he wasn't near as handsome as his son. His thin, unshaven face made him look older than he was. His over-alls were shiny from grease. A cigarette hung loosely from his mouth.

"Hey, Pop, I wish you wouldn't smoke while you work. You're gonna blow yourself up one of these days."

Sparky ignored his son's concern. "Tally-Boy, where have you been? I thought you were going to help me with this transmission!"

He took the butt from his mouth and dropped it on the floor. He pulled another smoke from a crumpled pack of Luckies in his chest pocket and lit up. Tal crushed the smoldering butt with his foot.

"Sorry. I had to work. I want you to meet someone. This is Gemima Renner. Gemi, Clyde Jinx."

Sparky stopped wiping his hands to offer Gemi a hand shake. "Please to meet ya." Then held out his pack. "Want a smoke?"

"No, thanks."

Sparky motioned towards the small office. "Let's go sit a spell."

Gemi showed her black, grease smudged hand to Tal. "It wasn't a very clean rag," she whispered.

Tal grabbed a paper towel from a roll by the door and handed it to her. The office wasn't much cleaner than the work area. Sparky's desk was piled high with bills, letters and work orders. The bureau behind the desk was stacked with parts books. Gemi hesitated sitting down on the dirty chair she was offered. Tal could see her unease so he sat down and motioned for her to sit on his lap.

"So tell me, Tally-Boy, where did you find this honey and what happened to Gracie?"

Gemi looked at Tal. "Who's Gracie?"

"Why, he didn't tell you? She's the mother of his children."

"Children? Tal, he's kidding, right?"

Sparky kept it up. "Nope. Ain't kidding. They're identical twins, a boy and a girl. Right, Tally-Boy? You ought to see them! The girl is as ugly as her mother."

Tal was getting impatient with the joke. "Stop it, Pop." Turning to Gemi, he pulled her close. "There is no Gracie . . . , and no twins. By the way, Sparky, how could a boy and a girl be identical twins?"

Sparky laughed then took a drag of his smoke. "Okay, you got me. Had you going for a minute, didn't I Girl?"

Gemi forced a smile. "I can see where Tal gets his sense of humor."

"Pop, Gemi and I are going steady. She's the one who stole my heart."

"I can see why. Girl, you got gorgeous eyes.

Gemi blushed. "That's what your son tells me."

She began to cough. Tal could tell the smoke was making her uncomfortable. Her discomfort put him on edge so he thought of an excuse for them to leave.

"Listen, Pop, we got some stuff to do and you need to get back to work. I just wanted you to know who I was with when I wasn't coming home."

They stood up.

"Okay, son. Why don't you take her to meet your mother?"

Tal helped Gemi pick her way towards the door. She watched her step carefully, still afraid of losing a shoe.

"Maybe I will, Pop. Have fun with that transmission . . . and don't blow yourself up."

They stepped into the sunny afternoon. Gemi took a deep breath of fresh air, glad to be out of the smoky, smelly garage.

As they walked back to the car Gemi squeezed his arm. "Tally-Boy? That's cute."

At first Tal didn't like her using that name. It was his mother's pet name for him when he was very young. It was a little boy's name. He figured he had out grown it by this time. She said it so sweetly, though, he decided to let it go. After a time, he grew to like the way she said it. "I'm sorry Gemi. Now you see why I was putting you off. He's a good guy. He just marches to the beat of a different drum."

"Yeah, in a different universe."

Tal didn't want to show her the house. He just wanted to go. His house was a cold, lonely, empty place. Her house was a home, a warm refuge, a place where he could find some semblance of a family he no longer had.

"C'mon, I'll take you to meet Katy, then we can go have some lunch."

Tal drove a few miles away from town then turned into a lonely, overgrown cemetery. Pulling around to the back, he parked under an old live oak. He led Gemi several feet up a gentle rise. At the top he stopped and pointed down at the tombstone.

"Mom, this is Gemima Brianna Renner. Gemi, this is my Mom, Katy."

Gemi held his hand with one hand, his arm with the other. They stood together for the longest time, neither one of them saying anything. Then Gemi read the inscription slowly, reverently, out loud.

"Katy Jean Linnitar Jinx. Born August 1, 1904. Died October 30, 1956. 'May the angels carry her to heaven.' Tal, that's beautiful. Did you write that?"

She looked up and saw Tal's eyes glistening. Gemi held his arm tighter and put her head on his shoulder. He waited several minutes to speak as he choked back tears. He chose not to answer her question. To him, it didn't matter who wrote it. It was a prayer he held in his heart. "I wish you could have known her. She was the opposite of Sparky . . . tender and kind, never crude."

Then he said nothing more. They just stood there, looking down at the stone, listening to the wind in the ancient live oak. Her understanding of why it was so hard for him to say, 'I love you' was becoming clearer.

Finally, he became aware of her shivering. He put his arm around her and pulled her close. "This wind's got a hard edge on it. Let's go."

He pulled out on the highway and headed for town. Gemi slide over and wrapped both arms around his arm. There was no acknowledgement of her gesture. He kept both hands on the wheel, looking straight ahead. Gemi looked at his face and squeezed his arm, trying to get his attention. His face revealed a new side of him. The town clown, the crazy goof-ball who liked to play tricks on her, looked cold, distant, and stoic, like nothing or no one could ever touch him, ever hurt him again. Yet, at the same time, she saw pain in the eyes of a little boy who wanted, needed a family. Finally, Gemi asked the question.

"How'd she die?" She spoke softly, gently, caringly.

He silently stared straight ahead. She began to think he didn't hear her. Just as she was about to repeat the question, he spoke.

"Don't know. Sparky said it was her heart. I don't know. Sometimes I wished I did. Try not think about it much. Don't matter. She's gone. I need get over it, need to move on."

His tone was terse, the words clipped. It had the tone of someone who was trying to perfect the art of stoicism. She wasn't sure if he was trying to convince her . . . or himself. She wondered, too, if he really didn't know or if he didn't want to know. She knew by his tone of voice, though, that the 'why' couldn't take away the pain of the reality of her passing.

"Do you think about her?"

"Everyday."

She wanted to ask more. Fear of stirring up more pain cause her to leave it be.

"Thanks for taking me."

Their song came on the radio, the song they danced to at Homecoming. Gemi reached to turn up the volume.

As they listened, Gemi could feel the tenseness drain from his body. He looked into her eyes, smiled, then looked back to the road ahead. She saw the Tal she knew reemerging. He put his arm around her and she snuggled into his side, softly repeating the words to the song. This was the most vulnerable he had made himself to anyone since his mother's death. Listening to her sing their song made him feel safe, at peace. He could feel his love for her deepen more and more.

When the song was over Gemi said, "Let's get something to eat. After dark we can go back to my house and park behind the barn. Maybe we can talk about us."

Ah, yes, the barn. "Great idea. Wished I'd thought of it."

The ease of his voice told Gemi the difficulties of the afternoon were going away. At that moment, all she wanted was to spend time with the boy she loved. She wanted to love away the hurt and loneliness he felt as he stood at his mother's grave.

All he wanted was to be in her presence, to feel her warmth and smell the sweetness of her being. In that place, there was no loneliness.

"One more thing, My-Gem, where did you learn to wear jeans the way you do?"

She gave him a puzzled look. "What do you mean?"

He chuckled. "Oh, nothing. Never mind."

He thought she looked cute when she looked puzzled so, at least for now, he would leave her in her puzzlement.

* * *

Tallet Jinx suddenly became aware of the sound of rain on the roof. Rain was always a welcome sound in the Texas Panhandle. Puzzlement. Don't that describe what was happening. Lost in his own puzzlement, he wondered out loud. "What on earth is going on?" He sat up and rubbed his chest, scratched his head. He felt groggy, heavy headed, and he didn't like it. "Maybe a shower will make me feel better," he thought. He rose from his bed to head for the bathroom. At the door he had to pause and lean on the wall as a wave of dizziness swept over him. He showered, shaved, put on clean, fresh clothes and combed his hair. He looked at himself in the mirror. "I sure don't feel better. At least I look better . . . . I think . . . , I hope." He decided to invest this little burst of energy in a trip to the kitchen for supper.

His sister turned to greet him as he shuffled through the door. "Hey, Bro, good to see you up!"

"Got any fresh coffee? What day is it?"

"You bet. Grab a chair. I'll get you some. It's Sunday."

"Sunday? I seemed to have lost track of time and that ain't like me. I sure wish I knew what was going on with me."

Bekka kept her suspicions to herself. She wanted him to talk. "I don't know either. You feeling okay?" She knew the answer. She hoped that getting him to answer on his own terms would help her understand more clearly, what else was ailing him.

He took a drink from his cup then looked down. "It's a puzzlement, Sis. I don't get it. I feel like I've been kicked by a mule. I feel weak, like I can't get my breath. If I stand to quick, I'm dizzy. In the past month I feel twenty years older. On top of that, I can't get this girl out of my mind. Why should

I be missin' a girl I haven't seen or talked to in so many years. I feel out of control an' I don't like it."

Bekka smiled to herself. She knew quite well how much he liked to be in control. This was new territory for him and he was not used to it. She demurred, wanting her brother to tell her more. And she knew what girl. "Who do you mean?"

He leaned back and stretched. He paused to choose his words carefully. "You remember when you brought me that Valentine card?"

"Yeah."

"Well, that name, Gemima, is someone who meant a lot to me once . . . a long time ago."

"Tell me more."

Tal took a drink of coffee, stalling for time. He found himself in a familiar spot. He wished her memory would go away yet he wished he could remember more. He didn't want to talk about her. At the same time, he wanted his sister to know everything about this girl and what she meant to him. He set the cup down and smiled a slight, sad smile. "She was someone I thought I loved a long time ago. Maybe I did love her or maybe it was just me and her, two kids who didn't know a thing about love and we couldn't keep it . . ." His voice trailed off. He put his cup to his lips for a drink then bowed his head.

Bekka saw his shoulders sag with pain and loneliness. She walked over and put her hand on his shoulder. "Keep what?"

Her question was met with a long silence. She let the silence hang in the air, giving her brother time to think. She wanted him to answer on his own terms.

"Oh, I don't know." He put his cup down, his voice tinged with hurt, or frustration, or maybe both. He shrugged to push her hand away. "What do a couple of teenagers know about love?!" Feeling a little too vulnerable he tried to change the subject. "What's for supper?"

"I'll make you some soup. Would you like that?"

"I suppose that would be good."

"Tal, I think I know what's going on with your body. I'm not sure what is going on in your head. I do know one thing. You need to talk about it to someone, if not me. It ain't going away by itself."

He knew, deep down inside she was right. He wasn't ready to admit it. "So what's wrong with my body?"

"We will find out tomorrow when we go see Doc Fagin. I think something is going on with your heart, and I don't mean Gemima."

He ate the soup she fixed, went to the fridge for some beer and headed back to his bedroom.

"You shouldn't be drinkin', Tallet Jinx!"

"Ah, shut up!"

He hated it when she called him by his full name. She sounded too motherly. Yet deep down inside he appreciated the fact that she had his best interest at heart. Besides, she was right. The alcohol didn't seem to help the pain in his heart. Maybe it would help him forget about Gemima. It hadn't worked yet . . . , left him with a headache, too. He did like the temporary numbness it provided.

"What time is my appointment?"

"Ten."

"I'll see you at 9:50."

He went to his recliner and flipped on the television, looking for something, anything besides the beer, to occupy his mind. He drank the first can quickly, to hurry the numbness. The second, slower, to make it last.

He found a program about the universe. "Great", he thought, "something innocuous to keep my mind occupied. I don't want to think of her."

It wasn't to be. The narrator began talking about meteor showers, and his memory went back, back to Gemi and the 'drive-in movie' that so astounded her. It was something a city girl had never seen. It was Thanksgiving, 1961.

VIII

Stardust Fell on November

Tal picked up the phone on the first ring. It was who he hoped it would be.

"Hey, Tally-Boy. Mom and G.B. want you to come for Thanksgiving."

"I can't, Gemi, I'm busy."

Gemi was surprised at his answer but then remembered, this is the town clown. And she was learning how to fight back. "Doing what, helping Sparky clean up that hazardous, nuclear waste dump you call a garage? People who fly over it think they see a glow."

"Wow, you're good! Guessed it. On the first try."

"Lucky guess. So are you coming or not?" Gemi feigned impatience. She wanted him to be with her for the holiday, more sooner than later.

"Okay. There's one condition . . . , only if I can take you to a special spot after supper."

"Will we be alone?"

"Just you, me and the stars."

"Deal, Cowboy, we eat at three. Don't be late or you'll end up with cold potatoes with a wish bone. And you can bring Sparky if you want."

It is not that Tal wouldn't bring his Father. If there were no other choice, he would. He was glad he didn't have to face that prospect. "Can't bring Sparky. He's on the road all week."

"Then come for lunch, stay for dinner." Secretly, she was glad Sparky was not available. She only invited him to be polite. She loved Tal but didn't think much of his father.

"I'll be there, My-Gem."

Thanksgiving morning came and Tallet tried to sleep in. The excitement of the day's promise's wouldn't let him. He showered, shaved, donned his cowboy casuals; pearl snap shirt and new denims. As he was leaving, he paused in the living room to listen. Nothing. Since Katy died, with Bekka and Sparky gone, all that was left was a vast, lonely nothing. Gemima took away the loneliness and filled his nothing. He couldn't wait to get into her arms. He stopped in the door way to look back into the dusty, dreary room that was no longer his prison. He had a place to go and he needed to get there. He locked the door and was gone.

The day was bright and cold. A north wind made it feel more like late December than Thanksgiving. The fall colors were beginning to fade and the winds of late autumn were doing their job, stripping the leaves off the trees. He liked to watch the wind swirl the leaves back and forth across the road as if they were playing 'tag'.

He dug in his jeans to see what kind of cash he had. "Just enough," he thought. The sign on the grocery store said 'Open 'til noon'. He went into the bakery section and found two pumpkin pies. "I'll lie to her and tell her I made them all by myself, alone, with no help from anyone," he thought to himself. "I know she won't believe me. I'll try to make my best case."

Gemima listened for the sound of Tal's car as she and Mom prepared the 'roast beast for the Thanksgiving feast'. Her heart leapt in her chest when she heard him in the driveway. She looked at the clock. It wasn't even noon yet. It made no matter to her. He was here and that's all that mattered. Gemima hurried to the door. She didn't want Tal to ring the bell and disturb G.B. He might grump about Tal coming four hours early for dinner.

Gemima opened the door just as Tal stepped onto the porch. "Hey, Tally-Boy, get in here out of the wind." She looked around to see if Mom was watching. Seeing no one, she gave Tal a long soft kiss, pressing him against the wall with the fullness of her body. Then she whispered in his ear, "Is this what you came for?"

Tal whispered, "Yeah, and some food. More of this first." He kissed her, slipping his hand under her shirt and caressing her bare back, holding her close. "On second thought, skip the food, this is enough for me."

Then Gemi heard Mom call from the kitchen door. She pulled Tal's hand from under her shirt and took a step away just before her Mother appeared.

"Tal, is that you, dear?"

"Yep, and I brought some pies." He went back to the car to retrieve the bag he forgot when he saw his girl. "Made them myself."

Any chance of impressing Gemi was dashed when Mom recognized the grocery store packaging. "Thank you, son. I'm sure you worked very hard picking them out."

The three of them laughed as they went to the kitchen. The sights, sounds and smells of a Thanksgiving dinner in preparation was something he had not experienced in a long time. He would have been content sit in the corner and watch. That was not to be. Mom and Gemi put him to work peeling potatoes and cutting up some of the ingredients needed for other dishes.

In the back of his mind, Tal already had the evening planned out. He was going to take Gemima to a drive-in movie, one she had never seen before. Tal thoroughly enjoyed the day. G.B. was his usual blustery self. Tal had gotten used to it so it didn't bother him much. Still, Gemi found her father's occasionally overbearing mindset a bit embarrassing.

After dinner, Tal excused himself. "I have to leave for a few minutes."

Mom insisted he stay. "You haven't had any of the pie you worked so hard to pick out."

"I gotta run home. I'll be right back. Promise."

Tallet rushed out the door, leaving everyone wondering about his abrupt departure. Tal had a plan. He needed to make preparations for the night. Half hour later, Gemi heard a roar in her drive way. She went to the door and saw Tal getting out of a beat up old pick-up.

"What on earth . . . ?", Gemi said with a sense of disbelief.

"After some pie, we are going to a drive-in movie."

"What are you, nuts? It's all ready freezing and the drive-in is closed."

"Au contraire, my dear Gem. This drive-in is open year around and it is the best movie you've ever seen."

The pie was cut and eaten. After what Tal thought was a respectful period of time, he asked Gemi's parents if he and Gemi could take a ride. He promised he wouldn't keep her out late, hoping that would swing the deal.

Permission granted.

With that, they were out the door. Tallet helped his girl into the old pick-up. It was past dusk when Tal turned west out of the drive. The faint orange remnant of the sun tapered off on either side to red, blue, then a deep purple. The sliver of the waning moon and the evening star hung just above the horizon.

"Ain't it beautiful," Tal exclaimed.

Gemima was impressed. Still, she wondered. "Where are we going?"

"It's a surprise . . . just for you . . . just for being so nice to me."

He put his arm around her and pulled her close. She was glad because either the heater wasn't working very well or there was a hole in the fire wall. Her feet were chilled from a cold draft on the floor. She curled up and nestled into his side, mostly out of love, partly to keep warm.

Tal drove west, then north out of town. They were out of sight of the city lights when he pulled off the highway and eased the truck up a rutted road. He had to stop three times to open and close cattle gates before going up a gentle rise. At the crest, he stopped and backed the truck around so the tail gate was angled down, facing southwest. By this time only the faintest rays of the quarter moon were visible across the hill tops to the west. And it was getting very, very dark. Tal reached into the glove box for a new stocking cap. He put it over Gemi's head and pulled it down over her face.

Gemi protested and lifted the hat up. "What are you doing?!"

"I'm getting ready for the show. Trust me. You'll love it."

He pulled the hat back down. She sat there in the dark, listening to snipping, swishing, thumping and bumping in the back of the truck. She jumped when Tal opened the driver's door.

"You better not be pulling another one of your famous tricks!"

He reached across the seat, lifted her hat just enough to reveal her lips, kiss her quickly then pulled the hat back down. "Can't. Promised you, no tricks, remember. Besides, if I did, you said you would kill me. Granted, this is a good place to hide a body. You don't know the way back. You'd get hopelessly lost. After a painstaking search, they would find both of our carcasses, or at least what the buzzards didn't get. The evidence of your strangling me would reveal your evil deed and both our reputations would be ruined. Then G.B. would kill me again. Be patient. Please? It'll be worth it! Promise!"

Gemi sighed and sat back. He was right about her killing him. She just wasn't sure if strangulation would be the most humane way to do it.

After a few minutes, Tal opened her door. "Take off your coat and blouse."

Gemi lifted her hat to see Tal standing there in the cold, naked from the waist up. "Now I know you've lost it. I don't have to kill you. Pneumonia will get you first."

"No, c'mon. The show is about to start. Take off your coat and sweater."

"No! All I got on is a tee shirt and it's freezing!"

Tal dug around for the thermometer he had put in the bed of the truck. "See? Look. It's not freezing. It's thirty-four degrees." Tal began to shiver in the cold. Deepening his voice to exude authority Tal said, "I'm going to stand here and shake until you obey."

Gemi rolled her eyes as she unbuttoned her blouse, knowing it was useless to resist.

"Take off your shoes, too. Keep your hat on. Don't want your ears to get frostbit."

Tal picked her up and carried her to the back of the truck. The glare of a flashlight revealed what all that thumping and bumping was about. She hadn't noticed the bales of hay in the back when she got in at her house. The noise she heard was Tal making a bed of hay, covered by quilts and a thick comforter. He stood her up on the tail gate while he got in. He lifted the top blanket and laid down, his back against a bale of hay. Then he motioned to Gemi. "C'mon, lay down between my legs and lean back. The show is about to start."

Too cold to do anything else, she followed his instructions. As she slide down, the tail of her shirt crept up. She leaned back then jumped. "Yeeow, Tal!!"

"What?"

"Your belt buckle! It's like ice!"

He grinned sheepishly. His large, Lone Star brass belt buckle had touched the small of her back. "Sorry."

He pulled his belt off so Gemi could snuggled in. Tal pulled the comforter over them and tucked it in down their sides, then he switched off the flash light. Gemi was stunned by what she saw. Nothing. Just an all consuming, inky blackness. She pulled the comforter up around her ears, more from fear than from the cold. He could sense her fear of the night as it consumed them. He waited until his hands had warmed against his body. He didn't want a repeat of the belt buckle incident. Then he slid his hands under her t-shirt to feel the warm, soft skin of her middle. She welcomed his touch by putting her hands on top of his. He pulled her close and whispered in her ear. "It's okay, My-Gem, you are safe with me. Just relax and watch the show."

In no time, they were both warm and cozy. It took several minutes for their eyes to adjust to the intense dark.

"Gemi, look up and tell me what you see."

She looked at the heavens and gasped. "It's beautiful! I've never seen so many stars! Look, is that the Milky Way?"

He was amused by her enthusiasm. He knew well the excitement and beauty of the stars. That's why he had brought her to one of his favorite places.

"Why did we have to come all the way out here? We're in the middle of nowhere."

"We're not in the middle of nowhere but you can see nowhere from the top of the next hill."

Gemi laughed because she knew it could very well be true.

"We had to come out here." Tal pointed to his left. "You see that faint glow just above the hills? That's Kayne City to our east about thirty miles. We had to come out here to get away from the lights of the city. They obscure the stars. The real show, though, is not the stars." Tal pointed towards the southwestern sky. "Watch out there. I've all ready seen two."

Just as Gemi looked up, she saw a white light streak across the sky. "Wow, what was that?"

"That is the main feature of our drive-in movie. Tonight there is a meteor shower named after you. That's why I was so excited at your house. I wanted to stay with your parents. I wanted you to see this more."

"What's it called?"

"We are watching the Geminid meteor shower. It is called that because astronomers believe it originates in the Gemini constellation."

Gemi protested. "I'm Gemima, not Gemini."

Tal paused with a deep sigh for the purpose of drama. Then, with great indignation, he said, "Okay, I'll send the National Astronomical Society a nasty-gram for misspelling your name."

As usual, Gemi wasn't sure if she should believe him or not. "Are you serious?"

"I am about the meteor shower. I read about it in a book. It happens about this time every year."

Gemi leaned her head against his chest and watched the show. They were seeing as many as two meteors a minute. Then the big one. An orange ball streaked across the sky for what looked like a thousand miles. It was so bright that, at least for a few seconds, it light up the night. It seemed so close that Gemi was sure she would hear a loud boom. To her surprise, all she heard was the silence of the cold, prairie night.

"How did you ever find this place?"

"The spread is owned by a rancher that Dusty worked for last summer. Dusty brought me out here because he knew how much I loved the dark. We've been here almost a half hour and you still can't see much of the land. Just the stars. Me and him would wait for the new moon then ride out here on horseback to take in all this dark, all this silence."

Gemi thought this to be a curious statement. "Why do you like the dark? Most people are afraid of the dark. I'm afraid of the dark."

"No, you're not. You're afraid of what's in the dark. You are afraid you might get hurt by something or someone hidden in the dark. In the dark, especially out here, I see the vastness of the universe and my troubles shrink by comparison. I don't feel so lonesome."

Gemi moved his hands around on her middle. She loved the feel of his hands on her skin. She pondered her next question carefully. She wasn't sure how, or even if, it would be answered. "Are you lonesome a lot?"

"More than I'd like to admit." His answer surprised her. It wasn't the least bit guarded. His responses no longer seemed guarded, and she was glad.

"Why?"

Tal paused to find the right words. Vulnerability was no longer a threat to him. He hadn't told anyone else as much about himself, as he did her, since his mother died. He trusted her. This was his Gem. He wanted to show her his love. He would tell her anything she wanted to know.

"I guess it's for the same reason I like it at your house. Since Katy died, nothin's been the same. My sister's in Amarillo, Sparky's gone all week and that little old house where I live gets too empty too much of the time."

"I thought you liked being on your own."

"I do. Being on my own and being alone, though, are two different things. You got my heart. Being on my own means that when I'm not working, I can spend my time with you. With you, I'm not lonely, even when we are alone."

Just then Gemi grew tense. She heard something.

"What's that?"

"Yeah, I heard it too. It's probably an armadillo." He remembered Ole Jim. "I mean, a harmless armadillo." Tal did not want Gemi to be afraid in any way. He wanted to protect her, to make her feel as safe with him as he felt with her. "Watch your eyes, I'm going to turn on the light."

They sat up as he switched on the flash light and scanned the scrub brush off to the side of the truck.

"There, see him, under that bush? He's rooting for grub worms. That's their favorite meal." Tal felt around the inside of the truck bed 'til he found a small rock. "Watch this."

Tal took careful aim and threw the rock as hard as he could. It hit the armadillo in the side. It jumped three feet straight up and came down running at full speed. They both laughed.

"That's their self defense mechanism. Their shell don't keep the coyotes from crunching them. It protects them from the thorns and brambles as they run through the brush."

Tal was just about to switch off the flash light when he saw a tiny sparkle in the air. He pointed the light straight up.

"Gemi, look!"

Suddenly the air was filled with what looked like tiny flakes of snow. There was no perceptible wind yet they swirled and danced in the beam of light as if guided by some inaudible music from the stars.

"Wow!!! What's that? Can't be snow. There's no clouds."

"It's star dust, falling from the tails of the meteors. It only falls on lovers. I guess the stars think you love me. Do you love me . . . truly?"

Gemi moved away from him. "C'mon, tell me what it is?"

Tal put his arm around her neck to pull her to himself. When they sat up to see the armadillo, they had disturbed their covers. She resisted.

"Tell me the truth. What it is?"

"Okay, okay. Cuddle up first. Our nest is getting too cold too fast."

Gemi settled back down into their nest and Tal pulled the comforter up around their ears.

"It's hoarfrost. The temperature must have dropped below freezing. When the dew point is below freezing and the temperature drops to the dew point, the dew freezes into tiny flakes in mid air instead of forming on the ground. What you see is tiny flakes of dew. It don't happen very often. When it does, it's really something to remember." Tal switched off the light.

"No, no, leave it on. I want to watch the magic stardust fall on us."

"So you do love me?"

She gave him a long kiss. "Yes, without a doubt."

He switched the light on so they could immerse themselves in the magic of this natural phenomenon. After several minutes it stopped. He switched off the light and Gemi turned to put her head on his shoulder. He pulled her shirt up and put his hand on the soft skin of her middle. She put her hand on his bare chest and they went back to watching the meteor shower. For a long time they didn't say anything. Gemi, at last, at home in the deep darkness, felt safe, content just to be in his presence. Tal wanted the night to last only forever and a day.

Then Gemi spoke. "Tal, do you believe in God?"

The question took him by surprise. No one had ever asked him that question before. "I don't know. Don't think about it much."

Gemi pointed at another meteor and all the stars that filled the sky from horizon to horizon. Then she spoke slowly, choosing her words carefully. "Do you think all this is an accident of happenstance or do you think it was created?"

Tal sighed deeply. "Well, to be honest, sometimes I wonder. I mean, well, we saw a spectacular sunset. I have watched many sunrises and the sunsets. I thought they were too beautiful to be by accident. I've wondered if there was a God someplace who could put on such a show. Still, I'm not sure about God. I am sure of one thing. He doesn't think about me and my little troubles. I tried praying . . . once . . . It didn't come to much."

Gemi was surprised by his answer. The town clown had a thoughtful, philosophical side. There was much more to him than she knew and she wanted to know it all.

"Do you think God brought us together, how we ended up at the same desk in the same class?"

"First God and now fate? What's next, predestination? This is a little bit too much philosophy for a dark night on the prairie."

She wondered if there was a tinge of sarcasm in his voice. Perhaps she had pushed the subject too far too soon but she wasn't willing to give it up yet. "I told you I had seen you around school last year. I didn't know how, when, or even if, I should approach you. When we went to Mass at St. Anne's parish, I remember praying that God would, some how, bring us together so I could at least know you and you could know me. I think God heard my prayer 'cause when you walked into class and sat down next to me, I was thrilled. I was sure my prayer had been answered."

Tal thought about that day. "Dusty made me late. If he hadn't held me back, I would've taken the last chair in the last row."

Gemi smiled. She turned to face him and put her arm around his neck. She pulled herself up. She kissed him and laid her head on his chest. "See, you've made my point. There must be a God. You walked in and there was only one chair left. Next to me. Aren't you glad?"

"Glad about God? Maybe. Glad about you. Absolutely! I suppose it is no surprise to you that I didn't want a girlfriend. I especially didn't want someone like you who would charm my socks off and steal away my heart."

"So you regret coming to art class?"

"I took art class for an easy credit. Finding you was a bonus. The easy credit is for now. You and me, we're forever. Okay, okay, I was wrong not to trust you. I hope I've made it up to you."

"You have, and I love you."

In the darkness Tal could barely see her broad smile of contentment. No matter. He didn't need to. He could feel it in the relaxed warmth of her body. She turned her attention to the heavenly display above their heads.

Tal slipped his hands back under her shirt to feel the warmth of her skin. Gemi laced her fingers into his and held his hands tightly against her. Neither one moved or said a word for a long time. They were soul mates. They were sure their love was as real and as forever as the stars they were gazing at. A coyote howled on the next ridge over. Two months earlier it would have scared Gemi. Now it seemed as though all of nature was singing, approving of their oneness. Tal turned to face her. He kissed her neck, her ear, her mouth. Then pressing his ear against her chest, he sighed and closed his eyes.

"Your heart. I can hear your heartbeat. I love to listen to your heart."

Gemi kissed the top of his head. She was his. He was hers. The stars streaked across the sky, as if to show that their love was celebrated by all of creation. They embraced one another and all seemed right with the world. It was a magical moment. They were alone in the universe and everything was theirs. Wrapped up in the warmth of each other, snug in their bed under the stars, nothing could hurt them. The darkness, the cold. Nothing. Except themselves. And the question of God? Well, that could wait 'til another day.

* * *

Tal heard Joey barking near the patio. Probably a rabbit. He looked at the time. An entire day wasted, lost in old, dusty memories. The movie he had found on the television was over. He had no idea how it had ended. Her memory had become a complete distraction. And he knew exactly how that ended. He looked down beside his chair. He had one beer left. He knew that one more beer would put him out for the night. He didn't want to dream because it might be about her. He knew there would be a price to pay in the morning. For now, it was worth it for a few hours of oblivious unconsciousness. Maybe the doctor could take away the pain in his heart. Only sleep could take away the pain in his soul. He drank the beer and went to bed. Sleep came quickly. A dark, dreamless sleep.

IX

A Wounded Heart and Soul

Tallet Jinx was up and dressed, but didn't want to be, when Bekka knocked at his door.

"C'mon, Tal, we gotta go. Don't wanna be late."

"Don't wanna go," he mumbled as he opened his door.

He stumbled down the hall and out to his truck, trying to keep his balance as waves of dizziness washed over him.

"Here, you drive."

The dizziness told him he was in no shape to drive. He didn't want to endanger himself or Bekka so he tossed the keys to his sister. She was surprised. He never let anyone drive his beloved old truck. As they got in she had to ask the question. "Why am I allowed this honor?"

He chose not to tell her the truth. "Don't wanna open my eyes. Don't wanna be awake." Tal reached for the door handle to get out. "Think I'll go back to bed."

Bekka hit the gas. "Oh no, we're going to see the doctor."

Doc Fagin's waiting room was empty when they arrived. Bekka checked in as Tal sat down to browse through the well read, well worn, magazines that are ubiquitous to any doctor's office.

Doc Fagin was an interesting man. Short and pudgy, his premature grey made him look older than his mid-forties. Those who didn't know him thought everyone called him Doc because of his profession. Those who did know him knew he would have been called 'Doc', even if he were a truck driver. If he were a little shorter and a little pudgier, he could well have been the identical twin, even down to the spectacles that were precariously perched on his nose, of the dwarf who roomed with Snow White and his six brothers. In spite of his somewhat comical appearance, he was a kind, caring, thorough man who knew his business. He was well respected and trusted in the community.

Tal was shown to an exam room by Doc's nurse. He told Bekka to wait for him. She insisted on going in with him. She knew her brother would try to minimize what was happening to him. Doc Fagin came in just as the nurse was finishing taking Tal's vital signs.

"Hi, Bekka, how are you today?"

"I'm fine, Doc. It's Mister Grumpy Pants here that I'm concerned about."

Tal gave them both a forced, sarcastic smile.

"So what's been going on, Tal?"

"Bekka thinks I'm dying. I'm sure I got a little cold or something. Just heal me and send me home."

"I knew he would say that," Bekka said. "Let me fill in the details. He's had shortness of breath, dizziness, and congestion. Sometimes he's very pale and sweaty. He has little, if any, stamina. The other day he went out to work in the barn. I found him, less than an hour later, on his patio, laid out in his recliner. Sometimes his breathing is labored. The other day I could hear fluid in his lungs. I think something's going on with his heart."

"See, I told you. She thinks I'm all ready dead. Just work your magic so I can get out of here."

Doc smiled at Tal's more than usual cantankerousness.

"Well, before we bring out the chicken bones, amulets and feathers, let's have a look."

Doc gave Tal a thorough examination. He was beginning to think that Bekka's instincts were right. Finally, he sat down and began to speak slowly, with great care.

"We need to run some more tests but I think your sister's right. I think you are in congestive heart failure. Right now, we don't know why. Until we do, you need to take it easy. We don't want to trigger a heart attack. I'll have my nurse call the hospital and arrange the necessary tests. In the meantime, I'm going to prescribe medications to help relieve the burden on your heart. No salt and no alcohol. It will only make the symptoms worse."

Tal could not believe his ears. Heart failure? Heart attack? Who are they kidding? Worse, now his sister will really be watching him. Burden on his heart? He thought of Gemi and the walk down memory lane that had been consuming a big part of his life. Maybe that was it. Maybe her memory was at the root of his problem. At least he hoped so. That would be the simple answer. No salt and no alcohol? That's a fate worse than death! Tal asked Bekka to leave the room. She was willing to leave Tal alone with the good doctor because her fears had been made known.

"I have a question. Suppose loneliness or hurt, or . . . something like that, kept me preoccupied. Could that be a cause?"

Doc looked over his glasses at his friend. He suspected that there was much more to the story than Tal was admitting. Well aware of the effects of the mind on the body, his instincts told him to press the issue. "I think you are trying to tell me something. Would you like to tell me more?"

Tal's immediate, inner response was 'no'. He didn't want to admit to anyone that he was grieving the loss of someone he hadn't seen or talked to in almost forty years. The whole scenario he had been living through bordered on the absurd. Yet, the feelings were real. And he knew he needed to talk about it with someone. At least, he was sure Doc wouldn't laugh at him, or worse, spread it around town. He told Doc what he had been experiencing everyday, all day, and sometimes in his sleep. He explained how the memory of Gemima Renner had come to dominate his life. He told Doc about his desire to self medicate with beer and Jim Beam because he didn't want to dream about this girl. And when he spoke of her eyes, those blue eyes haunting his soul, he had to fight back tears.

Doc stood up and put his hand on Tal's shoulder. "How long has this been going on?"

"It seems like my whole life, but really, since the end of September."

Doc gently patted Tal's shoulder. "Well, old buddy, I think the woundedness you are feeling in your soul is real. It will affect your heart. However, it will only make worse what is already there. This much we do know. You are in congestive heart failure. We need to find out why. Maybe then we can find a cure that can give back to you some sense of control in your life." Doc laughed and patted Tal again. "Until then, you need to listen to me and Bekka. I don't want to lose you. It wouldn't look good on my resume`. Have Bekka take you home and put you to bed. We'll get you through this. If I could make a suggestion, please? I can help heal your body, but not your soul. Maybe you should think about talking to a priest."

"Thanks for letting me bend you ear. I will take your advice about my body. The priest . . . well, I'm not so sure. I'll think about it."

Tal shook his friend's hand and went to the waiting room. Before they could leave, Doc called Bekka into his office.

"Bekka, I will get right to the point. I didn't want to scare your brother but I think he is in serious trouble. The tests will confirm what I think. I believe his heart is failing. Keep a close watch on him and don't let him do anything that is physically stressing. Do you know about the memories he's been having about this girl he knew in high school?"

"He's mentioned it a few times in passing. He insists it isn't much. I don't know anymore than that. You know how good he is at hiding his emotions."

"He told me that the memories were preoccupying his mind. As he spoke of her, I saw him fighting back tears. Something is going on and it needs to be tended to. I told him I could help with his body. Someone else would need to see to the pain in his soul. All this emotion he has been experiencing did not cause his heart problems. They will, though, make his physical problems worse. I suggested he talk to a priest."

Bekka laughed out loud. Tal? Talk to a priest? He didn't think he needed God. Why would he need a priest? "I'll push the suggestion."

"Good. In the mean time, I would suggest that some prayer for your brother would be appropriate. I'll be in touch."

Bekka took Tal home. She fixed him some lunch and then ordered him to bed. Had he felt better, he would have put up more of a resistance to the idea.

Well aware of doctor's orders, and not wanting to cross his sister, Tal waited until she stepped out of the kitchen. He went to the cupboard above the sink. Reaching towards the back, he found the fifth of Jim Beam he had been keeping there. As he shuffled off to his room he called back to his sister. "If I can't have any beer, can I at least have some lemon-lime soda . . . , on ice?"

Not suspecting a thing, Bekka brought him the other ingredient for a seven & seven. Soon the whiskey buzz had him floating on a cloud of relative painlessness. He tried to find distraction in his collection of western novels, or a movie, or looking out the window, or Joey, or a football game on television or, or . . . Nothing worked. He laid on his bed wondering what to do to pass the time. He got up and went to the patio door to look out at his beloved prairie, wishing he could get out on it. "Don't have to worry 'bout my heart. Boredom will kill me first," he muttered to himself.

He settled on an old western on television. Late in the day Bekka knocked on his door.

"Need anything?"

"Yeah, bring me the spaghetti strainer."

She stuck her head in the door. "Why do you want that?"

"I want to count the holes."

A look of complete puzzlement came over her face. "What on earth for?"

Tal was amused by her puzzlement. "Never mind. When's supper?"

She scratched her head and shrugged. "I'm making it now. I'll bring it shortly."

Tal ate his supper, watched another western, had another drink and went to bed. It didn't take long for sleep to come. His last thought before dropping off was, "I didn't think doin' nothing can be so exhausting."

X

Dusty's Concern

Tal awoke early, jolted out of his slumber by a coughing fit. The congestion in his lungs made breathing difficult. Bekka must of heard him because she knocked at his door.

"You okay?"

He didn't answer. She opened the door a crack and saw Tal sitting on the edge of the bed, with his face in his hands.

"Tal! Are you okay? I heard you cough and . . .

He stopped her in mid-sentence. Without lifting his head he snapped at her. "I'm fine. Go away." His brusqueness revealed how irritated he was by her presence.

"You're not fine. All I'm trying to do is help you. I'm not trying to make life difficult. I'm worried about you. I know Dusty would be worried too. Have you told him yet?"

"No, I haven't told him yet!"

Now Bekka was getting irritated. She paused to take a breath and gather her thoughts. She didn't want to start an argument by responding in kind. "Tal, I am not your enemy in this thing. I'm your . . ."

He stopped her in mid-sentence again. He lifted his head and motioned to her. "C'mere. Sit beside me."

She sat down next to him on the bed. He put his arm around her, his head on her shoulder. Choking back tears, he spoke slowly. "I know, Sis, I know. But I'm afraid. What's going to happen to me?"

She embrace him and held his hand. She sighed deeply and spoke slowly. "I don't know, yet. Just believe me when I say I'm here for you. I'm with you every step of the way. Okay?"

With his head still on her shoulder he nodded. "I'm sorry. And I appreciate your concern. I'll tell Dusty when we know something for sure."

"Thanks, Bro. I appreciate your trusting me. I am concerned and I want to help you get better. Try to rest. I'll check on you later."

She hugged him for a moment then rose to leave. Before closing the door, she flash him a smile and a 'thumbs up'.

"Dusty's concern? He had cause to be," he thought. "Guess I should've listened to him." He locked the door and got back in bed. Sleep wouldn't come. Even a few shots of whiskey didn't help. The memory of his friend's concern came rushing back.

* * *

It was almost dark when Tal pulled his into his drive. Mr. Corley had him close and lock the store. It meant sweeping and dusting. Tal didn't like that part of the job. It meant getting home late to call his girl. He missed the sound of Gemima's voice. As he turned towards the garage, his headlights fell on his friend's car. Dusty was missing his best friend and he figured the only way to see his buddy was to come and find him.

"Hey, Dusty, how the heck are ya?"

Dusty got out of his car, carrying a sack. "I wondered if you cared anymore. Haven't seen much of you since you fell in love."

Tal detected an edged of sarcasm in his friends voice. "Sorry I've been neglecting you lately. Let's face it. She's prettier than you . . . smells better too." Tal pointed. "What's in the sack?"

Dusty laughed. He reached in, pulled out a can. "Thought I would come over and have a beer with my best friend who ignores me."

"Cool! Where'd you get it? Ever since the sheriff shut down the road house, it's been hard to find."

"I went out to the truck stop, south of town. Found a driver who was willing to buy me a case if I gave him money for two."

Tal smiled. "I've always said necessity is the mother of invention. Let's go in and enjoy the fruits of your invention." Tal popped the top and took a long drink as they walked into the house. "Have a seat, pal, I'll be with you in a sec. I need to do something real quick."

Tal went to the kitchen phone and dialed her number. She answered on the second ring. "Hey, My-Gem, you miss me? . . . Yeah, I miss you too . . . yeah, I know . . . I'm sorry. I know its late. I had to close tonight and . . ." Tal's voice became muffled as the kitchen door closed.

Dusty sat on the couch watching the clock on the mantel, wondering how long he would have to wait. Five minutes, ten minutes. He finished his second beer and opened the third. Twenty minutes was enough. He went to the kitchen door and opened it. "Hey. You. Remember me? I came to see my friend. If you are too busy, I can come back."

"Gotta go, My-Gem. Yeah, Dusty's here. I'll see you tomorrow. Love you too. Bye." Tal took the last drink of his beer and tossed the can in the trash. "Sorry, pal, I guess I get carried away sometimes."

"That's why I'm here. I'm worried about you. We haven't gone out harassing girls for weeks now. Remember what fun that was? Seems as though you don't have time for me anymore."

"Oh, stop whining! We went to the Homecoming dance, didn't we!"

Dusty tossed Tal a refill. "It's more than that. I'm worried about you. You seem lost in this girl. Remember, no senior year romances? Remember, you don't want to get your heart broke again?"

Tal took a long drink. "Yeah, I know. Gemi's different. I feel like I can trust her."

"Maybe so. I've seen the way she looks at you. There's love in those baby blues, love that can break a heart."

Down deep, Tal smiled. Dusty had just confirmed what he thought. Someone else had seen what he had seen, the glow of love, love for him by another person. It only made Tal love her and trust her more.

"Listen, I know I've been neglecting you. We've been friends since, well, a long time. Now, we are growing up. I gotta do what I think is right, for me. We can still be friends, can't we."

"I guess. What about after graduation? She still has two years of school left. You hate school. All that's left is the military. You'll get drafted and leave town. She'll forget about you. She'll find someone else and still break your heart."

"Oh, I don't know. I thought maybe I'd ask her to marry me after she graduates. That way she can wait for me. We'll be all right."

Dusty gasped. "Marriage! You? Are you crazy?! I don't believe it! We go from 'no romantic entanglements' to 'marriage'? What on earth is wrong with your brain? Does Sparky know what you're thinking? Come on, Tal! I don't believe you!" Dusty put his hand on Tal's shoulder. "I'm telling ya, you need to slow down. She could break your heart . . . just like all the rest."

Dusty's vehemence was surprising to him. Tal would not let it deter him. He had been making his own decisions long enough. He believed he was ready to make this one. He offered Dusty a handshake. "Trust me, I know what I'm doing. Besides, by spring, I won't need Sparky's permission for anything. I'm on my own in reality now. In the spring, I'll be on my own legally. C'mon. Be happy for me. Somebody loves me for who I am. I know I got my heart broke before and I was glad you were there for me. Gemi is different. She's not like all the rest." Tal thought about that cold night in the back of his pick-up as the stars fell around them. He remembered the warmth of her body and the touch of her hands on his. He remembered the sound of her heartbeat. "She has given me something that none of those other girls ever did. I can see it in her eyes. We're soul mates."

Dusty went to his sack and pulled out two more beers and handed one to Tal. They popped the tops. Dusty held his can up to offer a toast. With a twinge of resignation in his voice, he began.

"Here's to you, my friend. May the wings of love keep you aloft. If they don't, may the parachute of our friendship give you a soft landing. I'll be here to catch you."

"Thanks old buddy, I knew you'd understand."

"I don't understand. I am resigned to your fate. Tomorrow's Friday. Wanna go to the square and have some fun?"

"Can't. Gemi's parents are going out and she wants me to come over and keep her warm. It's gonna be a cool night."

Dusty rolled his eyes. "I give up. Let's finish this beer so I can go home."

Tal went directly to Gemi's house after work. He arrived just in time to say goodbye to Mom and G.B. He and Gemi stood in the doorway and watched them leave. Their supper was leftovers from the night before. Tal went into the living room and sat down on the couch. Gemi laid down and put her head on his lap. They had turned off the television and put the radio on low. Tal pulled her up onto his lap and kissed her. She snuggled down into his arms like it was sanctuary.

"Last week you asked me about God and fate, remember?"

Gemi smiled. "I guess I got you to thinking, huh."

"Well, yes and no. I don't know about fate and I would rather believe it was God, I mean your prayer, that brought us together. Maybe God is real. Anyway, I'm glad you're here and I'm here and we're together."

He picked up her hand to look at his ring. She had wrapped angora yarn around it to make it small enough to fit her delicate finger. He wondered how long that took. He didn't ask. He had something else on his mind. "You know Dusty's mad at you. Says I spend too much time with you and not enough with him."

Gemi smiled, her eyes bright and cheery. "You mean I broke up the town clown duo? Believe me, there are a lot of girls who will rejoice when they hear the news."

Tal laughed and hugged her. He couldn't believe how much at peace he felt with her in his arms. "Dusty did bring up a good point last night. He asked if I'd thought about what we were going to do in the spring, you know, after I graduate."

"That's easy. You can go to the county junior college, so you can be near me."

"You know how much I hate school. If I don't go to school, I'll get drafted. I don't like that idea, either. Even if I do go to school, I still could get drafted. I've always liked the Navy."

Tal saw Gemi's face grow cold, her eyes lose their cheer. "Tally-Boy, I don't like this conversation. I don't like either option. I just want you here, with me. Can we think about it later?"

Tal wrapped both arms around her and kissed her again. "Sure, My—Gem, we got time. All the time in the world."

Gemi got up to make some popcorn and got some sodas from the fridge. She came back to the couch and settled in again. In the middle of snacking, their song from the homecoming dance came on the radio. They put the popcorn aside and laid down on the couch, her head nestled on his shoulder. They said nothing for a long time. Their kiss, their embrace said what was in their heart. All they needed was that song and to be in each others arms. The song said it all. Then Tal broke the silence.

"Do you suppose, well maybe, we could, you know, umm . . ." his voice trailed off.

Gemi had heard this approach before. Tal wanted to ask her something that was hard to put into words. That meant it came from his heart. He didn't stumble around if he didn't mean it and feel it in his heart. She waited in bemused silence as he tried to find the words.

"Well, I mean, maybe we, you and me, that is, ahh, could get married, you know, some day, in the future . . . , later . . . , I mean."

It was a question she had thought about in passing, late at night when she couldn't sleep. She hoped it was a possibility. She never expected it to come so soon. After all, this was the boy who was trying to chase her away just a few months ago. His demeanor was absolutely charming. She stifled a smile and paused to catch her breath. She wanted to leap at the prospect but decided to be coy.

"Sure, Tally-Boy, who did you have in mind? Is she pretty? Am I invited to the wedding? I hope you got a good guy for me, maybe someone rich. I hope they aren't on the same day. I want you to come to mine. You don't even have to bring a gift."

Tal was mystified by her answer. "No, no, I mean to each other."

Gemi laughed out loud. "I know, ya big clown, I was just giving you a taste of your own medicine."

She threw her arms around his neck and kissed him. A long, passionate kiss, the fullness of her body pressing into his was all the answer he needed. When she pulled back from his face, he saw tears of joy on her face.

He kissed her tears away. "I don't think we should say anything to anyone. Your Mom might understand, but G.B.? I don't think so. He'll go off on one of his 'he's too young, you're too young' tirades and never let us be together again."

Gemi knew he was right. He had come to know her father very well in a very short time. "Good idea. It's our secret."

She kissed him again, deeply, warmly, fully. Tal couldn't resist. He slipped his hands under her shirt and caressed her bare skin. There was no hesitation in their embrace. All he wanted was to feel her soft skin, her kiss. All she wanted was the warmth of his hands, his kiss.

Dusty's concern? That was the last thing on his mind.

* * *

Bekka's knock at his door brought him back to the present. Just in time, he thought.

"You okay? Need anything?"

"Well, I am thirsty. How about another soda?"

He went to his bathroom to wash his mouth out so Bekka wouldn't smell the whiskey.

She returned with the drink, on ice. "Tal, can I come in?"

Tal went to the door and unlocked it. "C'mon."

"Why did you lock your door?" Her suspicions were aroused.

Tal brushed off her comment. "Didn't know I did. I can't seem to think straight lately."

She believed him because it was mostly true. "I'm going to Corley's to get your drugs. You okay for now?"

"I'm fine. Go. I promise not to go out and run Paint around the prairie, although I'd like to."

He knew he would be fine as long as he had some whiskey to temper the ache in his soul. The memory was gone . . . for now. Some how, he knew it would be back because it was always there, lurking, waiting for another chance to surface.

The next few weeks were a blur for Tallet. Bekka kept him busy driving him to various health care facilities for all the tests that Doc Fagin had ordered. Tal suffered through machines that thumped, bumped, banged, clanged, hummed and whirred. All of them had too many blinking lights. He was sure some of those lights had to be there for no other reason than to impress the customer. After each session, Tal would ask the technicians what they saw and each time he was told that they didn't know. He would have to ask his doctor. Tal was beginning to think that if they knew what all those blinking lights meant, they had to know what the machine was telling them. Either that or they were glorified button pushers in lab coats. Whatever it was, it irked him that he wasn't getting any answers.

The good news was all this activity left little time to think about her. By the time he got home to his bedroom, he was tired and ready for a shot of whiskey in a cup of soda and a pillow. Bekka was glad to see him drinking lemon-lime soda instead of beer. She did wonder why he drank so much soda. She figured maybe he was thirsty. Tal was content to let her think that. It meant less oversight of his health problems by his well meaning sister. Maybe, whatever it was about Gemima, was past. Maybe her memory was returning to its place, in the deep recesses, in the back corners of his being. He even began feeling better. Bekka assured him that he was not better, it was the medications that were relieving the symptoms. He doubted her. He was fairly sure that the heartache he had been feeling was a result of that stupid Valentine's card. It was that card that brought back all these memories. He decided to help his recovery process. He decided to burn that card. Maybe most of her memory would go up in smoke and the torment would be in the past.

Tal waited 'til Bekka left for the store. He went to the desk and rummaged through the drawer 'til he found the card. He looked at her signature, faded with age. As he looked at it, he felt that pain starting again. He began to doubt he could burn it. He was sure nothing could make her memory die. He glanced down and saw the corner of another card. He put the Valentine card back and pulled the other card from under the miscellaneous stuff.

"Oh my God," he said out loud. He put his hand to his mouth in disbelief. It was a Christmas card. After all these years, why would he still have a Christmas card? From her. To him. He opened the card and read the signature out loud. "To Tally-Boy, my one true love. May this be the first of many Christmases together. Yours always, Gemi. P.S. I don't like you more than ever. Can't wait for spring"

Tal tried to put the card down in the drawer three times, but his fingers would not let it go. A flood of memories swept him away, back to that December, so many years ago. Tal took the card back to his room and set it up on a bookshelf, where he could see it from his recliner. He mixed himself a strong drink, sat down and kicked back the chair. He didn't want to look at the card, yet he couldn't look away. He found himself in what was an increasingly familiar place, torn between wanting to forget the hurt and remembering the love he still felt. It was becoming too much to endure. The difficulties he had been experiencing couldn't be the health problems Bekka had warned him about. He had not heard anymore about the tests that he had suffered through and the pain was nothing more than the burden of her memory. He was sure Bekka was wrong.

Doc Fagin, though? Maybe he was right. In matters of the heart, a priest could help. A priest? He found himself still resistant to the idea. He had always been able to take care of himself. He was always able to simply will himself to 'get over it'. "Yeah," he thought, "that's exactly what I need to do. I'm going to get over it."

He stood up and retrieved the card from the shelf. Unable to destroy it, he quickly took it back to the desk drawer. He came back to his room, mixed himself another drink, this one a little stronger. He found an old John Wayne movie and got it started in his VCR. He sat down in his recliner, took a long drink of forget-it-water and turned up the volume. He decided that he would drown out her memory with video, audio and a drink.

It didn't work.

And the memories flowed.

XI

The Christmas Presents

Tal came out of the drug store to find Gemi waiting for him. He hurried to the car, eager to feel the warmth of her lips, her embrace.

"Hurry up and get this thing started! I'm cold."

Tal started the car then wrapped her in his arms, kissing her gently on the cheek. "Let me warm you up."

Gemi relished the moment. It was a cloudy, cold and windy December day. On a day like this, nothing felt better than his touch.

"What are you doing Christmas? I want to spend as much of it with my Tally-Boy as I can."

Tal was warmed by her sentiment.

"I want to be with you, too. Unfortunately, Sparky wants to go to Amarillo to see Aunt Dori and Bekka Christmas Eve morning. I want to go with him because I miss my sister."

"Will you be back by evening?"

"I hope so. At least, I'm planning on it."

"Good. I want you to do me a favor. Remember our night under the stars? I told you how I prayed at Mass for the chance to meet you? I want you to go to Mass with me. We can pray about our future, together. Will you? Please?"

Tal hesitated. "Go where?"

"Midnight Mass. At St. Anne's church."

Tal had been to church only once in his life, his mother's funeral. He didn't like church. It made him feel uncomfortable, ill at ease. He was used to his independence. He liked getting things done his way. Most churches reminded their people that dependence on God was important. God had let him down too many times. He didn't know where God fit in his life and he was content to leave it at that.

"Oh, I don't think I want to do that. Can't we get together Christmas day?"

Gemi knew what to do. She knew how to bend his will. She kissed him and batted her baby blues. She pulled his head down to her breast so he could hear her heartbeat. "Please, Tal? It sure would mean a great deal to me. I think you will like it. And I bet G.B. will like you for it."

The warmth of her body, the beat of her heart, was too much to resist. He lifted his head and kiss her neck. "Okay, okay. I should be back in town by six. I'll be over by seven. Is that good?"

"Oh, yes. Thankyouthankyouthankyou!" She kissed him all over his face. "Come as soon as you get back to town. We can have supper together. It will be a special night, just wait and see."

Christmas eve day seemed to drag on forever for Gemi. And watching the clock didn't make the time go any faster. She was looking out the window when Tal turned into her drive. Her excitement bubbled over as she ran to meet him at the door. She practically knocked him over as she jumped into his arms.

"Kiss me, Tal! Tell me you love me."

"Shh! Your parents might hear."

"Tonight I don't care who hears me. Remember? We're getting married soon. Come on in. Supper's on the table. You hungry?"

"I could eat!"

Tal gave his seasons greetings to G.B. Mom gave him an extra warm hug. G.B. gave his usual handshake and a gruff 'Merry Christmas'. Tal took his place at the table, next to Gemi. He was beginning to feel like one of the family, something that both Mom and Gemi had hoped for. Mom had a deepening affection for Tal. She saw him as kind and considerate, especially with Gemi. G.B.? Not so much. Deep down he saw Tal as competition for

Daddy's little girl. G.B. didn't like the thought of his only daughter growing up and moving away. Tal was a catalyst for that.

After supper the two excused themselves from the table. Gemi took Tal by the hand and led him back to her bedroom. The only light was the soft glow of the pink shade on her bedside lamp. He stood at the foot of the bed looking at the complete femininity that was her room. Gemi closed the door halfway. She came up behind him and put her hand on his shoulder. As he turned towards her, she threw her arms around him and kissed him, knocking him backwards onto the bed, her on top. He could feel the weight, the warmth of her body on his as she pressed the fullness of herself onto him. Tal slipped his hand under her blouse to feel the soft bareness of her back. Her submissiveness meant love and trust of him. She was eager for the warmth of his hands on her skin. His touch meant safety, sanctuary, security and love.

She lifted her head and without taking her lips off of his whispered, "Welcome home, Tally-Boy."

"What do you mean?"

She smiled and kissed him again. "Don't you want a home? In my bed? With me?"

Her forwardness was both exciting and pleasing making it a thoroughly enjoyable moment. "I'd rather be anywhere with you as long as we're alone."

Tal remained lost in the moment, transfixed by her embrace until a thought flashed through his head . . . . like a lightening bolt.

Alone? They were not alone!

Parents . . . Mom and G.B . . . . In the kitchen. Twenty feet away. The thought made him jump.

"What's the matter, Cowboy? Don't you like me?" She spoke in a coy, innocent tone.

"Your parents!" He tried to roll her off and get up. The momentum left them on the other side of the bed . . . in the same position. He tried to sound assertive which is hard to do when you are whispering. "Your parents! What if they hear us? G.B. will shoot me if he catches us."

"Relax. It's okay. They trust us . . . well, at least Mom does. Besides, I'll protect you." She giggled with delight at his embarrassment. She kissed him again as she wiggled her hips into his.

"No! C'mon, I mean it. Let me up." He pushed her over and sat up on the edge of the bed.

"Scardy cat! You could pretend G.B.'s a poisonous armadillo. You're not afraid of those. Are you?"

She poked him in the ribs. He poked her back and after some minutes of poking, tickling, playful wrestling and giggling, they both wound up on the floor, out of breath.

Gemi stopped the play, sat up and leaned back against the bed. He sat next to her straightening his shirt. She turned away to reach for something she had hidden under the bed.

"Here, Tally-Boy, I have something for you."

It was a beautifully wrapped present with a big red bow. She placed it in his lap and began to straighten her blouse. He looked at the tag. It read 'Merry Christmas, from your Gem. A gift from the heart'. He looked at the box, then at Gemi three times before he could speak. Gemi could see his eyes glisten with thankfulness.

"Gemima, I . . . I . . . don't know what to say."

"Say thank you and open it."

Inside he found a beautiful long sleeve sport shirt. It was his favorite color, blue, like her eyes. It reminded him of the scarf she wore to the homecoming dance. The shirt had a flap of cloth that covered the buttons. It could easily be more dress than casual. This is something he never expected and of a value he could never repay. He held the shirt up as he searched for the right words to say. The last time he had received a present this nice was from his mother. And she had been gone for five years.

"Gemi, why? I can't take this. It costs way too much. And I don't have anything for you."

"I know. I didn't buy it for you because I wanted something in return. I bought it because I thought you would look cute in it and, as the tag says, it's a gift from the heart."

Tal started to take his shirt off. "I'm wearing it to Midnight Mass."

They spent the rest of the evening talking about their feelings for one another. They spoke of hope for their future, their dreams of love, of marriage and of their life together.

It was 11:30pm when Mom came to bedroom door. "Time for Mass, kids. I'm so glad you are going with us, Tal."

The parking lot was almost full when they arrived at the church. Gemi took Tal by the hand as they walked to the entrance. They paused at the door so Gemi could introduce Tal to the pastor.

"Fr. Williker, this is Tallet Jinx."

"Welcome, Mr. Jinx, we're glad you decided to join us tonight. Are you Catholic?"

Tal blushed as he hesitated in embarrassment. He wasn't sure if it was being called 'Mister' or the question about his faith.

Gemima jumped in. "He's my classmate, Father. I asked him to join me tonight."

"Well, I am delighted to meet you. And I'm glad Gemima invited you. Is this your first time in a Catholic church?"

Tal blurted out the first thing that came to mind. "This is my second time in any church."

Now it was Gemima's turn to blush. Fr. Williker put them both at ease.

"Mr. Jinx, you are more than welcome. The Mass may seem strange. I know Gemima will help you feel at home. Just do what she does. At communion, please come forward with Gemima. I would be pleased to give you a blessing."

As Father's friendly greeting settled into their hearts, Gemi put her arm in Tal's. She led him to a pew, towards the front. Tal sat down and looked at the beauty that surrounded him. The statues, the stained glass, the carved altar surrounded by poinsettias, the smell of incense were all so beautiful. It was so overwhelming, beyond words. Yet there was something beyond the visual, a presence of solace and consolation. He felt a strange sense of complete peace and contentment, like he had just come home to a place he'd never been before. He looked over at Gemi. She put a white veil over her head and knelt to pray. Tal listened intently to hear the words she was whispering.

"Hail Mary, full of grace, the Lord is with you.
Blessed art thou amongst women
and blessed is the fruit of thy womb, Jesus.
Holy Mary, Mother of God, pray for us sinners
now and at the hour of our death. Amen

He didn't know what she was saying or what it meant. He could tell, though, by the look of peace on her face, that it meant something special. The words were easy to understand but not the depth of their meaning. It didn't matter. He was just glad to be there.

Tal felt a spark, a stirring inside that he was totally unfamiliar with, a quiet, calm, reassuring voice saying to him, "Believe in me. I believe in you."

Tal sat back, squeezed Gemi's hand and sighed.

"You okay?"

She had to ask him three times before he finally heard her. Tal turned to look in her eyes.

"Oh, yeah. Couldn't be better." Then he smiled a huge, peaceful smile. Gemi smiled back, with the same kind of peace, a peace rooted in the knowledge she did the right thing, having Tal there with her.

Father Williker was right. The Mass did seem strange. Tal came away with as many questions as answers. He knew one thing for sure. He wanted to come back, to know more.

Tal got home late. He glanced at the clock as he passed through the kitchen, towards his room. It was half past two in the morning. He was glad for everything the whole day had brought, even though it left him very tired. He unbuttoned his new shirt slowly, carefully, preoccupied with thoughts about the hands that chose it and wrapped it just for him, with such love and thoughtfulness. Usually his clothes were thrown on the floor by his bed. Not this time. He carefully hung the shirt in his closet. Just as he was getting into bed, he heard a knock at his door.

"Tal, can I come in. I need to talk to you?"

He didn't like Sparky's timing. He was sleepy, but invited his father to come in anyway.

"You and Gemi have fun tonight? You sure spend a lot of time with her."

Tal yawned and stretched. "I don't think so."

"Son, you need to take it slow with her. You are both young and you don't know about life, love and commitment and . . ."

Tal interrupted him. "I know what I'm doing, Pop."

"I'm sure you think you do. Please listen. Y'all don't know what love is and I don't want you to get your heart broke again."

"You know, I wish people would stop telling me that!" His disgust was impossible to hide. "It's my heart. Let me worry about it."

Sparky ignored his son's tone of voice. "You could get this girl in trouble. It could be trouble for you and her. You could end up with regrets and years from now you . . ."

Tal cut him off again. The fullness of weariness washed over him leaving him with little patience for advice.

"Look, Sparky, you have left me on my own, to find my own way and that's exactly what I have had to do. I got this far without you, I can get on by myself. I'm in control. I know what I'm doing." He paused to yawn. "And so does Gemi."

Sparky's eyes darkened. He didn't like it when Tal called him by name. He knew it was Tal's way of rejecting him as a father figure. He also knew it was the price to pay for not being an attentive father. He wished he could make it up to Tal.

"Son, I know it hasn't been easy since Katy died. I miss her too. The reason you and your sister are here is because I loved her first. We loved you both into being. I know I haven't been much of a father. I'm not good at showing emotion. I know that. I want you to know, though. I do love you and don't want to see you hurt. Will you think about what I'm saying?"

Tal sighed and yawned again. "Sure, Pop. Sure."

Sparky knew his son was placating him just for convenience. He knew he would have to settle for that. Though it was late, he paused a moment. He smiled, patted his son on the shoulder, tucked him in like he was six again, kissed him on the head and moved towards the door.

"Good night, Son, and Merry Christmas. Would you, please, at least think about what I said?"

Tal grunted, turned over, and was asleep before his door was closed.

Christmas day dawned gray and cloudy. The low clouds that scudded on the north wind were a harbinger of the coming storm. The wind howling at Tal's window woke him up. He looked at his clock. It was well past nine. "Feels good to sleep in." he thought. He got out of bed yawning, stretching and scratching. He headed to the kitchen, stopping at Sparky's door for sounds of life. Silence. Tal grunted and mumbled, remembering the night before. "Can't be too concerned about me if he's gone this morning." Tal looked in the fridge for something to eat. Not much. Just some soda and some redskin peanuts. "Good 'a breakfast as any," he muttered. He looked at the thermometer outside the kitchen window. Thirty-six degrees. He knew that snow would be flying by sunset. The idea came to him in a flash. The perfect gift for Gemi. He took his breakfast and went back to his room. He found an inane movie on the television for company. He waited until noon to call her. It was hard to wait that long to hear her voice.

"Hey, My-Gem."

"It's about time you called me!" Gemi tried hard to sound angry.

"I didn't want to take you away from your family on Christmas morning. Hey, I've got a great present for you. Have you ever been swimming on Christmas . . . in the snow?"

Gemi was sure he was joking. "Yeah, once. I lost my left leg to frost bite so I never tried it again."

"No, I'm serious. I'll pick you up after supper. It's more fun after dark."

"Why don't you come for supper?"

The meager breakfast left him hungry. He jumped at the offer. "I was hoping you'd take the hint. Be there by five."

After supper, Gemi begged her parents for an evening out. Since the holiday was drawing down, Mom and G.B. agreed. As they got in the car to leave, the snow was already beginning to fall. Gemi didn't know what Tal had in mind and she didn't care. She was just glad to be alone with him. He turned east and headed out of town.

"Where're we going?"

"Swimming. Did you bring a swim suit?"

"Are you serious?"

"As serious as a train wreck."

"Train wreck is right. That's what swimming in the snow will be like. I'm not going to risk hypothermia. I'd rather watch you catch pneumonia. And you'd better not die 'til you take me home!"

Tal was confident in his judgment of her skepticism. That is why he brought along a t-shirt. "Open the glove box."

"Why?"

"Just do it.

She opened the box and saw the shirt. "What's this for?"

"Oh, ye of little faith. Put it on. We are about to have more fun than the law allows."

Gemi took the shirt. She stuck with a 'wait and see' attitude and held it on her lap.

In the months she and Tal had been together, Gemi had seen just about every back road in Kayne County. Where Tal was driving, though, was totally new to her. He headed east, out of town, then north. As they rode on, the snowfall grew heavier. She had grown to trust Tal because he had been very careful to respect and calm her fears. The snow covering the road began to shake that trust and she was afraid. She was in her usual posture, curled up against his side. He could feel her trembling in the warmth of the car. He knew it was because of fear. He pulled her close and slowed the car down.

"Relax, My-Gem, it's going to be fun. Really. Trust me. I don't want you hurt. Okay? We're not going very much farther. We'll head back before the snow gets deep."

Tal turned off the highway ten miles north of town. He followed a two lane black top up over a low rise. The paved road ended at a cattle guard. He crossed the guard, then down a narrow, gravel road into an arroyo. Even though it was dark and overcast, the countryside had an eerie, pale glow from a full moon that illuminated the clouds from above. The whiteness of the snow reflected what little light there was, making it easier to see. Tal followed the road as it wound back and forth. He slowed as he passed through a grove of pine. Gemi saw the white snow on the green branches and was entranced by the beauty. Tal flipped on the high beams. Gemi could see the road ending at a steep bluff. The bluff was partially obscured by what look liked steam rising out of the snow.

"See that, My-Gem? That's our destination."

"What is it?"

"It's a hot spring. It's where we're going swimming."

"Now I know you're loony tunes! If you think I am getting out of this car, in the snow, with nothing on but a t-shirt, well . . ."

Tal put the car in park and got out before she could finish. He left the engine running, the head lights and heater on. He undressed down to his shorts, then walked around to Gemi's door, in the snow, bare foot. He opened her door and invited her to step out of the car.

"C'mon, you little coward. No guts, no glory! The water's 103 degrees year around. And it feels great." He took her hand and tugged. "C'mon!"

Gemi resisted, wondering aloud why she had to fall for the town clown. Tal turned, ran to the spring and dove in. Gemi lost sight of him in the rising clouds of steam, but she could hear his voice.

"C'mon, My-Gem. It's getting lonely!"

Gemi took a deep breath. "It's now or never," she thought. She stripped and put her clothes in the backseat. She put on the shirt, opened the door and stepped out into the snow. Screaming, she ran on her tip toes, trying to keep her bare feet out of the snow. She jumped into the spring, almost on top of Tal.

"If I get pneumonia and die a painful, lingering death, I will come back to you every night and haunt your every dream. And I won't be a friendly ghost!"

Tal splashed her in the face and laughed. "Is that a threat or a promise? Either way, I can hardly wait. You'll be the prettiest ghost I'd ever seen!"

The snow continued to fall into the steam rising from the hot water. The steam and snow swirled together forming billowing, ethereal clouds that seemed to take on a life of their own. The wind pushed the clouds towards the car where the snow and mist danced and swirled in the soft, yellow glow of the headlights. It was as if angels from heaven were delighted to share the glory of creation with these young lovers. Gemi screamed with delight. The water was as warm and comforting as a bath. She floated on her back, hoping to catch a snow flake on her tongue. She mostly missed. They were hard to see in the steam. She looked up at the bluff rising behind them. The snow was gathering on the red rock outcroppings and the pines that had somehow found enough dirt to squeeze their roots into. The red rock, white snow and green pines seem to reflect all of the colors, all of the joy of this very special Christmas night.

Tal laughed and splashed as he swam around her. "I don't have money to buy you a gift so, I brought you out here. Remember the meteors? Well, here is another special gift of nature."

Gemi was caught up in the improbable joy of swimming in the midst of a snow storm. "This place is incredible! How did you ever find it?"

Tal pointed towards the top of the bluff. "If you climb that cliff and walk back about a quarter mile, you will come to the Boy Scout ranch where

Dusty and me spent our summers." Then Tal pointed the other way. "If you go out through those trees about a half mile you will find a Girl Scout camp. One summer day me and Dusty were out exploring the prairie. We heard girls laughing and splashing. We crept to the edge. Looking down from the top of the bluff, we saw a bunch of girls skinny dipping. Since then, we've come here a lot. It's an old Comanche spring. The Indians use to come here after a battle. They believed the water had special powers to heal." Tal pointed to the swirling mist. "They believed that the steam clouds were their ancestors coming back to heal them and prophecy about what was to come. Me an' Dusty used to dig around under the trees lookin' for arrow heads. We found many. Yep, we've had a lot of fun here."

Gemi swam to Tal and wrapped her arms and legs around him, kissing him and pulling them both under. They came up laughing in an joyous explosion of water and steam.

"This is wonderful, Tal. Can we stay here forever?"

"I'd love to, except I didn't bring any food. In a day or two, we'd be hungry and look like prunes."

They played, laughed and splashed. Tal stayed alert, keeping an eye on the accumulating snow. He knew that if they played too long, they could end up stuck. Finally he swam to Gemi and hugged her.

"We'd better go. The snow's getting deep."

Gemi swam towards the spot she jumped in. "Okay, Einstein, I hope you got a good way to get to the car without freezing."

"Yeah, just run fast, too fast for the cold to catch you."

Gemi gave him a playful slap. "C'mon, I'm serious."

Tal made a move towards the shore. "Okay, we'll run together. You get dressed in the back seat. I'll get in the front. There's a towel for you in the back seat."

They got out and ran for the car. The steam coming off their bodies made them look like they were on fire. They were into the car before the heat of the water wore off. She stripped off the t-shirt and began to dry herself. Tal turned the heater on high. As he dried his hair, glanced at his rear view mirror. What he saw took his breath away. Gemi had dried herself and was putting on her pull-over top. The dim light of the dash board glistening on her bare skin was mesmerizing. She finished dressing and jumped into the front seat. Still cold from her damp hair, she snuggled into Tal's side. He pulled her close and kissed her, feeling deeply the warmth of her body. He wanted to stay right where they were but he knew the danger of delay. He almost got stuck twice trying to turn the car around. The drive back to the highway took longer because of the deepening snow. He pulled out onto the highway slowly but fast enough for the tail of the car to spin around leaving them pointed the wrong way in the wrong lane. There was no traffic and they were in no danger. In an instant, Gemi panicked. She screamed, and dove to the floor board. Tal laughed and reached down to help her up onto the seat.

"Relax, we're okay. There's no one out here."

Gemi curled up on the seat, nestled against his side. Tiredness was beginning to overtake her. Her thoughts turned reflective as she thought about them, now and their future.

"When do you think we can get married?"

He thought about what he had seen in the mirror, smiled and let out a deep sigh. "Oh, I don't know. Sooner than later I hope. I'm, well, not sure. We got time, I suppose."

"I don't want to wait two or three years." Her voice was plaintive, impatient.

Tal tried to change the subject. "How many kids do you think we should have? I'm thinking six."

"Six? You seem to forget who's having them. How 'bout two, a boy for you and a girl for me?"

Tal liked that idea. "That's a start. I think we should name the boy Tallet Jinx Junior and the girl Tallette Jinx Juniorette."

Gemi made a face. "I like Patricia for a girl and Stinky Jinx for a boy."

"That sounds great. When he grows up and wonders why his schoolmates keep teasing him I will simply say, 'Go ask your mother'."

He poked her in the ribs to tickle her. She giggled and moved away, out of reach. All the way home they laughed and talked about their future. It was late when they got back to her house, not too late, though, for some time behind the barn. Tal pulled up close to the barn and turned off the car. They didn't need the heater. They had each other. There were no words to say. They embraced each other completely. The snow and the cold could not touch them. The past was gone, memories in the wind like the snowy mist. The future spilled out ahead of them like a book of blank pages on which they could write their hopes and dreams. The present was theirs and nothing could hurt them. Or so they thought.

* * *

The explosions and gunfire of his movie startled Tallet Jinx. The noise brought him back to the present and to the pain in his chest. As he rose to go to the bathroom, he heard Bekka at his door.

"Can I come in?"

Tal took his half empty glass to the bathroom with him. He quickly wash it out, and put it on the counter. He didn't want Bekka to smell whiskey.

"Yeah, Sis, come on."

Bekka came in and sat down on the end of her brother's bed. "We need to go see Doc Fagin tomorrow morning. He said it's very important. He has the test results and he needs to talk to us."

Tal sighed. He really wasn't interested in going anywhere, especially to Doc's office. It seemed to him to be an exercise in futility. All he needed was a pill to ease the pain until he could rid himself of her memory. He had convinced himself it wasn't his heart. It was her memory that somehow got stuck there. Maybe Doc Fagin was right. Maybe he needed to talk to a priest. Why a priest? The idea still seemed silly. He had managed to find his own way through sixty some years of life without God. Oh, he was thankful for the blessings of family when Christmas and Thanksgiving rolled around. The ranch? He had built it by the sweat of his brow. The friends were there because he wanted, appreciated them. Beyond that, Tal didn't see where God figured into his life. Nope, he got this far by himself. He could get beyond Gemi and move on . . . by himself.

"Look, Bekka, I really don't want to go. My heart is fine."

"Do me a favor? Just go along with me. Humor me this one time. Please?"

Bekka down played the urgency she felt inside. Her nursing instinct told her that Tal was in serious trouble. She didn't want to tell him. She knew her brother. She knew that he would not believe her, no matter how she said it. Her brother needed to hear it, as the say in the Panhandle, from the horse's mouth. And if it was what Bekka thought, maybe Doc Fagin could make it believable for Tal. In Bekka's estimation, her brother's life depended on it.

XII

A Broken Heart

Tallet set his alarm for six. He wanted to be up and dressed before Bekka, to show her he was better. When the clock went off, he was slow to arise, feeling groggy, heavy headed and short of breath. He forced himself out of bed and into the shower. When he stood, waves of dizziness washed over him, making him unsteady. He felt like he was back on the rolling deck of that Navy Destroyer. It took longer than he wanted, but he did it. He was shaved, dressed and ready to go when his sister called from the kitchen.

Tal put on his cheeriest face. "Good morning, Sis. Don't want breakfast. Not hungry. I'm going to the barn to check on Paint."

"Can't. There's no time. We need to go now."

"Doc's office don't open 'til nine."

"He's meeting us there at eight."

"Good", thought Tal, "let's get this thing over with."

Doc Fagin was in his office when he heard Tal and his sister come into the waiting room. He opened his door, greeted them warmly and asked them to come in and sit down. He poured coffee for all three of them then sat at his desk.

"Tal, I know there's been a lot going on with you lately. I had an idea what it was. I needed the tests to make sure. No need for false alarms."

"That's good, Doc. I don't want any either. I'm glad you found the problem. Just give me a pill so I can go home and get better."

Doc smiled and took a drink of coffee. Then his face grew serious and dark. "I'm afraid it's not that simple. There is significant cause for alarm. You are a very sick man. The reason you are doing as well as you are is because of your physical, outdoor lifestyle on the ranch." He paused for a deep sigh. "There is no easy way to say this. You are suffering from congestive heart failure."

Tal saw this a good thing. "Great, doc, give me a decongestant and I'm outta here."

"Oh, were it that easy. Tal, you need to listen to me." Doc took a sip of coffee, looked down at his cup as he leaned forward, then looked up, directly into Tal's eyes. "You have a very serious heart disease. It's called cardiomyopathy. Simply put, a virus has attacked the heart muscle causing it to enlarge. As the heart gets bigger, it has to worked harder but gets less done. As it gets less done, it has to work harder. Fluid builds up in your body and the cycle worsens. The result is congestive heart failure. Essentially, your lungs fill up and you drown in your own body fluids . . . . unless you have a fatal heart attack first."

Tal looked over at Bekka. She had her hand over her mouth, tears welling up in her eyes. He looked back at Doc and asked in a bewildered tone, "So what's that mean? You can't make me better?"

Doc shifted in his chair. In all the years he had been doctoring, this never got any easier. Saying it to a friend made it even worse. He paused looking for the right words. "I'm sorry. There is no cure. This is a disease we don't understand very well. We don't know why the virus attacks the heart. Once it does, its effects cannot be reversed."

Tal began to see the gravity of his plight. He was in some deep trouble. He looked at his sister. She was crying. He looked back at Doc. His eyes looked wet. "So what's the prognosis?"

Again, Doc paused to gather his thoughts, to choose his words carefully. "Listen carefully, my friend. I want your permission to enter your name into the national database for organ transplant. We need to try to find you a new heart . . . before it's too late."

"Transplant? A new heart?" Tal looked to Bekka for understanding. "Cardio . . . , what was it Doc said?"

Tal's thoughts were in a spin. How could this be? No, no, he must be dreaming. He thought of Gemi. Suddenly, her memory wasn't so bad. Suddenly, remembering her was easy. Her looked to his sister. "Bekka, what is he talking about? He looked back. "Doc, what are you saying?"

"You need a heart transplant to save your life. If we can't find a donor, well, there isn't much time left."

Tal took a deep breath, leaned back in his chair and sighed. His first thought was, "This would be a good time for a stiff drink." He could not believe what he was hearing.

"How much time do I have?"

He heard himself ask that question about others. Never, even in his wildest imagination, did he ever think he would be asking it about himself.

Doc looked to Bekka. "You are going to have to help me. We need to preserve and protect him. If we manage treatment of his symptoms, I figure three months, six at the very most."

Bekka nodded. It seemed to her that this moment needed a bit of levity. "I'll do what I can. You know this guy as well as I do . . . managing him is like herding cats."

They all laughed.

"So, Doc, you think I could die from this?"

"No. You will die from this. Sooner than later. I know it's a lot to take in right now. I need an answer, though, as soon as possible. I need your permission to put you on the transplant waiting list. In the meantime, I would suggest you get your affairs in order and make your peace with God."

This is not what Tal expected. He had gone from thinking a pill would give him a clean bill of health to dying. And soon . . . way too soon.

"So you are saying it's a new heart or six feet under?"

Doc nodded.

"Sounds like a no brainer to me."

"I was hoping you'd say that. You are my best, worst patient and losing you now would make my life way too easy. I've called in some prescriptions to Corley's. Bekka will go by and get them for you. In the meantime, go home and take it easy. Don't get excited and don't do any strenuous work. We need to take good care of what heart you have left. Okay?"

As they got up to leave, Bekka gave her brother a warm, reassuring gentle hug. Then she hugged Doc and thanked him for all his efforts. "I'll watch him like a hawk, Doc, and if he dies, I'll bring him by here on the way to the cemetery so you can kill him."

Tal protested. "Hey, I'm not that hard to manage!"

Doc and Bekka looked at each other then at him and said in unison, "Yes you are!"

All the way home, Tal sat and stared straight ahead. Bekka drove to the drugstore, then to the grocery store. He said nothing. He just stared. As Bekka pulled the truck into the drive, he finally spoke.

"Bekka, don't say anything about this to anyone. I need to figure out what to do. I need time to do that. When I do, I'll tell our friends and family. Okay?"

Bekka recognized her brother's attempt to hold onto the remnant of control he once enjoyed. It was quickly slipping away and he didn't like it.

"Sure . . . under one condition."

"Sure, Sis, what is it?"

"You do what I say and give me the whiskey you have hidden in your room."

Tal went agape. "How do you know about that?!"

"Well, to be honest I wasn't sure. I didn't think you really liked all that lemon-lime soda by itself. I thought I caught a whiff of it a few times. Still, wasn't sure . . . , until just now. Your guilty conscience just let the cat out of the bag."

Tal smiled a sheepish grin. "You got your devious streak from Sparky. I'll give it up. Don't ask where it's hid. I won't tell you."

"I love you too, Bro."

Tal went to his room, retrieved the bottle, brought it to the kitchen and set it on the table without saying a word. He didn't have to. The scowl on his face said it all. Bekka grinned at him and went back to making lunch.

"Go to your room and sit. I'll bring you your lunch."

Tal went to his room. He stood at his patio door staring out at the ranch he so loved. The thought of himself, Joey and Paint never again riding the high plains of the prairie or going out to Huerfano was . . . well, unthinkable. So much to do yet so little time. What does all this mean? It made no sense to him. How could this be happening to him? He was lost in his thoughts when Bekka brought his lunch. He sat down so Bekka could put the tray in his lap. She saw a strange, new look on his face, a look of resignation. And it frightened her.

"Tal, I don't want you giving up. You are a survivor. We can get through this. I just need you to mellow out for a while."

He smiled a weak smile and took a small bite of his sandwich. "I guess old age and heartache, real or other wise, can make you mellow."

Bekka smiled as she brushed back his hair. Her gentle touch was reassuring. "Promise you won't quit on me?"

Just then she heard Joey scratch at the door. She slid it open to let him in. She knew the old dog's presence would do her brother good.

"I promise. Besides, my dog and my horse need me."

He waited for her reaction.

"And me?"

"I don't know yet," he said in a teasing tone. "You took my whiskey. My dog and my horse let me drink."

"Yeah. They also let you cook, clean and do your own laundry. Would you rather do that yourself? I'd be glad to let you, if you want?"

Tal kept teasing. "You like to play hardball, Sis."

Bekka smiled. "Got to. Consider it payback for the boy friends you chased away."

Tal sighed. He knew she wasn't to be intimidated. He also knew she only protecting him like he tried to protect her. "Come here and give me a kiss."

She bent over, held one cheek and kissed the other. "Well, I guess I'll leave you two incorrigibles alone. I'll be back to check on you. Enjoy your lunch."

"Thanks, Sis. I really do appreciate and need you."

She smiled, blew him a kiss, closed his door and was gone. He ate slowly as he contemplated his fate. Now what? He had always been able to will himself to, well, 'to just get over it'. He still entertained the thought, however slim it may be. He finished his lunch and turned his mind back to Gemi. Her memory was strangely calming and unsettling at the same time. He wondered what the near future might hold. Maybe her memory could help him through it. After all, she was his first love. He remembered his love for Lucy. He loved her memory too, but not like Gemi. He had loved no one like he loved Gemi. He wondered if he could find her after all these years. He didn't know where to begin to look. What if she wasn't alive? He shuddered at the thought of the light going out of those incredible eyes. If he did find her, would she remember him? Would she even want to talk to him? Would she remember how she had hurt him? Probably not.

Probably not? The thought that only he would remember the 'we' that 'they' were so many years ago troubled him. His mood turned dark and somber. He wished he still had some of that whiskey. He was losing his heart. Again. Only this time it was for real. The pain was the same. Joey whined as he pushed his nose under Tal's hand. The dog wanted his ears scratched. Tal was glad to oblige. He needed the distraction.

After a while he rose from his chair to stretch and to take his lunch plate and glass to the kitchen. As he approached the sink, he heard music coming from Bekka's room. He couldn't quite hear the words, but the music was enchanting. He put his dishes on the counter and went towards her door to hear the words. He paused to listen to a song he had heard before so many times in so many different forms . . . songs about love that is won, songs about love that is lost, songs about broken hearts and painful memories. The events of the morning brought a whole new meaning to what he was feeling.

He had heard enough. He turned towards his room. One idea, one question penetrated his being. Where do broken hearts go?

He walked slowly back to his room. He sat in his chair, in silence scratching Joey 'til the afternoon was gone. Bekka brought him a supper he didn't want, citing no appetite. She insisting that he needed to eat to keep his strength up. When she left, he had a few bites then gave the rest to Joey. The room grew dark and he rose to let dog out. He slid the door shut and stood there. The night was creeping over the prairie he so loved. The land below and the sky above grew dark. Seeing the vastness of the universe above his head always made his problems seem smaller. Not this time. The growing darkness outside turned the glass door into a mirror. He saw his swollen, haggard face. He saw a broken heart, broken on so many levels. What he saw was simply too much to believe, too much to bear. He turned off the light by his chair, undressed and got into bed. He stared at the ceiling and whispered the last line of the song.

Hearts are made to last 'til the end of time.

Not his heart. Not her heart. The heartbeat that so enchanted him was gone, lost in time. Now he was losing his heartbeat . . . for real. He turned over and tucked his pillow under his head. Then he did something that he hadn't done since the night of his mother's funeral. He cried himself to sleep.

XIII

Winter's Chill

Morning came and Tal awoke slowly. He wondered why his pillow felt damp. Then he remembered . . . the tears. His memory turned back to that card, the Valentine card that started it all. His mind turned introspective as he mused about the past, the present and the future. How can memories mean so much? After all, in the end, what are they, really? Doesn't a man with moonlight and memories in his hand have nothing there at all?

Bekka came to his door. "Tal, you up yet? You ready for some breakfast?"

He thought of the perfect breakfast. "Yeah, I sure am. How 'bout three eggs, sausage, grits, and some biscuits and gravy. Butter soaked toast with grape jelly for dessert. And a big glass of orange juice."

Bekka opened the door. "Doc's orders are cereal with skim milk and some coffee."

"Yeah, and I suppose you agree with him."

"Yes I do, Mister Grumpy Pants. Get up and get dressed. I'll be back."

Bekka headed down the hall towards the kitchen. She could rule his diet but that was all. He pulled the covers over his head.

"Maybe if I pretended the world didn't exist, maybe I could find some quiet for my mind and some peace for my heart," he thought.

Sometimes thoughts and feelings take on a reality of their own. Trying to control those thoughts and feelings can be very difficult. Today it was impossible. His thoughts went back to January, 1962. It was the beginning of the end for Tal and Gemi.

* * *

The phone rang just as he was walking in the door. It was Gemi.

"Hey, Tally-Boy."

"I just dropped you at home twenty minutes ago. My good-bye kiss wear off already?"

"I forgot to ask you something. What are we doing tomorrow, for Valentine's day?"

"You won't believe it. I got a date with the cutest girl in the Panhandle. I was hoping you could come too."

Gemima laughed. "Sure, I would love to. What time are you picking me, uh, her up?"

"Right after breakfast. Love you, My-Gem."

Valentine's day fell on Saturday which meant the burden of school wouldn't mar the reverie of the day. The two lovers decided to spend the whole day together. Gemi asked him to take her out to the hot spring in the morning. The prevailing, southern wind had melted the snow days ago. The day was bright, clear and cool. Gemi wanted to see that special spot in the daylight. The spring had a rocky bottom which allowed the water to stay crystal clear. Gemi was amazed at all she could see, even in the deepest area. A long swim in the hot water felt so good.

They came back to town, had a light lunch and walked around 'til sundown. They shopped, laughed and teased each other as only young lovers can. They ate supper at a downtown café. He bought a bag of chocolate covered peanuts for them to share. It was after dark when he brought her home. He steered the car to their favorite spot, behind the barn. He didn't want to be apart from her. In fact, he wished he could take her home. For keeps. So did she. Gemi curled up in his arms and kissed him.

"I have something for you." She reached into her purse, pulled out a small envelope and gave it to him.

The card was a small red heart. Inside Tal read, "Can we be together always? Be mine forever, Tally-boy. I don't like you very much. Always have. Love, Gemi."

Tal was deeply touched, grateful for the sentiment. He had come to know her, to trust her, to love her, in the deepest part of his being. "I love you too, My-Gem. I can't believe how mean I was to you last fall. Can you ever forgive me?"

She crossed her arms across her chest and feigned a frown. "Yes you were and no I won't! I can't."

"Why not?" Tal was surprised by her answer.

"Because I already have.

She laughed out loud and poked him in the ribs. He tickled her back. By this time, he knew all the right places to poke. The mini-wrestling match ended with an embrace and a long kiss.

Then Gemima asked the fateful question.

"What are we going to do when you graduate? I'll have two years to go. I don't like the thought of life in Kayne without you."

His eyes grew dark, his face grew pensive as he searched for the right words.

"I've given it some thought. You know how much I hate school. If I don't do school, I'll get drafted into the Army. When I was in Amarillo last week, I went to see the Navy recruiter. Thought I'd join the Navy. I've only been out of Texas twice in my life and since I have to do military, I would like to see the world."

This was not the answer Gemi was expecting. "What about me? I can't go with you. I need you around! We were gonna get married, weren't we?"

He wanted marriage . . . now more than ever. It would seal and sanctify their life, their love. It meant that if he had to be gone, they would still belong to each other . . . no matter what.

"Yeah, we are. We can wait 'til you get out of school. I will miss you too. We can write. I'll be home once a year or so. After you graduate, we'll get married and you can be with me wherever I go." She put her arms around his waist and began to cry on his chest. He gently pulled her chin and kissed her.

"Why can't you stay here and find a job in town, or on a ranch, you know, somewhere close? G.B. will give you a job."

"If I'm not in school, I'll get drafted. You know that. Then I'll be gone anyway. Try to understand. I've always wanted to be a sailor. If I do it this way, we won't be apart for long. Come here."

He tenderly held her body against his, as close as he could. The car was getting cold. He could feel the cold coming down off the side glass, penetrating his soul. It seemed to be a metaphor, an omen of things to come. It touched an insecurity deep inside that he thought had died with the coming of her love. He brushed aside the shadow of fear and held on to her. She was with him. They were together and always would be, even if it were only in their hearts. He could feel the sweet warmth of her breath against his cheek. "Do you believe I will come back to you?"

She didn't hesitate. She pushed herself away. "I don't believe you are leaving!"

He gently tugged her hand to pull her back. "Shhhh, it's okay. The Navy isn't a done deal. We still have time together. All the time in the world."

Tal slipped his hand under her sweater and caressed her back. It was a touch that she needed. His hands, softly on her body, provided the reassurance she needed. He needed to touch, needed to have that intimacy that told him she was his and he was hers. Then he kissed her. Long and deep. He kissed her tears away and whispered in her ear. As softly as he could. "I love you, My-Gem. I really do. And I need you too." He felt her body soften in his arms. "It'll be okay. We'll be okay."

He eased her down on the seat and kissed her lips, her neck. Then he pressed his ear against her chest and stroked her head.

"I hear your heartbeat. I love your heartbeat. We've got time, My-Gem, all the time in the world."

For the moment, she was okay, they were okay. He downplayed his decision to enlist. And he was sure he could manage her opposition. The sense of foreboding that was the shadow of fear was gone. At least for the moment.

* * *

Bekka's knock at his door caused him to open his eyes.

"Come on in, Sis."

"Here's your breakfast."

Her voice was bright and cheery but the meal wasn't. He sat in his chair and looked at what she had brought him.

"That's the breakfast you threatened me with. You expect me to survive on quarter rations?" The question reeked of sarcasm.

"Yes. As a matter of fact I do. You heard the good doctor. You need to take care of your heart. I'm here to see that you do." Bekka turned to leave. "Call me if you need some thing else."

Tal muttered under his breath. "Yeah, like you'd really bring it."

"What?"

"Nothin'. Don't need nothin'."

Bekka closed the door to leave him alone with his meager breakfast and abundant memories. All the time in the world? How ironic! All the time in the world had dwindled down to a few remaining days and the distraction of Gemi's memory. Bekka was back at noon with some lunch then at sundown with soup and milk for supper. The three small meals left him hungry. He didn't care. His mood was too dark, too somber to worry about a little thing like hunger. The day grew dark. He looked at the clock. Nine-thirty. Another day wasted with useless memories. He didn't like going to bed at nine-thirty, until tonight. Her memory, his heart. It could all wait. In sleep there was no pain. And that is what he needed most, no pain.

As tired and worn out as he was, he couldn't sleep. He laid in his bed staring at the ceiling. He tried to make sense of what was happening to him, trying to understand the 'what' and the 'why'. Nothing made sense.

He thought about the failing heart in his chest and what that meant. Death. His death. The death of who he was and what he had left to accomplish. The thought of a life time of work coming down to naught made him shudder.

Then there was Gemi. He thought about his wife, Lucy, and the years they had together. In the end, he had made his peace with her. Her passing was made less painful by that peace. He and Gemi? There was no peace because there was no closure. He began to understand the importance of closure. The question remained the same. How can you call someone, after years of silence, and say, "Hi, this is Tal. I loved you once until you hurt me. I need you to apologize to me so that I can forgive you because I want to die in peace."

Suddenly the need for closure, the need for peace, the fear of dying melded into a single black thought. And a sense of panic swept over him.

It was time to make his peace. It was time to heed Doc Fagin's advice and put his affairs in order. He needed to prepare for the worst and plan for the best. That decision helped sleep to come. Not so, peace. He slept a fitful, uneasy sleep that provided little rest.

The next several days were excruciatingly slow. Tal had always been a man of action. Everyday of his life he did something. Even when he was sick, he would go out to his barn and do something just so he could say it had been a productive day. Now, restricted to his room, his bed, by a disease he didn't understand made each day seem like a week.

Bekka purchased a cell phone. She explained to him that if and when a donor became available, they both needed to respond immediately because every second counted. Each second lost reduced the donated organ's viability. Tal had his western novels, his movie collection and satellite television. After a while, even that couldn't keep his mind occupied.

He did make every attempt to put everything in order. He called a meeting with his sons. He tried to be as upbeat as he could, choosing his words carefully so as to minimize what was happening to his body. His sons laughed at his attempt.

They all asked him the same question. "Dad, how do you minimize a heart transplant?"

They had him stumped on that one. He explained the will he had drawn up that week. All three sons would share equally in the land. Bekka would get the house and two acres around it. The sons understood. They remembered the tornado had that destroyed what Bekka once had.

After the meeting, after they all left, Tal went to his dresser. He shuffled through the scraps of paper 'til he found what he was looking for. He peeked out his bedroom door towards the kitchen. The light was off. Good. That meant Bekka had gone to her room. He quietly crept to the phone in the kitchen and dialed the number. Dusty answered on the third ring.

"Hey, hello, old buddy . . . . Yeah, this is Tal . . . . I'm good. Well, no I'm not. I need to talk to you. Can you come over? . . . Yeah, I know it's late. We need, I mean, I need to talk . . . Thanks, Dusty, and could you bring some beer? And don't ring the door bell. Come around the end of the house to my patio door. I'll leave the light on for you. And listen, I need you to be quiet. I don't want Bekka to hear anything . . . . Yeah, I know it sounds mysterious. I have my reasons. I'll explain when you get here."

Tal went back to his bedroom. He switched off his bed lamp and switched on the patio light leaving that the only light in the room. As he waited for his friend he thought about endings. He thought about the end of Gemi and him.

XIV

The End

Tallet Jinx came home late, very late, even for a Saturday night. He went directly to his room and turned on the radio, looking for distraction. He sat down on the edge of his bed and put his box of beer on the floor, between his feet. He cracked a can and took a long drink. Unfortunately, the first song he heard was their song.

He switched off the radio. He didn't want, couldn't bear, to hear the rest of it. He muttered to himself as he unbuttoned his shirt, his voice a little slurred from the evening's refreshments. "Those stupid wise men. They know what they're talkin' 'bout. Should'a listened to 'em."

Just then he heard a knock at his door. It was Sparky.

"Son, can I come in?"

"Yeah, if you want."

The first thing Sparky saw when he opened the door was the beer. Tal offered one to his father. Sparky frowned and hesitated.

"I heard you come in. Kind'a late, don't cha' think? You know I don't approve of you drinkin'. You're only eighteen."

Sparky did disapprove. Ever the pragmatist, though, he accepted his son's offer. He pulled Tal's desk chair around and took a beer from his son. "Gemi called. Twice. Says she needs to talk to you."

Tal's face grew dark, tense and foreboding. He put his hands to his face and rubbed his eyes. He looked at the floor and wiped his mouth with his sleeve.

"Gemi called and wanted . . ."

Tal threw his empty can across the room and spoke in a tone Sparky had never heard before. "I Heard ya!" He sniffed as he took a drink from a fresh can. "Don't want to talk to her. If she calls back, tell her I went to Amarillo to see Aunt Dori. Tell her I don't want to talk. Tell her anything, just don't tell me she called."

Sparky took a drink of beer. "Trouble in paradise, eh?"

"Should've listened to you. Me an' Gemi . . . , we're over."

"You want to tell me about it?"

The question caught him off guard. It had become uncommon for his Father to show any interest in his troubles. Only one other time did he have anything to say about Gemi. He tried to think his way through the alcohol cloud that had dulled his senses. Finally he found the words he needed.

"Well, Pop, I've tried to make her understan'. Tried an' tried. It ain't workin'. Remember two weeks ago, I went to Amarillo to sign my Navy enlistment papers?"

"Sure do, son. I'm proud of you."

"Told Gemi. She burst out crying. She wants me to stay in town and go to school. You know how I hate school. If I go to work, I'll end up drafted. Don't want the army. She wouldn't listen. I told her we could still be together and I'd be back for her when she graduated. She still thinks I'm leaving her behind." Tal stopped to take a long drink from his beer. "Last weekend I found out she had accepted a date with 'Mister Football', Seven Stevens." His voice dripped with venomous sarcasm. "I called her and told her that if that was what she wanted to do, well it was just fine . . . yeah, just fine with me. Tonight Dusty told me she cancelled the date. She only did that to make me jealous."

Sparky smiled. "Women . . . , can't live with 'em, can't shoot 'em."

"She didn't have to do that." Sparky could hear the anguish and hurt in his son's voice. "Pop, I need to get out of town and see if I can find my own way, my own life. She don't understand! Why won't she understand?" He finished his beer and opened another.

"Trying to drown your sorrows, huh?"

Tal took a long drink then wiped his mouth, and his tears, with his sleeve. "Whatever works. Problem is . . . the real ones can swim."

Sparky smiled. "A wise observation son. Where'd you get the beer?"

"Dusty's got a fake ID and we know where to use it."

"Son, I told you last fall to take it slow. My advice is if you love her, try to make up with her. I'd hate to see you regret it down the line. Chances for love like this don't happen like we want or expect. If you let something like this get in the way, you could regret it . . . more sooner than later. In the mean time, drinkin' ain't gonna help."

"That's what you think. Wanna 'nother beer?"

Sparky accepted his son's offer. "Get some sleep. We can talk tomorrow."

Sparky put the chair back and left, a beer in each hand. Tal closed his door, finished undressing and got in bed. Lying in the dark, he tried to gather his thoughts through the beery haze. Staring at the ceiling, he felt tears on his cheek. He muttered to himself, "This is the last time. No one is going to hurt me like this again. No one. Not ever. Never!" He felt his resolve stiffen as he built the protective shell back around his heart, thicker and harder than ever. Too many hurts from too many girls in too short a time. Gemima would be the last one to wound his heart to such a depth. He wiped his tears away, finished his beer, turned over and went to sleep. "Yep, this is it. No more hurts . . . ever again."

The next morning Tal woke up in a decidedly foul mood. His first thoughts were about pain. He hurt in every part of his being. His heart hurt for Gemi, his spirit hurt from loneliness and his head hurt from beer. He rose slowly, sitting on the edge of his bed, holding his head. Sparky was gone and the house was quiet. "This is good", he thought, "I won't have to suffer through another 'I told you so' talk." He found no comfort, though, no respite in the silence. Noise would have been a grateful distraction. The break-up, still very fresh, still echoed in the forefront of his thoughts.

Finally he rose and stumbled to the bathroom to relieve himself. He washed his face with cold water, hoping it would wake him up and help his headache. He was only half right. He went to the refrigerator to see what he could find for breakfast. Not much there. He grabbed a can of cola, went back to his bedroom and got back in bed.

"What to do?", he thought. "Maybe I'll stay in bed all day. Nope, bad idea. I'll be wasting my time thinkin' about her."

Just then the phone rang in the kitchen. His first impulse was to go answer it. Then he remembered. It could be Gemima. He laid back down and counted the rings. They stopped at twenty-three. "Whoever it was," he thought, "they sure were persistent."

"What to do?," he thought again. "I don't need to spend Sunday inside a cold, empty house." The idea came in a flash. He decided to get out onto the prairie. He would drive out to the Boy Scout ranch. Maybe a horse-back ride into the hills of the Panhandle would clear his mind. The wind and the sun always helped his mood.

He headed out to the ranch, stopping at a drive-in for some breakfast to eat on the way. The road leading into the ranch was long. He drove past the main building, around the back of the barn, and parked his car near the corral. He saw his old friend filling the feed troughs.

"Hey, Pete!"

Pete Thomas had been the wrangler on the ranch for as long as Tal could remember. He was tall and thin, narrow at the hip and broad in the shoulders. His skin was like leather from years of ranching in the Texas sun. He was tough too. Tal had seen him break a finger trying to wrestle a steer to the ground. Old Pete didn't even flinch. He simply pulled the broken digit to aligned the bones, taped it to a good one and went back to work. Some say he held his pants up with horse shoe nails. Tal almost believed it.

Pete turned around. "Hey, Tal, ain't seen ya for a while. How the heck have you been? What brings you out here?"

Tal didn't want Pete to see his dark mood. He walked tall and found his cheeriest voice. "I'm finer 'n frog hair . . . and I need to borrow a horse for a few hours."

"Sure thing, pal. Take Peaches. She ain't been out for a while. She could use some exercise."

Peaches was an unusual horse, a palomino mare. What made her different was she had the size and muscle of a stallion. Her yellow color had some red in it making her peach colored. She was gentle with the children, yet when spurred, she could run like the wind. Tal knew the horse from when he and Dusty spent their summers on the ranch.

"Thanks, Pete. I owe you one."

"You mean one more, don't 'cha?"

"Put it on my tab."

"Can't. There ain't no more room."

They both laughed.

Tal quickly saddled up. He headed west out of the corral. The valley floor rose gradually towards the west to meet the rim of the cliff that overlooked the hot springs. Tal steered Peaches down off the high point towards the mesquite forest on the valley floor where a trail led off towards the Girl Scout camp. He hadn't gone very far when he heard a horse galloping up behind him. Before he could react, the rider pulled up beside him, grabbed his hat, let out a whoop and took off down the trail at a full gallop. The sudden noise startled Peaches. She reared up and spun around. Tal tried to hang on to no avail. He found himself on his back side in the dust. The rider stopped about fifty yards down the trail. He got to his feet quickly, dusting his jeans with hand slaps. He was glad that nothing was broke except his pride. It was his broke, though, and that made him mad. He looked to see a young woman waving his hat.

"What happened, Cowboy, did ya fall down?" She said it with a teasing laugh which made him even angrier.

"You come back here with my hat, you little brat!"

Tal jumped on Peaches and spurred the horse down the trail after the woman . . . and his hat. The woman turned and spurred her horse too . . . , and the race was on. They sped headlong through the mesquite. Peaches was faster than the other horse though not by much. Before Tal could catch her, they broke into a clearing near the Girl Scout ranch. The woman sped towards the back of the corral. Tal thought he had her. She would have to stop at the fence. No hesitation. The woman spurred the horse over the fence. Tal tried to get Peaches to jump also. The horse balked and stopped so quickly that Tal almost went over her head and into the dirt. The woman rode back to the fence. She got down from her horse and held out Tal's hat, just out of his reach.

"Want your hat back?" She smiled coyly as if she had just found it and wanted to return it to it's rightful owner.

Tal dismounted and walked up to the fence, still fuming.

"Yeah, I want my hat back . . . and I want to give you a good spanking for what you did."

The woman giggled. She pointed towards where she had grabbed his hat, but Tal knew she was referring to him. "Hope you didn't break something important back there."

Tal jumped on the fence. The woman quickly stepped back. "Gimme my hat! Now!"

The woman threw the hat down in the dirt, just far enough inside the fence so that Tal would have to climb over into the corral. "Here's your dirty old hat Mr. Tallet Jinx." She feigned indignation, as if it were his fault all along.

"How'd ya know my name?"

Tal picked up the hat and dusted it off against his jeans.

"It's in your silly hat."

Tal began to cool off. He took his first good look at his tormenter. She was tall, almost as tall as he was. She was thin built and full figured, curvy in all the right places. Her hair was auburn and curly in every direction. She had fair skin, freckles dotting her high cheekbones. Her green eyes sparkled with a mischievous glint. She had a broad mouth and a little turned up nose. All in all, she was easy to look at and hard to stay mad at.

"Okay, brat, you know my name. What's yours?"

"Lucy Jane Morgan. My friends call me L.J."

"What do you enemies call you?"

"Don't know. Don't have any."

Tal reformed his hat and, none the worse for wear, put it back on his head.

"Well, you do now. You are a menace!"

She walked up and gave him a playful punch on the shoulder.

"Oh, lighten up, will ya. Just wanted to have a little fun. Don't be such a grump. Will you forgive me?"

Tal smiled and ignored her question. "I don't know you. Are you new in town?"

"I'm from Lubbock. My cousin lives in town. She invited me up to help open the Girl Scout ranch for the summer. Maybe you know her. Her name is Anni. She dates some guy named Dusty."

Tal laughed out loud.

"What's so funny?"

"Oh, nothing. Let's just say it's a small world."

"So you gonna forgive me?"

"I suppose."

Tal offered a handshake as a sign of peace. Lucy took his hand, thinking it was nothing more than a friendly gesture. He grabbed the hand, pulled her to himself, put his other arm around her back and held on tight as he gave her a big, wet kiss. She quickly stiffened and struggled to get away. Finally he relaxed his embrace and she pushed him away. She reached out to slap him. Tal anticipated her move. He ducked her swing and used the fence to vault himself onto Peaches.

Now it was her turn. She was indignant, this time it was for real.

"You shouldn't have done that, Tallet Jinx!"

"Now we are even, Lucy Jane. Maybe I'll see you in town tonight."

He turned to gallop off.

"Not if I see you first!"

He let out a whoop and spurred the horse faster.

She hollered after him. "If I see you, I won't talk to you!"

Tal laughed as he rode off. He had found the distraction he had looked for. The rest of the day he didn't think much about Gemima. He thought about Lucy.

At sundown, Tal walked into Jim Bob's Burgers. Dusty, Anni and Lucy were sitting at a table in the back corner. Tal walked up behind Lucy and grabbed her hat.

"Hey!"

She turned around and saw Tal, smiling and spinning her hat on his finger.

"How ya doin', little Miss Menace?"

Tal tried hard to hide the gloat in his voice.

Dusty stood up to greet Tal with a handshake. "I suppose you two have met."

Lucy stood, grabbed her hat and sat back down. "Yeah, I stole his hat, he stole a kiss. It was all very . . . well, shall we say . . . what's the word? Distasteful. Yeah. That's it! Distasteful."

Anni spoke up with a smile. "She told me what happened today, Tal. Sounds like you two were meant for each other."

Tal pointed to everyone at the table as he spoke to Lucy. "Told you it was a small world."

Tal joined them at the table. It was an evening of fun and frivolity. It was just what he needed. Tal and Lucy teased each other mercilessly all evening, not because of mutual dislike. It was because of a mutual attraction. Lucy was completely at home on the prairie and fearless on a horse. Some people saw her as a tomboy. Not Tal. He liked her self-confidence. Lucy was drawn to Tal for different reasons. She like his western flair. She also saw a sad, wistfulness in a young boy with a lonely heart. She didn't know about his very recent, painful break-up with Gemi. The pain was there, though, just below the surface and Lucy could sense it. She could see in his eyes someone who was lost in his fear of losing. That endeared him to her. Maybe it was her mothering instinct. She thought she could fix him, make the hurt better. At the end of the evening, Tal offered Lucy a hand shake. Remembering the stolen kiss, she put her hands behind her back and stuck her tongue out as she turned to get into the car. As Dusty drove away, Lucy rolled down the window, smiled and blew Tal a kiss.

"See, you around, Cowboy!"

Tal smiled and waved back. "Not if I see you first!"

Tal went to his car to head home. Just as he was getting into bed, the phone rang. He didn't count the rings this time. He didn't care. He turned off the light and closed his eyes. His last thought was not of Gemima. It was of Lucy.

* * *

A noise on his patio brought Tal back to the present. Dusty slid open the patio door and stuck his head in. He saw Tal sitting in his recliner holding a small brass statue of a palomino. He remembered how Tal came to own it. Lucy had given it to him at his going away party the night before Tal left for boot camp.

"Thinking 'bout Lucy?"

"Yeah, I suppose so. Remember how mad I was that you had given her my Navy address? C'mon in and have a seat."

"Yeah, I sure do. Thought it was the end of our friendship. She insisted, though, and I knew it was the right thing to do."

"Who'd a thunk it . . . a mail order courtship that would actually come to something."

"I guess you did love her."

"Love?," Tal said with a chuckle. "Oh, I don't know. I needed her and she was there. I did grow to love her. I never loved her, no one, like Gemi."

"I remember when she followed you to Treasure Island, California. You didn't come home for a year and a half."

Tal smiled a wry smile. "Didn't need to. Guess I didn't want to. Did you bring the beer?"

Dusty gave him the sack. "So what's the emergency?"

Tal cracked a can and took a long draw. He looked at the floor long enough to gather the words. Finally he spoke softly, slowly. "Dusty, I'm dying."

"Yeah, I know, I can tell by the smell."

"I'm serious. The doctor said I got cardiomyo . . . something or other. I can never remember the name. No Matter. It's a virus in the heart. If I don't get a new one, I'll be dead in six months, maybe less."

Dusty went pale. He grabbed a beer, cracked it and took a long drink. "I can't believe it. I'm stunned. We got too many things left to do."

"Well, I ain't done yet. Doc Fagin's got me on the transplant list. In the mean time, I really need you to do something for me."

"Shoot, man, whatever it is, I'll do it!"

"I need you to try to find out where Gemima Renner is. I need to talk to her." Tal got up and put the horse statue on his bookcase shelf.

"Man, I don't know. That was a long time ago. She could be any place, if she's still alive."

"I know. The same thought occurred to me. This is important, though."

"You remember, she broke your heart."

"Yeah, I know, that's why I need to find her, to talk to. Lucy and I were at peace with each other when she passed. Gemi and I never made our peace. I need to find closure with her, with her memory. I don't want my life to end wondering about her, and what happened to the 'us' we were once. I need to know why we broke up. I need to know what happened. Do you get what I'm saying?"

"No, I don't." Dusty scratched his head. "But I'll try help you. I'll do some web research. What was her parent's names?"

"I don't remember her mother. Her dad was George Renner. Remember, he owned the oil road construction business?"

"Oh, yeah, that helps. I'll see what I can do."

They finished the six-pack as they talked. The congestion in Tal's cough told Dusty just how sick his friend really was. It grew late and Dusty needed to leave.

"Take it easy, Pal, don't want you to wake up dead some morning."

"Take it easy?" Tal gave Dusty a wry smile. "That's all I do. Gotten good at it, too."

Dusty gave his friend a pat on the shoulder. "I know you don't like sittin' around but, consider the alternative. At least you're sittin' around alive."

Dusty smile and waved as he slid the patio door shut. Tal laid down on his bed, in the dark, and stared at the ceiling. Feeling just as lost, just as alone, just as afraid, still feeling like crying, he remembered the Midnight Mass so many years ago. He remembered the peace he felt as he sat next to Gemi while she prayed. He remembered the priest. Maybe it was time to talk to a priest. The little flash of peace that came to him at that moment brought him some hope. Tomorrow he would go to Saint Anne's and find a priest. The beer had helped him relax. He drifted off into deep, painless sleep.

XV

Looking for Answers

Tallet Jinx awoke very early. He came to consciousness slowly, gathering his thoughts. His first thought was not about Gemi. His first thought was about his health, about his heart. He rolled over on his back and stretched. The room was still very dark. He looked at his clock. Five-thirty. Maybe he was getting back to normal. Five-thirty was the usually get-up time for a rancher. He looked towards the patio door. No sign of dawn.

He arose slowly, pausing on the edge of his bed, waiting for the light-headed feeling to pass before he stood up. He went to the bathroom to relieve himself and to wash the sleep from his eyes. He looked at himself in the mirror. It was hard for him to believe that his heart could make him look this old. He never wanted to look this old, yet there he was, looking older than Sparky did at this age. He switched off the light, went to the patio door and put his hand on the glass. Cold, very cold. He picked up a blanket that hung over the back of his recliner. He wrapped it around his body and slipped on an old, beat-up pair of shoes he always kept by the door. He slid the door open and stepped out onto his patio, closing the door securely behind him. He walked out to the edge of the patio, leaned on the fence and looked up at the stars. Small, puffy clouds drifted on a gentle, persistent northwest wind. The clouds and the stars seemed to be competing with one another, playing peek-a-boo for his attention. Just then a small meteor shot through the dome of the sky as if to scare and scatter the clouds. He looked towards the east. The first faint glow of dawn began to paint streaks of pink and purple across the bottom of the drifting clouds. He could feel the chill of the wind penetrating his blanket. The cold was not uncomfortable. In fact, it felt good. It made him feel alive.

Alive. He wondered how much longer? How many more days or weeks would it be?

The vast, emptiness of the sky, his memories of Gemi, thoughts of his family and friends all conspired to create a deep, aching loneliness in his soul. He spoke out loud. "Why God, why? Why is this happening?"

He looked back towards the east and saw the purple and pink glowing brighter into orange and gold as the sun neared the horizon. His mind went back to the 'drive-in' he had taken Gemi to, that night under the stars. It was just as cold then, he remembered. He also remembered her question.

"Tal, do you believe in God?"

He also remembered his answer.

"Not really. Sometimes when I see the colors of sunrise and sunset, I wonder. This all can't be by accident. It's too beautiful to be an accident or a fluke of nature. Maybe there is a God."

Tal laughed to himself. What a way to start the day he decided he needed to talk to a priest. Just then he heard Joey barking out beyond the barn. He whistled, beckoning his old hunting pal to come. It was barely a minute 'til Joey came bounding over the fence, eager for Tal's attention. Tal rubbed the old dog's ears and scratched his back. The cold was becoming uncomfortable now and he began to shiver. He moved towards the patio door, urging the collie to follow. Back inside, he sat down in his recliner to watch the sunrise, his dog by his side.

The beauty of nature and the love of an old dog. Yes, maybe there was a God who was good and loving and would somehow provide some peace and comfort in what may be his last days. Yes, it will be an interesting day. He had lots of question for the priest.

Tal heard Bekka in the kitchen. He looked at the clock. Seven-thirty. The sun was up, the day bright. He went out to see what his sister was doing, Joey close behind. Joey hoped he could score some of the bacon he smelled cooking.

"Good morning, Sis, I hope you don't mind if I invited company for breakfast."

Bekka looked at Tal. He looked so much older. She tried not to worry about him. When she saw how quickly the disease was aging her brother, she couldn't help but worry. She glanced at Tal's companion. "I thought you didn't like him eating in the kitchen."

"I don't. He's jealous. Says I've been spending too much time with my sister. Says we need to saddle up Paint and head out across the prairie, to el Huerfano. Told him you were holding me prisoner. He needed to talk to you or bite your leg or somethin'." Tal turned to Joey. "There she is. Go get her."

Bekka laughed at her brother's lightheartedness. "Okay. I'm not setting a plate for him!"

"That's all right. He can eat off mine."

Bekka didn't mind the dog's presence. She knew her brother needed a diversion from his health problems. Bekka put Tal's plate on the table. Joey got the first piece of bacon. After Tal finished his breakfast he went to the mud room entrance to retrieve a grooming brush. He sat down against the wall by the kitchen door and called Joey. The dog came and sat in front of him. As he began to brush the snags and burs out the dog's coat he spoke to Bekka.

"I need to go to town today."

"What for?"

He hesitated, afraid of his sister's reaction.

"Well, . . . I want to go to Saint Anne's church to see if I can find a priest to talk to about prayer an' God an', well, you know, stuff like that."

Bekka had to turn away and stifle a smile. Normally this would have been the perfect place for various jokes about hell freezing or God fainting or the sky falling. Bekka knew better. This was not a place for jokes. She knew her brother was trying to settle his affairs and if this was the way to find the inner peace he would need in the coming days, so be it.

"Well, okay, but you can't drive. Doctors orders."

"Then you need to take me."

"Sure. What time?"

"I need to finish Joey's overhaul, here. Maybe in an hour or so."

"I'll be ready."

Tal brushed the dog 'til all the snags and burs were gone. Joey enjoyed every minute of it. He took the dog back to his room and let him out through his patio door. "Go catch me a rabbit!" He jumped the rail and was gone in a flash.

Tal dressed and went to the kitchen and called Bekka. He said nothing as they drove toward town. He thought about his meeting with a priest. He had so much to say and didn't have a clue where to start. He wasn't sure a priest would even talk to him, especially if the priest found out the last time Tal had been to any church. Whatever happened, he knew he had nothing to lose.

Bekka stopped in front of the church. "You need me to go in with you? Just in case the roof starts to fall or something . . ." She couldn't resist one little poke.

"Nah, I'll be okay. Don't know how long I'll be. Come back in an hour or so."

Tal stopped in the door way to look back as Bekka drove away, still a bit unsure this was right. He took a deep breath and turned his attention to what he came for. He walked in and paused at the back pew. He looked around at the stained glass windows, the statues, the altar, the candles. Then it all came back to him. Midnight Mass and Gemi so many Christmas' ago. He even remembered the place where they sat as she prayed the 'Hail Mary'. He walked up toward the front and sat down in that same spot hoping to find the same peace. His mind was in a spin. What do you say to God when you haven't talked to Him in forty some years? What was the name of that priest who welcomed him so many years ago? Father Williker. Yeah, that's it. Surely, though, he would be gone by now.

Tal sat in silence trying to clear his mind. He found himself swirling within the bounds of an unholy trinity of anger, longing and fear. He was angry at God for ending his life too soon. He longed to see, or at least talk to Gemima. And he was afraid of dying. He was afraid of the unknown, of not being able to be with the friends and family that he had known so long. He was also afraid of living with the pain of the loss still dominating his heart. The peace he had hope to find in this peaceful place seemed so elusive. In exasperation he lifted clenched fists and cried out, "Why, God? Where are you?"

"Those are very difficult questions."

Tal turned in surprise. He had thought he was alone. He saw a forty something man, thin and tall in build. He had thick, black, bushy hair and a mustache to match. He was dressed in an old sweatshirt and faded blue overalls. He wore socks and sandals on his feet.

"Did I say that out loud? I'm sorry. I thought I was alone."

The man's voice was kind and loving. "Hi. I'm Father Frank Norbert. I don't think we've met."

Tal looked at him suspiciously. The man didn't look anything like a priest. "Ah . . . , I'm Tallet Jinx and I've come . . . well. I've only been here once before and I need to, ah, well, talk to . . . Do you know Fr. Williker?"

"Oh my, that was a long time ago. Long before I came here. I didn't know him. I've seen his name in parish records. Have you been away from church that long?"

"No, Father, I'm not Catholic. I came here for Midnight Mass once with a friend and it seemed so peaceful. I was hoping to find some of that same peace." Tal looked at the man's clothes. "Are you sure you are a priest?"

Fr. Frank smiled as he offered a welcoming handshake. Tal saw a gentleness in his eyes and felt a welcoming softness in his grip. He sensed that he could trust him, talk to him.

"God lets us dress in civilian clothes sometimes. No matter what your faith, you are welcome here."

Tal bowed his head and spoke lowly, almost in a whisper. "I need to talk to someone. You got some time?"

"Sure, Mr. Jinx, come with me. Let's go to the rectory. There is a room where we can sit and have some privacy.

"Great. You can call me Tal. Everyone else does."

"You can call me Fr. Frank. Everyone in the parish does."

Father escorted Tal into the rectory and invited him to sit down in a small side room next to his office. "Would you like something to drink?"

"No, thanks."

"So tell me, Tal, what's on your mind and why do you need to know where God's at?"

Tal told Father about his heart condition and the transplant waiting list. Then he paused for a moment to choose the right words. "I told you I came here with a friend. Well, she was more than a friend. She was someone

I loved . . . once, . . . I think, and I, well, I wish . . ." Tal's voice trailed off as he buried his face in his hands.

Fr. Frank watched Tal as he searched for words. "Wish what, Son?"

Tal's voice grew dark and edgy. "I wish I could talk to her one more time before I die, but she hurt me. I don't know what I would say to her."

"How did she hurt you?"

"I was seventeen, a senior, and she was fifteen, a sophomore. We went steady for most of the year. I had enlisted in the Navy because I didn't want to be drafted. She didn't want me to leave. Back then, the choice was simple . . . school or the draft. She tried to make me stay by making me jealous. I resented her attempt. I left town and, well, we never spoke after that. There wasn't any closure. By the time I got home she was gone, moved away. Lucy and I were married then and, well, life went on. Lucy died a few years back, leaving me a lot of time for loneliness. Bekka, my sister, found a reminder of the girl. It was an old Valentine card. Her name was Gemima Renner. When Bekka showed me the card, I went spinning off into her memory. Her memory has been haunting me ever since. It's made the loneliness even harder to deal with. I want God to take it away."

Father could hear an echo in Tal's voice. He thought it may be more than loneliness. Maybe remorse was also a part of Tal's struggle. "Have you wondered why her memory has become so strong?"

"Only everyday. That's why I'm here. She brought me to that Midnight Mass so long ago. I felt a peace I had never felt before, sitting there next to her. I came looking for that peace. It isn't here anymore."

Father smiled and leaned back in his chair. "Your quest is not unusual. Many people, especially those who don't know God, or how to pray, make this search. Unfortunately, what you are looking for is not in that building." He pointed to the church. "It is in here." He pointed to his heart. "Peace comes from knowing and loving God. Peace enables us to be reconciled with those we have hurt as well as those who have hurt us. Peace is not the absence of conflict. Peace is reconciliation and restoration of relationships so that we can live in harmony with each other and God."

"So what do I do? Call her up and say 'Hi, what cha' been doing the past forty years'? Oh, by the way, you hurt me and you need to ask me to forgive you."

The depth of Tal's anguish was becoming more evident. Father paused to gather his thoughts. The questions posed by Tal were age old. They were questions he had heard many times. Each time they were asked, they were accompanied by the same anguish. They were asked by different names, different faces, different times, different places. It was always with the same anguish because the pain emerges from the same human frailty, imperfect love. It is what happens when people love without God's grace. Father Frank began speaking slowly, quietly, hoping his words would be taken to heart.

"Tal, I would be glad to counsel with you, to pray for and with you, as you face the end of your days. I also hope you will come back to visit. I have a feeling that remorse is a part of this puzzle. Somehow, you are going to have find closure with Gemima. If you like, I could check the parish records to see if the Renner family left a forwarding address. Perhaps if you could call her just to say 'Hello, how are you, been thinking about you'. Maybe that could soften your heart. In the meantime, you are welcome to join us for Mass any Sunday."

Father's words did have an effect. Tal smiled and began to relax. "Maybe you're right. What would it hurt to talk to her? And I would like to come back sometime. And closure? I've already thought about that.."

Tal stood up to leave. Father Frank said a prayer of healing and asked God to give Tal the strength and grace needed to face the days ahead. He ended his prayer with a blessing. Tal gave Father a heartfelt 'Thank you' and left to find Bekka waiting for him at the curb in front of the church. He got into the truck.

"How was your meeting?"

"It was okay."

"Who did you talk to?"

"A priest named Fr. Frank Norbert."

"What did you talk about?"

"Closure. And some other stuff."

His tone of voice was terse, his words clipped. Bekka could tell he really didn't want to talk about it. She decided to try one more time. "Were you able to find some answers?"

He did not respond to Bekka's question. Bekka assumed his lack of response was an unwillingness to talk. They rode in silence for several minutes. Finally, Tal broke the silence.

"Sis, I don't quite know how to take this God thing. All I know is that since I've had to confront the possibility of dying, I've needed to bring closure to several areas of my life. Some how, God fits into all that. I just don't know how. I need time to figure it out. That is something I don't have much of. Fr. Frank said he could help and I am going to take him up on the offer. If anything happens to me, please call him and ask him to pray for me. Okay?"

Bekka reached over and squeezed Tal's arm. "Sure, Bro, I would be glad to. My job is to help you get well. Whatever it takes, I will do it."

Tal smiled and patted her hand. They both had a new, deeper understanding of each other. And both of them found a higher level of consolation in that understanding.

Tal said no more. They drove home in silence. He ate lunch and went to his room for the remainder of the day. If Dusty found where Gemima was, then Tal would call her . . . just to say hi, how are you, just to hear her voice. Maybe that would help bring closure. Yeah, that's what he needed to do. Bekka came to his door late in the evening to ask if he wanted supper. Too many emotions left him tired and without an appetite. He chose sleep over food. The day's decisions made sleep easier, more restful.

Tallet Jinx awoke feeling better. He glanced out the window as he got up. The first light of dawn had colored the sky outside his bedroom window. He showered and dressed, taking his time. The hot water on his face and chest felt good. He reflected on his conversation with Fr. Frank. The priest's suggestion that he call Gemima lightened his mood. As he warmed to the prospect of talking to his first love, it seemed as though his heart didn't hurt so much. The sound of Bekka in the kitchen and the smell of breakfast beckoned to him. He looked for Dusty's phone number on his dresser then headed for the kitchen.

"Good morning, Sis."

"Have a seat. I got your breakfast. What are your plans for this day?"

He took a sip of coffee as Bekka placed his plate on the table. "I thought I'd call Dusty and ask him to come by. Maybe we can figure out why we keep lyin' to one another."

Bekka laughed at Tal's joke. His lightheartedness was a pleasant change from the dark moodiness she had been living with since Doc Fagin's grim diagnosis. The drugs the good doctor had prescribed had eased the symptoms of Tal's body. Bekka was sure that the talk with the priest had eased the symptoms of his spirit. She decided she needed to encourage her brother's out reach. "Ask him to come late morning and stay for lunch. I'll make some filet of skunk sandwiches."

"Um, um, my favorite. Throw in some warm, stale beer and you got a deal."

They both laughed at each other. Bekka was glad to hear laughter in the kitchen. It had been a while.

Tal finished his breakfast and went to the phone. As he dialed the number, the big question came to the forefront of his brain. Gemima.

"Hey Dusty. It's Tal . . . Yeah, I'm good, finer than frog hair." Tal stepped down the hall so Bekka couldn't hear his conversation. "Did you find that info I asked about? . . . Yeah, Gemima . . . You did? Great. Can you come for lunch today?" Tal lowered his voice. "Bring some beer and come to my bedroom door like last time . . . Great. See you 'bout eleven."

Tal hung up the phone and went to his room. He glanced at the clock as he took his heart medicine. Nine-thirty. He had some time before Dusty came. He put an old movie into his VCR and sat in his recliner to watch. The breakfast and the medicine relaxed him. As soon as he was comfortable, his thoughts turned to Gemi. What did she look like? When should he call? What should he say? Should he ask her for a photo? They were both forty some years older. The last time he looked in the mirror, he could see that he hadn't aged very gracefully, even though he knew it was the disease process that had made him look older than his years. He hoped she looked younger than her years. Oh, the possibility of her having grey hair didn't bother him. It was the thought of those eyes fading away. "I would hate it if her sky blue eyes had lost their sparkle," he whispered. He closed his eyes and imagined what she looked like. The next thing he knew Dusty was knocking at his patio door. Tal looked at his clock. Eleven-ten. He had napped for over an hour. He rose as quickly as his sleepy head would allow.

"Hey, old buddy, get your carcass in here." They greeted each other with a warm, brotherly hug. Tal looked at his empty arms. "Did you bring any refreshments?"

"You bet. How can I say no to my brother from another mother who can't buy his own? It's on the patio. Thought I'd let the January wind keep it cold." Dusty went out to get two cans.

Tal pulled his other chair around so they could sit face to face. They opened their cans and Dusty offered a toast.

"To healing for my life long friend. May this day be the first of many more."

They clicked cans and took a sip.

"Thanks, Dusty. I want you to know how much I appreciate you and our friendship. I don't think I've told you that enough."

Dusty smiled. "No, you haven't. What's been going on that you need to wax poetic before the third beer?"

"I went to see the pastor at Saint Anne's parish yesterday."

"So that's what that rumble was. I thought it was a rip in the space-time continuum."

Tal expected the tease. "No, really. Remember I told you that Doc Fagin said I needed to get my affairs in order?"

Dusty's smile faded when he remembered the seriousness of the situation. "Sorry, Tal, I was just kidding. What did the good Father say?"

"I told him that I had made peace with most everybody and everything except for one person, one memory."

"Gemima." Dusty reached into his shirt pocket for a crumpled peace of paper. "Here's the info you asked for."

Tal unfolded the paper and read. It was the address and phone number of Darbi Lincoln. "Who's this?"

"That's as far as I could get. I went on the web and searched for Renner Construction Company. I found three. Only one listed a George Renner as founder. I went to their web site and found a list of company personnel. The roster included a Darbi Renner Lincoln. Hers was the only number I could find in the phone book of Cottage Grove, Illinois. My guess is she may be a daughter or maybe a granddaughter. The business still seems to be family owned because most of the names were Renner. Anyway, I figured you could take it from there."

Just then Bekka opened the bedroom door. "I thought I heard voices. Hello, Dusty. I came to see what you two juvenile delinquents were up to." She looked at the beer in their hands. "Just as I thought, you're up to no good."

Tal held up his beer. "Care to join us, Sis?"

Bekka showed her disapproval with a frown and a tone of frustration. "I'll bring your lunch in a while, that is if you're not too drunk to eat it. You ain't doin' yourself any good, Tallet Jinx." She closed the door.

"Hope I didn't get you into trouble, Tal."

Tal waved off Dusty's concern as he took a long drink from his can. "Lead me not into temptation, I can find it by myself." He held up the scrap of paper. "I owe you for this, my friend. Thanks."

Dusty reached out and patted Tal on the knee. "Here's what I want most in the whole world. I want you fit and well enough that we can go hunting rabbits in the spring."

Bekka brought lunch. They ate and talked most of the afternoon. Finally the shadows outside grew long. Dusty got up to leave. "I'm going to leave what's left of the beer outside the door for you. Take it easy, will ya. And let me know what happens with this phone number." Dusty patted Tal's shirt pocket.

"Will do. I'll keep in touch."

Dusty left and Tal went back to his chair. He sat down and took the paper out of his pocket. He read it over and over, until he had it memorized. He wondered, who was Darbi Lincoln. Did she know who Gemima was, or better yet, where she was? Tal decided to wait 'til tomorrow, or the next day to make the call. As quickly as he made his decision, a glimmer of fear made its reappearance in the back of his mind. Did he really want to do this? Perhaps the status quo was less painful than dialing that number. He got up and opened the patio door for another beer. All he found was a note from Bekka, under a rock. "Doc said no alcohol." That's all she wrote. The flash of anger quickly turned into a smile. His kid sister outsmarted him again. It was okay. It was for the best. He knew that. He closed the door and went to bed feeling relaxed and at ease. Tomorrow would be soon enough to face the ghost of her memory. Tomorrow would be soon enough to go looking for her.

Tallet put Dusty's note under his pillow. Sleeping with the possible solution to his problem under his head was a source of peace. He had made his decision. It was no longer if he should call. It was when he should call. Finally he decided Sunday evening would be a good time. Chances are there would be someone at home, someone to answer his call

XVI

The Fateful Call

Sunday evening came. Tal retrieved the slip of paper from under his pillow and made his way to the kitchen, to the phone. Bekka had retired to her room. He was glad to hear her television. He knew she would not be able to hear him and come check on him. He did not want any interruptions. He could feel his heart quicken as he dialed the number. He hope that maybe Darbi Lincoln would point him toward Gemima.

"Hello."

"Ah, ... hi, ... hello. Is . . . is this Darbi Lincoln?"

"That's me. Who's calling please?"

Tal was not ready to identify himself. "I am an old friend, a classmate of Gemima Renner. Do you know her?"

His mouth went dry and his hands began to tremble. He felt like a schoolboy calling his first girlfriend for the first time.

"Yeah, she's my mother."

Tal's mind began to spin. He couldn't believe that it was this easy after all these months of thinking and wondering about her.

"Do know where I could find her?"

"Yeah, she's right here. Mom, telephone."

Click.

Tal panicked and hung up the phone. It was all too sudden. He wasn't prepared for this twist of fate. Emotionally, he had prepared himself to locate her, not to talk to her. He felt his control slipping away as the pain of betrayal mixed with the confusion of not knowing what to say. The excitement of actually talking to Gemima was trumped by a loss of words. He felt lightheaded and breathless as his heart raced. Suddenly the pain in his chest was excruciating. He needed to sit down. He grasped his chest as he reached for a chair at the kitchen table. The room started to spin and grow dark. The last thing he remembered was losing his balance.

Bekka heard a crash in the kitchen and came to investigate. She found her brother on the floor. Unconscious.

Tal woke up slowly. He felt groggy, disoriented. He heard a low beep-boop, hissing and the jumble of muted conversation. He wondered what was going on and why all these people were in his room. He opened his eyes and struggled to focus. Where was he? As his vision cleared he recognized a hospital room. The beeping was a monitor and the hissing was the oxygen tube in his nose. He turned his head and saw Bekka talking with Dusty and his sons. He tried to speak but his throat was dry and raspy. His words came out in a barely audible whisper.

"Bek . . . Bekka. I . . . I . . . I'm thirs . . . ty."

She turned to see her brother reaching for her arm.

"Tal! Dusty, go tell the doctor Tal's awake. Hurry!" She leaned over her brother and caressed his brow. "I am so glad you are awake."

"What's going on? Why am I here?"

"You're in cardiac ICU. You've had a heart attack. You've been in a coma. We were afraid we were losing you."

It slowly came back. Tal remembered. The phone call.

Bekka continued. "I don't know what you were doing but something stressed your heart."

Dusty came back with Doc Fagin. The good doctor checked Tal's heart with his stethoscope. "You scared us!"

Tal grunted. "I could say I scared me too. I don't remember anything."

"Don't talk now. You need to rest." Doc turned to the people in the room. "Say your goodbyes for now. Our patient needs rest." He motioned to Bekka. "I need you to stay for bit."

The sons and Dusty gave Tal a caress, a pat, a word of encouragement, then left for the outer waiting room. Doc Fagin took Bekka's and Tal's hand.

"Tal, Bekka already knows this. Now that you are awake, you need to know. You have had a serious heart attack. Your heart is failing fast, faster than we first believed. We need to pray for a miracle. If we don't get an organ donor soon, it may be too late. I don't want to scare you but I knew you would want the truth."

Tal squeezed both their hands and closed his eyes. "Bekka, c . . . call Fr. Frank . . . for me."

"I already have. He's been here twice. I'll let him know you are awake."

Tal managed a weak smile. "What time is it?"

Bekka looked up at the clock. "It's 9:30 . . . Wednesday night."

Tal closed his eyes and groaned as he tried to shift positions. It wasn't easy with all the tubes and wires running across the bed. The last thing he remembered was hanging up the phone. He squeezed his sister's hand and spoke haltingly. "Are . . . are you sure? It's Sunday, right? Just after supper. Right? I wanted to call . . . someone . . . who . . ."

Bekka leaned over and kissed his forehead. "That was three days ago."

"No, no it was . . ." A wave of weariness washed over him. He closed his eyes and started to drift off but he fought off the sleep. "What happened?"

"I was in bed reading. I heard a crash-bang. I found you on the kitchen floor, out cold. I called 9-1-1. They kept you alive 'til we got you here."

Tal grimaced. "Oh no, no, no . . . I need to talk to Fr. Frank."

Bekka kissed him again. "Shh, quiet yourself. It'll be okay. You're in good hands. We'll get through this. Father assured me he would be back tomorrow. I will call him and tell him you asked for him. Now you need to rest."

"Can . . . can I . . . have . . . some water?"

Tal took a sip and mouthed 'thank you' as he closed his eyes. He was asleep in seconds. Bekka brushed his hair back out of his eyes and pulled the cover over his arms. She leaned close to Tal's ear and whisper. "I love you, and we will get through this."

Tal stirred a bit, as if he heard her. She was sure he did. She wiped the tears from her eyes and left the room to meet the others. She hoped she had the inner confidence to assure them. The problem was she had her own doubts to grapple with. It's hard to sound convincing when you're not sure yourself.

She took a seat in the circle of her family and friends. Doc Fagin came in and sat with them. They all leaned forward, eager to hear what he had to say.

"I've checked the latest lab reports. For now, he is stable. The drugs I have prescribed have had their effect. I am optimistic that Tal will be okay . . . for now. I have called the organ transplant folks and told them we are approaching a critical time. They have agreed to moved his name to the highest priority. All we can do now is hope and pray. Tal needs rest and quiet so as to gain as much strength as he can. If, I mean, when we find a donor, he will need that strength to survive the transplant. I've told him as much as I want him to know about his condition. We need to be upbeat and positive when we visit with him. All of you need to go home and rest. Bekka, you have been here all week. Go home and go to bed. I will call all of you if Tal takes a turn for the worse. For now, I do believe he'll be okay."

They all thanked the good doctor, said their good-byes and left for home and some well deserved rest.

XVII

Waiting for a Miracle

Bekka undressed and went directly to the shower. The hot water splashing on her body was restorative. She spent several minutes just standing there, eyes closed, water beating her back and shoulders. It wasn't until she felt the water cooling did she realize how long she had stood there. She had used all the hot water. Stepping out, she dried and put on her night clothes. She sat on the edge of her bed to finish drying her hair as she thought about her brother. Putting the towel to her face, she began to sob. All the emotion she had held back for his sake came pouring out. The urge to despair was strong. For now, though, she was able to push it back. She appreciated Doc's attempt to temper the news about Tal. It didn't help. Her years of nursing experience told her exactly how critical the situation was. At long last, the emotion past. She hung up her towel then went to her purse. She dug to the bottom to find the rosary Fr. Frank had given her the first night Tal was in the hospital. She didn't know the prayer that went with it. Just holding it was enough to comfort her. She got into bed and pulled up the covers. The emotion of the whole week washed over her bringing with it an incredible weariness. She wanted to pray for her brother. All that came out was, "Help us, God. We need a miracle." She was asleep in seconds, still holding the rosary.

Tal awoke early Thursday morning. He knew he was doing better. He was hungry as well as thirsty. He was about to ring the call bell when the door opened. It was Fr. Frank.

"Hey, Father, how are you?"

Father smiled and put his hand on Tal's shoulder. He could hear the lingering weakness in his voice. "No, how are you? You look a bit better."

Tal got straight to the point. "I found Gemima. I could've talked to her. She was there. Before I could say anything, though, all the hurt came back. The last thing I remember is hanging up 'cause I didn't know what to say."

Father looked at Tal. Tal could see love and concern in his eyes and it was comforting. He could hear the hurt in Tal's voice. He knew Tal needed to talk about the phone call. He wasn't sure this was the time. He wasn't sure Tal's heart was strong enough to endure the stress needed for the healing of his heart and soul. Tal would need strength to move forward, to find peace and wholeness. Father chose his words carefully.

"Listen, what's most important is that you get well, physically, I mean. When you are better, we can talk about your heart and soul. In the meantime, I'm here for you and your family whenever you need me."

Tal smiled and patted the hand on his shoulder. Father gave Tal a blessing and a prayer before leaving.

Tal grew stronger as the rest and medical treatment gained ground. It was almost two weeks before Doc Fagin decided Tal could go home under two conditions, the first being strict bed rest. Doc was afraid that any moment of stress would be the last for Tal.

Bekka doted on her brother, seeing to his every need. Dusty came by about every other day, without beer (no alcohol was the second non-negotiable condition) to check on his lifelong friend. They kept each other company and it kept Tal from dwelling on his declining health which is what he frequently did when he found himself alone.

When he was alone his thoughts often turned to Gemima. He wondered if he should try to call Darbi again, to try to talk to Gemima. He was afraid to. Afraid for more reasons than his weakened heart. If he tried to find her, tried to talk, would he find a warm welcome or a cold shoulder? He was still feeling the pain of losing her once. It was something he did not want to experience again. It was safer to think of what could have been. "There is no risk in dreaming," Tal thought.

His mind went back to the first time they parked behind the barn, the first time he put his ear to her breast, the first time he heard her heartbeat. He hoped it wasn't too late. He hoped he could get better. If he could get better, maybe he could take the time to search her out, to go see her. Maybe hear her heartbeat . . . one more time. Maybe. If he could some how get past the hurt. He hoped so. He hoped Fr. Frank was right.

XVIII

A Miracle

Bekka sat bolt upright in bed. The first ring of the phone by her bed jolted her awake. She glanced at the clock. Three-ten. She picked up the phone before the end of the second ring.

"Hello."

"Bekka, Doc Fagin. We have a donor. Get Tal up. I'm sending an ambulance now. We need to get him to the Heart Hospital in Amarillo as soon as possible."

"Okay, okay. Bye."

Bekka rushed toward Tal's room then stopped in the hallway. She decided to let him sleep until the ambulance arrived. She went to the front door and opened it. She switched on the outside and inside entrance lights. She went back to her room and dressed quickly. She retrieved a small suitcase she had packed and placed in the closet. She put it by the front door so she wouldn't forget it. It was barely fifteen minutes before she heard the sound of the ambulance in the driveway. She showed the EMTs to Tal's room. She switched on the light and went to his bed.

"Tal, wake up! We gotta go."

Tal was groggy and disoriented. Who are all these people and what were they doing in his room? "Bekka, wha . . . ? Who . . . ?"

"It's the ambulance. The Doc called. We have a heart donor. We need to leave. Now!"

Bekka and the EMTs helped him out of bed and onto the gurney. He was quickly strapped down and they were gone. Bekka rode in the cab so she would be out of way of the EMTs as they began preparing Tal for surgery.

The ambulance pulled up to the emergency room entrance at the first glimpse of dawn. Tal was rushed directly to pre-op where Doc Fagin met them.

"Doc, where did the heart come from?" Bekka's voice had a sense of urgency.

"I don't know. The family of the donor has asked for complete anonymity. All we know is it was someone who died as a result of a car wreck."

Bekka gasped. It was a moment of complete contradiction. Her heart ached for the tragic loss of the family as she rejoiced in the fact that this tragedy would mean life for her brother.

"What day is it?"

Doc looked at his watch. "February 29th. I didn't realize it. This is leap day. This date should be easy to remember."

Bekka smiled in spite of a deep sadness. It would be easy to remember by two families for two very different reasons.

Just then a priest walked in. "Is this the Jinx family?"

"Yes, I'm Bekka and this is Tal."

"I'm Fr. Millikin. I got a call from Fr. Frank. He asked me to pray with you and bless you before surgery."

Bekka looked puzzled. "How'd you . . ."

Doc Fagin broke in. "I called Fr. Frank right after I called you."

"Thanks Doc. And thank you too, Father."

The nurses had finished preparing Tal for surgery. The anesthetist entered and spoke quietly, quickly. "Say your good byes. Any last words Tal?"

"Yeah, don't say 'last words' an' 'good bye' to someone going for heart surgery. Sounds too grim." He looked at all the people gathered around his bed as they all laughed. "Doc, thanks. Bekka, I love you and appreciate you. Father, thanks for coming and for the prayer. I'll see y'all in a few hours. I guess with a new heart, I'm going to have to be nicer, huh?"

Bekka laughed as the tears welled in her eyes. "I hope your sense of humor is in your brain and not your heart. Don't want you to lose it."

"Oh, yeah," Tall added, "call Dusty and your nephews. Let them know I've been kidnapped. Tell 'em I'm being held against my will for medical experiments."

The anesthesia quickly took effect. Tal was asleep. Bekka and Doc went to the waiting room for the long wait. Before Father left, Bekka asked him to bless her. She didn't like feeling helpless and for the foreseeable future, there was nothing she could do. Except pray. She went to a corner chair, found the rosary in her purse and held it close to her heart. She closed her eyes and whispered, "Thank you, God, for miracles. Console and thank the family who gave my brother a chance for new life."

Noon came and Doc insisted she eat some lunch. Bekka tried to eat some. The worry that preoccupied her every thought didn't leave her with much of an appetite. Occasionally someone would come out of the surgical suite to give a thumbs up so they all knew that, for Tal, it was 'so far, so good'. As time passed, more families came into the waiting room as others left to see their loved ones in the recovery room. Some people tried to ease the tension by talking. Bekka was not that kind. She preferred to stay quiet. She was irritated by the low jumble of multiple conversations. Early afternoon brought with it a crushing weariness. The early reveille and emotional stress took its toll. She curled up on the floor in a corner behind a row of chairs using her coat as a pillow. She was asleep in seconds in spite of the noise.

It was late afternoon when Doc shook her awake.

"Bekka, wake up. He's out of surgery."

Doc helped her up as she rose quickly, shaking the sleep from her head. "C'mon, we can see him in recovery but only for a few minutes."

Doc took her through the double doors into the recovery suite.

The surgeon met them at Tal's bedside. He spoke quietly. They found comfort in his upbeat, confident voice. "Everything went quite well. Tal's physical strength worked in his favor. He is in very serious condition. That is to be expected. The next seventy-two hours will be critical. Every hour that he remains stable increases the chances of a full recovery. We will just have to wait and see. Please, rest assured, he's in good hands."

Bekka went to her brother's side and took his hand. She was encouraged by the color of his face. He already looked better. She began to share the surgeon's optimism.

Everyone's optimism was well founded. Tallet Jinx surpassed everyone's expectations. Within one day, he was awake and alert, sitting up in bed and eating. By the seventy-two hour mark, he was up walking and wanting to go home. His days were filled with a disciplined diet and a steady pattern of exercise, rest and rehab. Tal grew stronger each day, and each day he became more aware of God through the loving kindness and care of all those around him.

Both Bekka and Tal tried to learn the identity of the family whose loved one was the donor of the heart he had received. The organ donation office remained adamant. No information would be released without the consent of the family of the deceased and the family insisted on remaining anonymous.

The time came for Tal to go home. And he was thrilled. So was Bekka, his sons and Dusty. Everyone involved wanted to be back in the friendly confines of Kayne County. Late April was spring time in the high plains of the Texas Panhandle. Tal was home in time to see the bluebonnets and Indian paint brushes in full bloom. The first morning he was home Tal decided to have breakfast on his patio. It is in the springtime that Texas puts on her prettiest dress.

He wasn't home long before his thoughts turned back to Gemima and that aborted phone call. The thought brought back the pain of her betrayal. The pain still couldn't be his heart. He had a new one. He came to understand that the pain was in his soul and his soul hungered for healing and peace. Tal called Fr. Frank. The priest was very glad to hear from him.

"Good morning, Father. I was wondering if you had time in your busy schedule to come see me? I need to talk about a few things."

"I would love to. How about tomorrow after lunch?"

"Why don't you come for lunch? I'll tell Bekka to fix something special. She has me on a heart healthy diet so I am sure she won't try to poison us."

They both laughed.

"It's a date, Tal."

As he drifted off to sleep that night he tried to make a mental list of what he wanted to talk about when he sat down with the good Father. Everything he thought about began and ended with one common theme, one person. Gemima. That was where Tal needed to start. He was fairly sure that it wouldn't be where he would finish.

XIX

A Search for Healing

It was a beautiful Panhandle morning. The crystal clear blue sky and bright sunshine made it impossible to stay inside. Tal dressed in his favorite old denims, boots and hat then headed for the barn. His best barn friends, Joey and Paint, were glad to see him. It had been awhile. Joey was so excited that Tal couldn't keep him from jumping all over him, eager to get his ears scratched. Paint whinnied and nuzzled Tal's neck as he brushed the horse's mane. Tal didn't do much work. He was still in the process of healing, regaining his strength. In fact, what little work he did do meant little to the overall upkeep of the barn. It was doing something, though, and that something meant everything to someone who had worked every day of his life. "Doing something, however small," he thought, "was infinitely better than doing a lot of nothing." Late morning Bekka came out to check on him. It did her heart good to see her brother active again.

"I got a table set up on the patio. Father will be here soon. Why don't you come on in and wash for lunch?"

Tal put away the few tools that were still out of place. He gave Joey a heaping bowl of kibble, Paint a quart of oats, and headed for the house. He went to his bathroom to wash, then sat in his recliner to rest a bit. He felt a little weary. It was obvious he still didn't have his stamina back. Over all, he felt good. "It felt good to feel good," he thought. He knew his stamina would come with time and exercise.

The door bell rang just after eleven. Bekka looked at the clock. Father was right on time. Bekka showed Father to the den then went to call Tal.

Tal came to the den immediately. "Good morning, Father. I sure am glad to see you. Hope you're hungry. Bekka made us a great lunch."

Tal showed Father to the main patio. The afternoon was warm and pleasant. A gentle breeze rustled the leaves of the ancient live oak that had stood watch over Tal and his patio for so long a time. The leaves filtered the bright sun, providing dappled shade. Bekka brought out a tray of sandwiches, chips and a pitcher of lemonade. Both Father and Tal bade her to join them but she demurred. She knew that Tal needed to talk and that she would only be a distraction.

"This is great, Tal. I have been looking forward to seeing you. You do look a lot better than you did in February."

"Feel better too. I've lost about twenty pounds. That has aided my recovery."

Tal poured the lemonade and they both dug into the plate of sandwiches and chips, chatting as they ate. The in-depth discussion would come later. Tal knew what he wanted to say. Talking about it on a full stomach would be easier. Finally, Father sat back and rubbed his stomach.

"Thanks, that was delicious. Why don't we get to the real reason you called me here?"

Tal took a sip of lemonade and leaned back in his chair. He paused to collect his thoughts. He had thought about God more than Gemi. He thought about his longing for peace and healing. He had received a great gift from a loving stranger. The gift of a new heart was a miraculous healing for his body. He knew he still needed healing in his soul and somehow, instinctively, he knew that Gemi, her memory, was at the core of that. Tal began to speak slowly, choosing his words carefully, hoping to speak more from his heart than from his head.

"Remember when we first met, in the church?"

"Yes, I do."

"I had come there looking for peace, the same peace I felt when I came to Midnight Mass with Gemima so many years ago. This search for peace was driven by my failing heart but it was also driven by a memory. There was this girl once . . ."

Father interrupted. "Ah, yes, a common lament."

Tal smiled. Lament? Indeed it is. "Well, I have always been able to make my own way. I've always been able to do it my way, to control my life. This heart thing has made me realize that maybe I need to find out how God fits in my life. Control is not so easy to hold onto, especially in the midst of life's frailties. As I said, it is her memory, Gemima Renner, that had me spinning out of my comfort zone. I got a new heart. I still have an old memory and an old pain of loss. How can you, or God, or both of you, help me with that?"

"I do remember our conversation then. I remember suggesting that you try to contact her. The reason for that suggestion is that sometimes our imagination looms larger than reality."

Tal nodded.

"Maybe if you could talk to her, the memory won't seem so bad. Maybe the hurt won't loom so large. Who knows, maybe she still has feelings for you. I remember you told me you tried to call her."

"Yes, I did. Dusty found out where her family had moved to. He had found the name and phone number of Gemima's daughter. It took me three days before I finally came to the decision to make the call. It was that call that triggered the heart attack that landed me in ICU."

"Was that call hard for you to make?"

"Well, yes and no. It was easy for me to pick up the phone and dial the number. No risk, no pain in that. As fate would have it, Gemima's daughter, Darbi, answered. I asked her where I might find Gemima, if she had a phone number. Then the unbelievable happened. She said her mother was right there, with her. Before I could say anything, Darbi called her mother to the phone. I didn't know what to say. I wasn't ready to talk to Gemima. I thought I needed time to steel myself for what might happen next, for what she might say to me. I needed to think about, to rehearse, the words I would say to her. I couldn't do it. I panicked and hung up. The thought of being a few seconds away from speaking to the person who hurt me was too much to bear. The next thing I knew, Bekka was staring down at me in a hospital bed."

Father could see the depth of the pain Tal had been facing. He paused for a moment of silent prayer. He knew that only God could heal a broken heart and a broken soul. In his prayer he asked for the right words to say. He had seen the pictures on the wall in the den. He thought that maybe if he knew more about Tal's family, he might find a doorway to healing. "Is that a photo your wife in there?" He pointed to the den.

"Yeah, that's her."

"Tell me about her."

Tal paused to search his memories. He and Lucy had lived many good years together. He wasn't sure where to start. He also wondered why it mattered to Father or to his memory of Gemi. If it would help though, he was willing to answer the question. Finally he spoke. "She was a good woman, a good wife. We had a lot of good years together. Losing her was hard. You love and care for someone for so long then they're gone. Makes you wonder what to do next."

"Did you think about Gemima much before you lost Lucy?"

"Yeah, on occasion. I'd hear her name or a old song. Only in passing did I think about Gemi."

Father paused for effect. "So, do you think that maybe your loneliness for Lucy is driving the memory of Gemi?"

Tal wanted to say 'no'. Deep down inside he knew that Father Frank was onto something. He leaned forward to reach for his glass. He took a sip of lemonade, put the glass down and leaned back in the chair. He looked up at the blue sky through the branches of the old live oak. He wondered how many secrets the tree knew about him.

Father asked again. "Do you think the loss of Lucy brought back the memory of Gemi?"

Tal suddenly felt the control that gave him peace begin to slip away. He was at the mercy of the memory of Lucy and also of Gemi. He didn't like being at the mercy of so much emotion. He wanted to turn away, to change the subject. He couldn't. He knew that Father was right. He also knew it was time to face it, no matter how 'out of control' he felt.

"Yes and no. I had closure with Lucy. I didn't have closure with Gemima. I think that's the issue."

Father smiled. He knew an understatement when he heard it. "You want to tell me more about it? Tell me about what happened to you and Gemi back then."

Tal crossed his hands and looked down at his lap. He paused trying to think where he should start. Father Frank let the silence be. His years of experience taught him that silence was when God spoke to the soul. After some time Tal started to speak slowly, choosing his words carefully as if he was walking through a mine field. The memories were there. The question was which one would do it? Which one might explode? Which old memory could lead to a new pain?

"Actually, it started way before 1961. Katy, my mother died when I was twelve. Dad fell apart. He was an 'over the road' trucker and I suppose his being away eased his pain of losing her. It left me alone to fend for myself and Bekka. Finally, Dad sent her to live with Aunt Dori in Amarillo. Then I was alone almost all of the time. It got lonely so I made a habit of trying to hook up with a girlfriend to keep me company, you know, someone for me to love and to love me back. I guess maybe I wanted, expected too much. Maybe I demanded too much emotional support from them so I got my heart broke. That's easy for someone who wears his heart on his sleeve."

Tal stopped to take a drink.

"It must have been difficult for you. Did you ever see your Dad?"

"Yeah, he was usually home on weekends. I'd work with him in our garage. If I didn't do that, I wouldn't see him at all. By that time, he wasn't much of a father. I didn't get much parental guidance so I did a lot of fending for my self. I did learn a lot about cars and trucks. I could drive anything on wheels by the time I was thirteen."

"I'll bet that was something to be proud of."

Tal smiled, nodded and went on. "Anyway, by the time I got to my senior year I decided no more girls. I hated school and wanted to get out as quickly and as easily as possible. I met Gemima in art class. Her eyes captured my imagination. I was immediately drawn to her and I could tell she seemed interested in me. I think was afraid of being hurt again so I pushed her away at first." Tal paused to consider what he just said. He remembered trying to scare her with Ole Jim. "No, I'm sure it was fear. Anyway, she didn't fit in my senior plans. Her persistence and my desire to get lost in her eyes wore me down. I fell in love with her. We talked about a future together, you know, marriage and kids. I really thought she was the one, that we were soul mates. I trusted one more time. One more time I took the chance and one more time, I got my heart broke. Only this time it was fatal, at least to a part of my heart. From then on, I kept my guard up. I wasn't going to let anyone hurt me like that again. It affected my relationship with Lucy. I wish I had her back long enough to say 'I'm sorry'. Does this make any sense to you, Father?"

"Yes. What you are experiencing is a common difficulty in human relationships. How do we love unconditionally without being hurt? The truth is we can't. Hurt is inevitable because human love, in the end, will always fail. That's where Christ comes in. His unconditional love helps us to forgive. Unconditional love and forgiveness brings us healing, if we let Him into those wounded areas. Letting Him into our hearts, though, requires we experience the pain anew. He heals us in the midst of our pain."

"I don't understand. We need to let the memory hurt us to heal us?"

Father continued. "We have to revisit those painful memories so that we can forgive the person who hurt us. Once we forgive, then the healing can happen."

He wanted to believe Father. His calm demeanor indicated his sincerity. It made no sense to Tal. "You are saying the memory doesn't go away?"

"No, it doesn't. The memory is transformed into something new. Think of it this way. The memory is resurrected to a new life. You remember the event, not the pain."

"How can the pain go away but not the memory?"

Tal was lost. Father could see the look of complete puzzlement on Tal's face.

"It's a small miracle, I suppose. It is hard to explain. Once you've experienced this transformation, this healing of memory, you will understand. Healing begins with your willingness to forgive those who have hurt you. Healing cannot happen without forgiveness."

Tal remember how Gemi used a date with Seven Stevens just to make him jealous. It was Stevens' ingratiating self confidence that brought into focus Tal's negative self image and his inability to compete. He remembered how betrayed he felt. He remembered thinking she didn't have to do that. He loved her. He had told her so many times. He would have made her a permanent part of his life. He really would have married her. She had hurt him. Would he let that go? He felt the anger growing inside of him. He was angry with Father Frank for suggesting that he should forgive when it was she who hurt him. Tal chose his words carefully, trying to contain the anger that was smoldering inside of him. "Father, she hurt me. I didn't hurt her. She pushed me away after I trusted her. This is her doing, not mine."

Father Frank saw Tal's whole demeanor change. His face grew dark and foreboding, his rising voice betrayed the depth of his anger. Father knew that he had hit a nerve. He looked at Tal with love in his eyes and spoke in a calm, peaceful voice.

"Are you sure? I used to fight with my brother. When our mother would pull us apart, I would complain loudly that the fight was all my brother's fault. She would be quick to point out that it takes two to make a fight. In the end, none us are completely innocent. You are not responsible for her behavior, only your own. She is not responsible for your behavior. Only her own. You cannot blame her for what you did anymore than she could blame you for what you did. That begs the question. What was your role in the break-up?"

Father's calm voice was disarming to Tal. He wanted to argue more. What happened between him and Gemi was all her fault. Not his. Father's sincerity told Tal it was fruitless. Still, there was something more. A vague, growing awareness deep down inside that suggested Father might be right. All Tal could say was, "I'll think about it."

Father was satisfied with that. He knew the discussion was over for now. He knew Tal needed time to digest what had been said by both of them. He told Tal he would pray for him as he contemplated what was happening in his soul. The next time they got together, they could talk about it more.

The two parted with an air of cordiality that belied the anger that Tal felt deep inside. As Father left for his afternoon appointments, he gave Tal one parting suggestion. "Think about the last time you and Gemima were together. You may find a clue to where forgiveness may be offered."

Tal went back to his room, to his recliner, to sit . . . and think . . . and remember. He remembered the last time they were together. It was a memory hidden deep in the recesses of his mind because it was simply to painful to remember. With Father's blessing and encouragement, he decided to take it on. It wasn't the hurt he wanted to remember. If there was healing and reconciliation to be found in that hurt, then it must be done.

XX

The Last Date

Tal came out of Corley's Drugs Store at dusk. The sun had ignited the low clouds in the west painting the horizon a brilliant purple, orange and red. He was delighted to find Gemi sitting in his car, waiting for him.

"Hi, My-Gem! How ya doin'? I was just going home to call you."

"I was going to ask you the same thing. Where have you been? I've being calling you for three days."

"I had to do something. I needed to go to Amarillo. I called your Mom and told her. Didn't she give you the message?" Gemi sounded miffed. "Yeah. I didn't believe her, though. I didn't think you'd really be gone three days."

"I'm sorry, My-Gem. I didn't mean to worry you."

"Well, you did."

Tal put his arm around her and pulled her close. She resisted to show her hurt feelings. She didn't understand why he had left town without telling her. The truth was that Tal didn't want her to know he was going to Amarillo. She would want to know why and he wasn't ready to tell her. He wanted to pick the right time and place to spring the news, hoping it would make it easier for her to accept his decision.

"Why did you go? To see Aunt Dori?"

"Yeah. And I wanted to see my sister." Tal tried to kiss her but she turned away.

"C'mon, Gemi, give me a break. I did call you. I did leave a message with your Mom. Ask her. She'll back me up."

He took her chin and gently turned her head back. He kissed her lips, her cheek. He could taste her tears and he realized she really was upset. He wasn't sure what to say to make it better. He knew one thing for sure. She wasn't going to feel good about the real reason he had gone to Amarillo.

"Tell you what. I got paid today. Let me take you out for supper then we can go to your Dad's barn and talk about it."

Gemi smiled as Tal wiped her cheeks. She did love him and couldn't stay angry. She put her arm around his neck and kissed him. He put both arms around her and held her tenderly.

At supper they talked about school, the latest hit songs, movies and all the other things that teens talk about. Occasionally, Gemi mentioned the end of the school year and what they would do in the summer. Tal skillfully changed the subject. He wasn't ready to tell her the real reason for his trip to Amarillo. After supper, they went for a ride around the square to see if there were any friends out for the evening. They stopped to visit with a few, then Tal pointed the car towards Gemi's home and the barn. It was after dark when Tal stopped the car and turned off the lights. The moon hadn't risen so the only light was the dim glow of the radio dial. The second song they heard was the song they danced to at Homecoming, the song that sealed their love for one another. Tal saw it as fate, a stroke of luck. Gemi turned to lie across Tal's lap. He embraced her and kissed her. He slipped his hand under her blouse, to caress her back, to feel the soft warmth of her skin. He hoped the touch of his hand would reassure her. It had worked before. Tal decided this was the best moment to tell her the rest of the story.

"My-Gem, I did something else while I was in Amarillo. I signed my enlistment papers for the Navy. I will be leaving for boot camp shortly after graduation."

Gemi's reaction was swift and loud. She sat bolt upright and moved towards the passenger door of the car. "No! You said you wouldn't do that! You said you wouldn't leave me here . . . alone!"

"No, I never said that. I said we could talk about the possibilities of what we could do after I graduated. I told you that I would not go to school or to the draft."

Gemi put her hands to her face and started to cry. Tal moved closer to her and put his hand on the back of her neck and tried to pull her towards him. She resisted and tried to move farther away but her back was already against the door.

"I don't want you to go! I need you! I need you here. With me. We're going to get married. You told me we'd be married and I believed . . . ."

Her voice trailed off, lost in the emotion, as tears continued to fall. Tal reached into his pocket for his handkerchief. He tried to dry her cheeks. She jerked the handkerchief away and covered her eyes. Tal searched for some words, something to say that would comfort her, something that would reassure her that he wasn't going away for good.

"My-Gem, honey, please understand. I'm not leaving you. This is something I need to do. We can write each other. I'll be home from time to time. When you graduate, you can come to where I am. We'll be married. It'll be okay. Honest." Tal slid over to her side of the car, kissed her cheek and whispered in her ear. "We'll be okay. Don't you believe me?"

Gemi wiped her eyes, her nose. She wanted to believe him even though the possibility of being apart for two years was her worst nightmare. She began to relax and respond to his nudging. She moved closer to him and put her head on his shoulder, her hands in her lap.

Tal put his hand on hers, trying to reassure her as much as he could. "I need you too. We can work it out. I really need to go. I need to do this. I've always wanted to be a sailor. Can't you understand?"

Her anger flared again. "No, I don't understand. You could stay here and work for my Dad. Then we could be together!"

Tal was beginning to think there was no way to comfort, no way to reassure her. He slid back over to the driver's door and crossed his arms on his chest.

"I'm sorry you won't understand. This is important to me. You are important to me. The Navy is important to me. I gotta get away from this town for a while. Not for good. This is home and I will be back. I don't want to get away from you. I just . . . I don't know. How else can I do what I think is the right thing!"

Gemi stopped crying as she remembered the one weapon in her arsenal that had never failed. Deep in the silence of the night, they were alone and time was on her side. She opened the top buttons of her shirt. She put her arms around him and pulled his head to her breast. The warmth of her skin against his cheek was so real, so mesmerizing. She bent down and kissed the top of his head and whispered in his ear.

"Can you hear my heartbeat?"

He nodded slowly. He could feel her warmth deep inside of him as he embraced her. Lost in the dark, he couldn't see her eyes. Deep in his soul, though, he could feel those eyes burning holes in his resolve to leave. He could smell the sweetness of her breath, feel the gentleness of her touch.

"It beats for you, just for you. You can't hear my heartbeat if you're miles away. Can you?" Her voice was soft, sensual, hypnotic.

"I guess not, My-Gem,"

For this moment, she was his everything. For this moment, she was the one thing in his life that made him want to love again, to risk his heart. And for this moment, he wasn't leaving. He would stay there and love her as long as she would let him.

The next morning Tal picked up Gemi for school at the usual time.

"Good morning My-Gem. Sure had a good time last night. Couldn't wait to see you this morning."

"Couldn't wait to see you, too." She slid close to him and put her arms around him as he headed out the driveway towards school. Then she asked that fateful question. "Did last night help change your mind about leaving me?"

Tal paused and took a deep breath. He wished she would let it go for now. Graduation was still almost two months away. "Do we need to talk about that now?"

"I need to know. Last night was very special. I would like to have many more just like them. I don't want you to go away. Ever."

"Look, I need you to understand something. I didn't want to love you last September when we first met. You, your eyes, convinced me to try. I didn't think I could love someone like I love you. Now I do. We have time before graduation to be together. Can't we just let it be for now?"

Gemi didn't like the direction their conversation was going. She feared his answer because of his evasiveness. She pressed the issue.

"I want to love you too. How can I when we are far apart? That's why I don't want you to go away. I need you to be around so I can talk to you, so I can be with you."

Tal stopped at a red light. He put his arm around her neck and tried to kiss her. She pulled away and asked again.

"What have you decided? What are you going to do after graduation?"

The events of the night before were a great temptation, a very good reason to stay. As much as his heart wanted to love her, a part of his heart also needed to find its own way. Part of his heart knew he needed to grow up and his instincts told him he couldn't do that in Kayne County. He hated school and that's the only thing that would make him ineligible for the draft. He wanted to stay but needed to go. He looked into her eyes. They were waiting for an answer. The driver in the car behind him blew the horn. The light had turned green and Tal was too distracted to notice. He put both hands on the wheel and hit the gas. He searched for a way, for the words he needed to say. He needed words that would ease the disappointment he knew his decision would inflict on her. He pulled into the school parking lot and switched off the car. He turned towards her and held her hands.

"Gemi, I have to go. I can't stay in Kayne County. I have to get away for awhile. I told you, that doesn't mean we can't be together. I'm not leaving you. I will come back. And after you get out of school, we can find a life together. We will get married. Promise."

Gemima's reaction was swift and strong. She slapped him. Hard. As hard as that first time when he scared her with the armadillo. Then she burst into tears. She got out of the car then turned and screamed at him. "I hate you! I hate you! You promised me and now your breaking your promise! I hate you! I never want to see you again!" She took his ring off of her finger and threw it at him. Then she slammed the car door and stomped away.

Tal sat in the car for a long time. A seething anger rose up inside of him. He never promised her he wouldn't go away and he resented her lashing out at him. He could feel his heart harden against her. She couldn't, no, wouldn't understand what he needed to do. He was determined not be swayed, manipulated by her emotional blackmail. He resolved to take her at her word. He would not to call her or talk to her until she apologized for hurting him. It had happened again. He risked his heart and lost. This would be the last time. He swore an oath to himself. This would be the last time he would risk his heart. He resolved to remember the pain he was feeling at that moment. It would help him keep this promise to himself. He spoke softly, out loud. The softness belied his steely resolve. "Never again. Never, ever again."

He started the car and left. He knew that going to school held a serious risk. He might encounter her in a hallway or lunch room. That was a risk he could not take. He needed the silence of the open prairie. He headed towards the Boy scout ranch. He wanted to get lost in the vast, rolling hills of the Panhandle he loved. That was sanctuary.

* * *

Tal heard Joey scratching at his door. He got up to let him in, then went to the bathroom to relieve himself and get a drink of water. He looked at his clock. Three-thirty in the afternoon. Too early for supper. In his present mood, he didn't want to talk to anyone. He sat down in his recliner. Joey hopped up and sat across his legs, his head on Tal's lap. Tal rubbed the dog's ears and thought about time. Two years. She didn't, couldn't wait for two years? That was forty some years ago. I guess two years is an eternity when you are fifteen and seventeen. It was a puzzlement. She could've waited those 'two years' for him. Why did she have to break it off? Why did she have to try to manipulate him by making him jealous? He had come to a point that had bothered him for the longest time. What happened to them? Why was there never any closure? He felt the need for peace return, peace in his heart, his soul and his mind. He knew that that peace would be impossible without answers to those questions. He needed answers to those questions and for the first time in his life, he was willing to search them out, no matter what the cost. He had a new heart, a new life. He wanted, needed to make it count. Hopefully Father Frank could help him.

He looked at the clock again. It was now after five. He heard his sister in the kitchen and began to smell supper cooking. The emotional journey of the afternoon had left him with little appetite. He thought he would go to the kitchen anyway. He put Joey out and headed for the kitchen. He slowly wandered in silently.

"Good evening to you too," Bekka said.

Tal just grunted. Bekka tried to get her brother to talk.

"What cha' been doing?"

Tal hesitated before he answered. "Nothin'. Just thinkin'."

Bekka tried to get Tal to smile. "Hope you didn't hurt yourself."

He ignore her comment. He got a cup of coffee then sat down. Bekka tried again.

"You hungry?"

"A bit, I suppose."

Bekka sat down across the table from him. "What's going on, Tal? I haven't seen you like this since before your surgery."

"I'm okay." Tal's voice was quiet, subdued.

Bekka didn't believe him. "You want to talk about it?" Bekka wanted her brother to talk. At the moment it seemed like pulling teeth.

"No."

"You want to eat?"

"I suppose."

Bekka gave him a plate and Tal ate in silence, picking at his food. He had not eaten half of his plate when he got up and headed down the hall towards his room without a word.

Bekka called after him. "Don't forget to take you pills."

Tal waved over his shoulder and in a dismissive tone said, "Yeah, what ever."

By now, Bekka had learned to take it in stride. Tal needed to work it out. She could help heal his body. The rest was up to God and Father Frank. She would leave Tal in his puzzlement. She instinctively knew that that is where he needed to be.

XXI

Facing Reality

He went to his recliner and sat down. He was angry at himself and Gemi's memory. It was her that so consumed his life and he wanted to think of something, anything. Just not her. He switched on his television for some noise. Maybe that would be the 'anything' to distract him from the present day. He scanned through the channels. "It's amazing," he thought. "Two hundred channels and nothing of interest on any of them." What wasn't noise was inane dialogue or silly humor. He switched off the television and stared at the ceiling. The room was almost dark. He looked out his patio door at the last rays of twilight streaking across the sky as the sun slowly sank below the horizon. In the silence he listened closely. He could hear his heartbeat. Or rather, someone's heartbeat. He wondered about the heart that he had been given. What family's act of unselfish love had given him new life? How could he ever repay such a singular act of love? He wanted to contact the family to tell them 'thank you'. The hospital, though, was adamant. The family insisted on anonymity. He spoke in a low whisper. "I don't know who you are. I hope God will let you know how grateful I am for your gift of love, your gift of life. I shall pray for your family everyday. May God console you in your loss."

God? It's funny, he thought. For so many years God was a mere afterthought in his life. Any meaningful mention of God made him uncomfortable. Yet here he was, praying to God. What was most amazing, it seemed to come so easily. It was if he had prayed every day, every moment of his life. He felt as if it was the most natural thing in the world.

Tal mused at this conflict in his life. On one hand there was the anger and resentment about Gemi. On the other hand was the peace he felt as he prayed his prayer of thanksgiving for his new lease on the life. He needed help sorting it all out. "I've come as far as I can by myself," he thought, "I need to go see Father Frank again." That decision gave him enough peace so as to calm his mind and provide a temporary escape. He fell asleep in his chair.

It was just after midnight when he was awakened by a loud bang. A northwest wind had brought in a line of heavy, late spring thunderstorms. These were the storms that often reached epic proportions. He rose from his chair and went to his patio door to watch the light show. The lightening was beautiful as it lit up the night. He loved to watch these storms, the glory and power of nature. At the same time, he wished they weren't so destructive. Having to repair the damage done by high wind and hail was usually painful and difficult. He remembered the tornado that ripped his sister's life apart. In the aftermath of these storms, though, there was always good. Bekka living with him was a great blessing. The water and wind brought renewed life to the prairie. Good coming out of pain and struggle. The metaphor came to him slowly. The storms were like Gemi's memory, so beautiful yet so painful to be immersed in. He had lived through many storms over the years. He had lived through her memory for several months. The storms always brought new life, new growth to the land. Her memory could bring newness to his life . . . if . . . yes, if . . . he could face it head-on. He waited until the thunderstorm had passed then undressed and went to bed. He smiled as the reality of the metaphor began to take root in his heart, mind and soul. What Father Frank had told him began to make sense. Healing of memories from the storms of life. Sleep came back quickly. He dreamed about spring flowers, new life and new beginnings.

Morning came and Tallet awoke feeling refreshed, full of energy. His first thought was his need to see Father Frank. He was excited and eager to talk about what had come to mind the night before. He was sure he was on the right track. He came to the kitchen as Bekka was putting breakfast on the table. He went to the phone and called Father Frank. The good Father could see him at ten o'clock. Tal hung up the phone and sat down with his sister.

"You sure seemed to be in a better mood today. You were a world class grump last night."

"Yeah, I know. Sorry about that, Sis. Had a lot on my mind. I think I'm finding my way out. Right after we eat I'm going to St. Anne's to see Fr. Frank."

Bekka was glad to hear this. She was skeptical at first, thinking that Tal's resistance to church would overwhelm the hunger for God he had found in his disease and recovery process. She wanted to do whatever she could to encourage Tal's choice. "You want me to drop you off?"

"No, I would rather drive myself. It would do me good to be out on my own for a while. It feels good to have some of my strength back."

Bekka smiled. "You have fun and tell the good Father hello for me. Don't forget to take your medicine before you go and be home for supper."

Another place and another time Tal would have been irritated by his sister's attempts to mother him. He knew, though, that the love she had shown him was not mothering. It was her concern for him and her desire to have him around a few more years. He accepted her comment for what it was . . . a sincere love and concern. He couldn't resist one little tease as gave her a farewell hug.

"Yes, Mommy dearest."

Bekka laughed. "Shut up and get out of here."

Tal drove into town slowly, thoroughly enjoying the warm sun. He opened the side and back window of his pick-up. The air was fresh and warm smelling faintly of sage. The midnight rain had left the sky a beautiful, crystal clear blue. The wild flowers and green pastures made the Panhandle absolutely glow with new life. He felt a deepening sense of gratitude for his new lease on life.

He pulled up and parked in front of the church. He looked at his watch. Ten minutes early. He decided to spend those ten minutes in the church. This was only the third time he had been inside. The first time was at night. The second time, late afternoon on an overcast day. Today was different. Today the brilliant sun lit up the stained glass windows. Tal walked up to the front, near the altar. He turned slowly to take in all the beauty of the stained glass. The window on one side depicted the crucifixion. The other side was Mary and the Christ child. He stood there, transfixed by the glory of the ancient tradition. He was truly amazed.

Tal looked at his watch. Five minutes late. He rushed out the side door to the rectory. Father Frank answered the doorbell promptly.

"Good afternoon, Tal. How are you doing?" Father gave him a hand shake and a hug.

"I'm well, thank you! It is great to get out and enjoy the spring weather. I've been cooped up too long."

Father showed Tal to the room next to his office. It was a small, pleasant room, decorated in pastel colors. The colors were meant to induced a sense of calm contemplation. Two large recliners faced each other. Father closed the door and they both sat down. The sense of privacy Tal felt helped him to relax and open up. Father began the conversation.

"When you called for this appointment, you sounded excited. Have you given any thought to the questions I left you with a week ago?"

"Yes I have." His tone was bright and cheery. I have come to a contradiction I need explained. Whenever I think about my new heart, my new life, given to me by a singularly generous family, I am filled with a sense of gratitude and thankfulness. Then I seem to feel a bit closer to God. When I think about Gemima and how her actions hurt me, I feel a sense of anger and resentment. Then I feel distant and alone, like God is nowhere around. I'm not quite sure what to make of it."

Father smiled and nodded. "Do you remember when we talked at lunch? You had come to that awareness then."

Tal smiled and nodded. "Yeah, I do."

"I told you then, about this truth. It is a spiritual truth that is found in the Psalms. 'The lord loves a humble, thankful heart.' In your thankfulness, you have a sense of God's blessing. In your resentment, your hardness of heart pushes God away."

Tal nodded as a sign of his understanding. "I can see what you are saying. Still, what do I do about her memory? She hasn't asked me for forgiveness. How can I give it?"

"It isn't that simple. Forgiveness is not something we give only when we are asked. Forgiveness starts by your understanding the hurt you have inflicted on her."

Tal furrowed his brow as his cheeriness faded. "Here he goes again," he thought. This is what Father had alluded to at their lunch a few weeks earlier. He still had no idea how he could be responsible for her betrayal. "So you are saying I need to ask Gemima for forgiveness because I hurt her?"

Father put his head back against the recliner and looked at the ceiling. He knew what he was about to say was going to be very difficult for Tal to accept. Yet, understanding what he was about to say was a necessary, non-negotiable part of healing. He needed to help Tal see the truth.

"The short answer is 'yes'." Father saw anger flash across Tal's face. He knew he had hit a nerve but he continued on, saying what needed to be said. "You don't believe you hurt her, do you?"

Tal recalled the metaphor of Gemi's memory and the storms. Its meaning seem to fade as his anger flared. Tal's voice grew hard. His tone of voice barely contained the anger he was feeling. "Well, maybe one or two times. They were little slights, nothing to break-up over."

"Tell me about the last time you saw her."

Father posed the question then rose from his chair to look out at the warm spring day just outside the window. This was a deliberate move. He didn't want Tal to see him as he listened. Any unintentional facial reaction might be a distraction, something that may break Tal's train of thought.

Tal thought back to his last date with Gemima. "I had picked her up for school as I had all year. When we got to school, I told her I would be leaving for Navy boot camp right after I graduated. She didn't want me to go. She wanted me to stay in town, find a job and wait for her to graduate so we could be together 'til we were married. I told her I couldn't do that because I needed to get out of town and . . ."

Father interrupted. "Why not?

"Why not what?"

"Why weren't you willing to stay with her? Why did you need to get out of town?"

"Because I . . . well, I always wanted to be a sailor and I needed to find my own way and . . ."

Father interrupted again. "Are you listening to your own words? Do you hear how many times you say 'I'? Have you thought about how your unwillingness to consider her request to stay may have hurt her? Did you have to leave right after graduation? Could you have waited six months or a year?"

Tal felt his pulse quicken as the anger flared inside of him. He had come looking for peace. All he found was conflict. He sat up and pushed in the foot rest on the recliner. He began to regret his visit. He wasn't in the mood to defend himself. It was Gemima who had betrayed him by trying to make him jealous. "I think we are done here, Father."

Tal got up to leave. Father turned from the window and caught Tal's arm as he reached for the door knob.

"Please don't go. I know how much you hurt. I can tell by the sound of your voice and the tension I see in your face. It is no accident that you are here today. God wants you, in fact all of His people, to be whole, healed and content with themselves, their family and their neighbors. The healing you seek requires you understand that both of you, you and Gemima, were young, foolish and ignorant about love, life, and the commitment of marriage. You hurt each other. You want peace as we all do. That peace will only come when you are able to ask her, or her memory, to forgive you."

Tal stopped but didn't turn around. Father's words had hit a chord. It had already occurred to him that immaturity had been a big part of what happened to him and Gemima. He stood there facing the door wanting to leave, needing to stay. He wanted silence but needed to hear Father's wisdom. Finally, Tal slowly turned and looked Father in the eyes. Father spoke again about hurt and peace.

"I wish you could see you, hear you, as you speak. When you talk about your new heart, the gift of new life given to you by an anonymous stranger, there is a sense of gratitude, humility and peace about you. When you talk about Gemima, your whole demeanor changes. You sound harsh and angry. If you want forgiveness, you must be willing to give it."

Tal paused to gather his thoughts. What Father was saying was becoming clearer. He went back to the memory of Gemima's outburst.

"What happened next I guess kinda' sealed the deal for me. When I told her I couldn't stay, she slapped me and told me she hated me an' never wanted to see me again. She took off my ring and threw it at me. She slammed the car door and walked away. At first I wanted to go after her. The slap, the words, they stung. So I sat there and watched her go."

"You believed her when she said she hated you, didn't you?"

"Well, I didn't understand how she could love me the night before then hate me the next day."

"Don't you think that maybe she was speaking out of her own hurt and disappointment? Do you think that she hated, not you, but what you were doing? And you reacted within the rejection of the previous people in your life?"

Tal sat back down in the recliner and put his face in his hands. It was finally sinking in. He realized how right Father really was.

"Was that the last time you talked to her?"

Tal realized he had been holding back. There was one more time and he didn't want to talk about it. He sat with his face in his hands.

Father waited. The sound of silence was deafening. He let it be. He had learned long ago that silence was necessary for people to sort out what was going on in their head. After several minutes, he walked over to Tal and put his hand on his shoulder. He asked Tal the question again, in a soft, almost a whispering voice.

"Was that the last time you saw her, talk to her?"

Tal dropped his hands and sat back in the recliner. He gathered his courage and, finally, began to speak. He answered Father's question, his own voice now subdued. He was resigned to his fate.

"No. There was one more time."

"You want to tell me about it?"

"No." Tal looked at Father and smiled. "But I doubt I could get out of this room until I did."

They both laughed. The laughter seemed to break the tension they both felt. Tal paused again to gather his thoughts, trying to decide where to begin as he related the last verse in the 'Ballad of Tallet and Gemima'. It was many years ago but he could see the whole scene in his mind's eye like it had happened yesterday.

"I had been away for almost a year and a half. The Navy had taken me to the west coast and to the Far East. I missed my family and Dusty. I wanted to see them so I came home on a ten day leave. I didn't think about her much while I was gone. The sense of adventure and discovery in foreign lands occupied most of my time when the ship was in port. At sea, the seemingly endless hours on watch made for very long days and very short nights. Most of the time I was too tired to think about high school memories. I had met Lucy shortly before I graduated and left for boot camp. She became the light of my life. I had proposed marriage and she accepted."

Tal paused to take a drink from his water glass. He looked past Father Frank to the sunlit window. It was a beautiful day. Tal thought he would rather be out there in the sun than in that room digging up bones. Father's comment brought him back inside.

"Tell me more. What happened next?"

Tal shifted in his seat and began again. "When I got home, I went to see Dusty. It was a great reunion. As the days passed, though, I began to see Gemima's face in all the old places we'd go to. The reminders got to be a nuisance. I thought about calling her, but I couldn't bring myself to do it. I guess it was the fourth or maybe the fifth day I had been home when Dusty came by with some beer, wanting to talk about, well you know, 'shoes an' ships and sealing wax, cabbages and kings', just idle stuff. He asked me about the Orient and about life on the bounding main. Then, almost out of nowhere, he said he had seen Gemima and told her I was back in town. He said she seemed excited and wanted to see me, to talk to me. It took me a few days to make the call. She asked if I could come over for awhile. I hesitated because I wasn't sure how close I wanted to get to the fire, if you get my drift."

Father nodded. Tal appreciated his understanding. Frank could see Tal grow tense as he got closer to the moment of encounter with Gemima. Tal took a deep breath and continued. "Gemima gave me her new address. Her family had moved shortly after I left for boot camp. It was almost dark when I rang her door bell. When she opened the door, everything, all the memories came rushing back. She was just as pretty, her eyes just as blue, as I had remembered. She welcomed me with a hug and a kiss. She seemed genuinely glad to see me as she asked me in. The smell of her hair and the warmth of her body stirred the desire in me. It took all I had to resist. She sat on her couch and patted the cushion next to her, bidding me to sit near to her. I didn't want to because it was the couch we used to . . . well . . . ah, I mean . . ."

Tal blushed a little. His voice trailed off as he realized what he was about to say. Father sensed Tal's spasm of discomfort.

"That's okay, Tal. I know about couches. I was young, too . . . and in love . . . once upon a time."

Tal managed a sheepish grin as he paused to pick the right words to continue.

"I sat in a chair opposite to her. I felt very uncomfortable. I wanted to not be there. At the same time, couldn't take my eyes off her. We talked about where each of us had been, what we had been doing with our lives. She said she hadn't dated much and had missed me. I told her I had missed her too, trying very hard not to sound sincere. Finally, I decided it was time to leave. Lucy was waiting for me. She didn't know where I was and I was already late. As I stood up to go, Gemi approached me again as if to hug me. I moved towards the door before she could. She caught my sleeve as I opened the door. She put her arms around my neck and kissed me. She asked me to write. She said that if I would write her, she would answer. I could feel the resentment of her manipulations simmering in my chest. I touched her cheek, said good bye. As I drove away, I brushed back the tears from my eyes. I wanted to turn around and go back . . . , back to her arms, back to those mystical, magical eyes. I couldn't. I just couldn't. As real as her eyes were, so was the pain. I never saw her or heard from her again. I was really glad to get to where Lucy was, I needed a reminder of why I had asked her to marry me. Being with Lucy helped me forget Gemi."

Tal lowered his head to hide his expression. Father let the silence be, not sure if Tal wanted to say more. Father Frank waited a minute or so then sat up in his chair and leaned forward.

"You said she asked you to write her. Right?"

"Yeah."

"Did you?"

"No."

"Why not?"

"Because she, I mean, I was still hurt and I . . . . I was . . . afraid . . ."

Tal's voice trailed off. He remembered why he didn't write her. He was unwilling to say it. Father leaned forward and touched his knee.

"Why? What were you afraid off? You were afraid, weren't you? All these years you have been blaming her for breaking off the relationship when all along it was you who ended it because you were afraid. What were you afraid of?"

Father knew what Tal was afraid of. He also knew it was necessary for him to say it, to vocalize what was in his heart and soul. The healing he longed for could only be gained that way . . . and it was within reach . . . if only Tal would stay the course.

Tal lifted his head and looked at Father. Father saw the tears fall as the revelation began to sink in. Tal leaned back in the chair and stared at the ceiling, tears streaming down his cheeks, saying nothing for the longest time.

Father sat in his chair praying, letting Tal wrestle with the emotions that were bubbling to the surface. After several minutes, Tal rose from the chair and went to the window, partly to look out at the spring growth, mostly to hide the tears that kept coming. He did what most men would do in this situation. He wiped his face with his sleeve. He took a deep breath as if to steel himself to say what he was feeling. He turned to Father and began to speak slowly, quietly, almost in a whisper.

"I was afraid. I was afraid of her. I was afraid what she could do to me again. I had no reason to believe she would. The emotional cut was deep and I was afraid." Tal paused to take a breath. "I walked away from her, didn't I?"

Father rose to stand next to Tal. He put his arm around his friend as if to comfort and encourage him.

"The hurt you are feeling today is not because of what she did or didn't do. You are feeling hurt because you have chosen to keep the wounds fresh through unforgiveness. Just like repeatedly picking at a scab keeps a physical wound fresh, unforgiveness keeps the wound on your soul fresh. Do you see how your hurt and anger blinded you to Gemima's attempt to reach out to you, to somehow begin a reconciliation?"

Tal looked at the floor, the ceiling, out the window, then into Father's eyes. The truth came suddenly, completely. A lightening bolt flashed in his heart and the thunder rumbled, echoed down through the years, through his mind and deep into his soul. Suddenly, everything was crystal clear. Every word Father spoke was the essence and purity of truth.

"No!! Oh, no, no, no. It was me. It really was me, wasn't it? It was my fault! After all these years. It was, I mean, it is my fault. You are right. I was too young, too hurt, too afraid to see how she wanted to . . . to . . . get back together and . . . oh no . . . . I can't believe I let her . . ." Tal sobbed. "I . . . I can't believe I let . . . let her . . . go."

Tal's voice trailed off again. After a few moments he began again, his voice rising in anger and frustration. This time it wasn't directed at Father or Gemima. His anger and frustration was directed at himself.

"This knowledge is all well and good for today. She, I mean us . . . , we were a long time ago. Okay, so I did it. I broke it off. Now what? Do I just go home and get over it? It's too late for us, I mean, me and her. I need to know. Now what?"

Father Frank smiled as he patted Tal on the arm.

"That, my friend, is the million dollar question. You are not the first person I have counseled in this area. Everyone, though, eventually comes to that question. You are right. It is too late to begin anew. However, it is never too late to reconcile. Think about trying, again, to contact Gemima. Maybe you two could talk. Maybe she is just as hurt and afraid of you. Who knows? Maybe God wants to bring forgiveness to both of you at the same time?"

The freedom of forgiveness was beginning to set in. The metaphor made complete sense. Forgiveness makes something good come out of the storm. Tal smiled broadly.

"You are be right, Father. I need to go home and think about what I should do next."

"Tal, let me say a prayer and give you a blessing before you go. What God has revealed to you is meant for the good, for healing. We don't know what may lie ahead for you. I do want you to go forward with a spirit of joy, not a spirit of foreboding. What is happening to you is for the good of everyone."

Father put his hand on Tal's head to say a prayer and a blessing for the future. Then Tal was off, headed for home to consider what's next. Whatever it was, he would not be afraid to face it. He knew that it would be for the good. A new, unfamiliar joy was rising in his heart. Yes, there was nothing to be afraid of. He remembered what Father had said about healing memories. For the first time ever, he understood completely. He remembered her and their time together. He remembered the love they shared. Not the hurt. He was glad, eager for her memory. Before he got home he resolved to call her. Soon. He felt no pain. No fear. Just an ever deepening joy.

XXII

A New and Improved Tallet Jinx

Tallet Jinx got into his pick-up and headed home. His mind was still a blur with all that the day had wrought. So much to think about. So much to wonder about. He knew he had a lot to sort out. Just as he turned into his driveway, he had an idea. He needed someplace quiet, someplace remote, someplace where he could contemplate what to do next. He backed the truck out and headed back into town, then north, out into the Panhandle. It took him a while to find the turn-off. It had been many years since he had been this way. He drove slowly up the washed out, rutted and overgrown paths until he found what he was looking for. The clearing. The place where he had brought Gemima to meet Ole Jim, the place where Gemima had jarred his emotions with her mighty slap. He parked the truck, switched off the engine and listened to the silence. He got out and walked to the spot where he and Gemi sat on the log. He found a rock and tossed it into the grass near the same tree wishing, hoping, that maybe Ole Jim was still around. So much of it had changed yet so much of it was still familiar. It was obvious no one had been there in a long time. Kids now-a-days weren't interested in finding the secrets of life in the glory of nature. They would rather stay at home with their video games, text messaging and satellite television subscription movies. The clearing still had the quiet charm he remembered. He walked around, looking, trying to recall the exact spot where her held her and kissed her for the first time. Then, a glint of something in the dirt caught his eye. He reached down and picked up an old friendship ring, a remnant of another relationship that may have been won, or lost, in this lonely place. He went back to his truck, opened the tail gate, sat down. The clearing was mostly overgrown with prairie grass. A few rusted beer cans could be seen here and there. Camp fire remnants were mostly gone, washed away by years of flooding rains. He sat there fingering the ring, listening to the wind and to his heart. The mesquite trees that were still there were had grown huge and graceful. He watched as their branches danced with the wind. The wind in their branches made a strange, lonely sound as if to recall and repeat all the words that were said by the many couples who had found and lost love, . . . or lust, . . . on a blanket under their branches. He listened intently, wishing and hoping that maybe the wind in the leaves would remember and repeat her voice. He wanted to hear her voice again. He remembered that night. He remembered his fear of love. He remembered why he tried to scare Gemima away. The fear he evoked in her worked against him. He remembered how it backfired on him. Her fearful scream and the slap that jarred him out of his world. It was her fear that shocked him. She won his heart in spite of his fear, he lost her heart because of his fear.

His fear. He had been afraid of love all of his life and it had cost him dearly. Now he knew he needed to face his fear and do whatever it takes to remove it from his life so he could live freely and, more importantly, love freely.

As he sat there, enjoying the late afternoon sun, what needed to be done next began to coalesce in his mind's eye. He needed to go. He needed find Gemima. It had become a matter of when, not if, he would try to find her.

Yeah, it was too late for them. Certainly Gemima was married and had a family. He had spoken to her daughter, Darbi, if only for a few seconds. It would be wrong to make any demands that would disrupt her family, selfish, too, at least on his part. He knew that this quest was not about re-establishing or renewing old relationships. It was about healing memories. This sentimental journey was not about reconnecting with the past. It was about disconnecting with those destructive emotions so that everyone could move forward. It was about forgiveness and finding closure. Hopefully everyone could then live in peace and harmony.

He took one more walk around the perimeter of the clearing, one last look for Ole Jim, or at least Ole Jim's grandson. All he found was old memories of a bygone era. Time to move on, he thought. He dropped the friendship ring where he found it. He closed the tailgate, got into his truck and headed home.

Bekka heard her brother open the front door. She glanced at the clock. He was over and hour late for supper and she had been worried.

"Where have you been! I've been worried. I called Father Frank and he said you had left the church hours ago and . . ."

Before she could finish her complaint, Tal walked up to her, embraced her and kissed her gently, on the cheek. He held her close and spoke, almost in a whisper. "Bekka, I don't think I have told you how much I love you and how grateful I am for all that you have done for me, especially during this time of my illness and recovery."

Bekka pushed him away and stared at him, up and down, with a look of suspicion. "Who are you and what have you done with my brother?"

They both laughed. Tal realized his actions were out of character for him. "No, no, it's really me! Well, the new me."

"C'mon and eat. I've kept your supper warm." Bekka put Tal's meal on the table. "I will leave you in peace to eat. I'm going to my room."

"No, no", Tal protested. "Sit with me. I need to talk to you about something."

Now Bekka really was wondering what was going on. She could not remember the last time her brother wanted her opinion on anything, except an occasional health question.

"What on earth happened to you today?"

Tal laughed again. "Love. Love happened to me. And forgiveness."

Tal related all that had happened in his conversation with Father Frank. He told his sister what he had come to understand about himself and what he needed to do next.

"Tomorrow I need you to call Doc Fagin and ask him if my heart is up to a road trip. Would you do that please?"

"Where? Why?"

"I need to try to find Gemima."

"Sure, Tal, I'll call. Do really think this is what you need to do?"

Tal reached across the table and held his sister's hands. He looked deep in her eyes. As he spoke, she knew one thing for sure. She had never seen this much sincerity in her brother eyes.

"Listen to me, Bekka. This comes from the heart. I have been less than honest with you because of fear. I was afraid to tell you what has had my mind so occupied for so many months. Do you remember last fall when you asked me about a Valentine card and a girl named Gemi?"

"Yeah, vaguely."

"Well, that opened a flood of memories full of love and betrayal, happiness and pain."

"I'm really sorry, Tal. I was just curious about . . ."

Tal interrupted her.

"No, no, it's okay. Really. What you did made me angry at first. Now I know it was for the good. I mean, very good because it brought me to a place that needed the healing grace of God."

Tal saw a look of confusion and doubt in his sister's eyes.

"Look, let me explain it this way. I loved Lucy with all my heart. She was the mother of my children. She was my light in a difficult life. Then I lost her. She is gone and all I have is her memory. I was able to tell her good bye. In my grief and mourning, I found closure. Lucy, though, was not my first love. My first real love was Gemima and I lost her first. All these years her memory has been a source of pain. All these years I have blamed her for the hurt, for pushing me away when it was me who pushed her away. When she tried to reach out to me, I was unable to respond because I was blinded by my own hurt . . . my own insecurities. I never understood what happened between Gemima and me because there was no closure for us. We never said good bye. I hope I can find closure. This is about finding peace and closure in forgiveness. Does this make any sense to you?"

Bekka saw something in her brother's eyes she had never seen before. She saw vulnerability, sensitivity and, most of all, a genuine need for love. She rose from her chair and walked around the table to where he was sitting. She wrapped her arms around his head and pulled it to her breast. She held him tight as she bent down and kissed the top of his head. Tal felt a warmth, a motherly love in her embrace and leaned into her as if to say thank you for the gesture. Then Bekka began to speak in a low gentle voice filled with love.

"We have been through a lot. When Mom died, I got the better of what happened. At least I had Aunt Dori to take her place. You had no one. Well, you had Sparky."

Tal sighed. "That wasn't much. He was gone most of the time and when he was here, he was in the garage. I worked with him mostly for the company."

Bekka went back to her chair and sat down. Tal ate as she spoke. "That's what I mean. I lost a lot when we lost our family. You lost so much more. We loved each other as kids. Living apart as teenagers, we lost that family relationship. As adults, we were more like strangers than siblings. When you came home from the Navy, I didn't know you. Sometimes I was even afraid of you. I wanted a big brother to help me. I thought you didn't want me around. You were this big, independent guy who could do anything and wanted no one. No matter what I did or said, you ignored me. So we stayed strangers."

He reached across the table to take her hands. "I'm so, so sorry, Sis. I didn't realize . . . , I mean, how can I make it up to you."

Bekka wiped a tear away and squeezed her brother's hands.

"In some ways you have. You let me come and live here and take care of you. You let me nurse you through the most serious event in your life, your transplant. And just now, you let me love you and you let me feel important to you."

Tal was still uncomfortable with his new vulnerability. He tried some humor to ease the moment. "Yeah, I guess I've let my guard down."

"Yeah, you have. Thank you. I like the new you. Very much."

They both arose from their chairs and embraced each other. In the silence of the moment, one thing became very clear. They needed each other as family now more than ever. And they were very glad they had each other.

"So will you call Doc Fagin for me tomorrow?"

"Sure, I'd be glad to."

Tal finished his supper and Bekka cleared the table.

"Thanks Sis. This has been a long day. Too much emotion. I think I'll hit the sack."

Tal started down the hall to his room. He paused at the kitchen doorway, turned back to his sister and gave her a wink. "One more thing. I love you, Sis."

Bekka smiled. "I don't know who you are and what you did with my brother but I love you too."

Tal closed the door behind him, sat down in his chair then switched on his reading light and television. He found nothing of interest to watch and the light was distracting so he switched them both off. The room was dark as the last remnant of day faded to black. He rose from his chair and went to his patio. The first sliver of a waxing moon was beginning to fall behind a low layer of deep purple clouds on the western horizon. A slight breeze out of the northwest brought the hint of a chilly night ahead. Joey must of heard Tal's door slide open. He came bounding over the rail, his tail wagging furiously. The dog missed Tal's hand on his head.

"Hey how ya doin' old buddy?"

Tal sat down in his lawn chair and Joey was immediately on his lap, eager for his ears to be scratched. Tal put his head back and gazed at the stars. The clear, black night seemed to make them glow with a brighter intensity, or maybe it was his new awareness of love. As he contemplated the vastness of the night sky, he was reminded of a deepening emptiness within his heart. He began remembering the faces of people. And there were so many. He remembered the people whose love he refused. He remembered people he wanted to love and how he pushed them away. Sometimes it was fear, sometimes he didn't know how to love them, sometimes it was both. As their faces came to mind, the emptiness he felt inside seemed to grow until it felt like all of the vastness of the cosmos would fit inside his heart.

Her memory came to the forefront because it was Gemima who was the catalyst for this new awareness. Everything he was feeling and thinking in terms of love seemed to begin and end with her memory, her face. This time, it was different. He welcomed her memory. Her memory brought no pain. Gemima was present to him in a new way. There was no pain or anger. Just regret. He mused at how different life would have been if he hadn't pushed her away. Pushed her away? Yes, he thought. He pushed her away. He was afraid to love her, afraid to let her love him. A wave of remorse swept over him as he relived that moment when she said she would answer if he wrote her. That was her reaching out to him. And he completely missed what she was saying. Now, that moment was forever gone because of the fear of love's hurt. Now, it was too late for remorse or regret. The years were gone. Forever. He knew the best he could hope for, if he found her, would be to tell her how sorry he was and how much he still loved her. And how much he would like to hear her heartbeat . . . one last time.

XXIII

Where is She?

Tal thought about tomorrow and what Doc Fagan would say about the road trip. Suddenly he wondered aloud, "Where would I go". It had been several months since Dusty had told him where he might find Gemima. He pushed Joey off his lap and stood up to look at the clock by his bed. "Not too late", he thought. Joey didn't want Tal to go in. He whined and curled up in the chair Tal had just vacated, having to be satisfied with his scent.

Tal went to the kitchen. He went to the phone and punched in the numbers. One ring. Two rings. Three rings. Four rings. Five.

"Hello."

A sleepy voice answered.

"Hey, Dusty, it's Tal. You in bed?"

"Well, yeah. It's almost midnight and some of us do have to work tomorrow."

"No, it's not. It's just past eleven. Still early. There was a time we were just getting started about now."

Dusty laughed. "Yeah, I remember. Not all of us don't have a new heart to keep us going."

"Okay, okay. I'm sorry I got you up. I need your help. Do you remember when you were able to find where Gemima might be?"

"Her again?" Dusty began to sound a bit irritated. "What do you need now?"

"I need you to do it again. See if you can find a contact, find out where I might find her. And bring it to me."

Dusty rubbed his sleepy eyes.

"Is tomorrow soon enough or do you want it by midnight?"

Tal didn't hear the tinge of sarcasm in his friend's voice.

"Tomorrow is fine. Please do this for me. Tell you what. Meet me for breakfast in the morning. Yeah, at the truck stop on the highway. I'll buy. It's the least I can do for getting you up in the middle of the night."

"Deal. Now unplug your phone and go to bed."

Tal smiled. "Thanks, pal, I knew I could count on you."

He went back to his room, undressed and got into bed. He laid on his back, put his hands behind his head and stared at the ceiling. Sleep came slowly as the excitement of what the days ahead may hold captured his imagination. He knew one thing for sure. No matter what the future may hold, he was going to be better.

He turned over and, as he drifted off to sleep, he had one last thought. He remembered the first time he pressed his ear to Gemima's breast to hear her heart. He wished, hoped, that maybe she would allow him one last chance to hear her heartbeat. If she would allow him that one favor, he would know that she had forgiven him for the hurt he had inflicted on her. Then he could live out the remainder of his life at peace with himself and her memory. That thought allowed sleep to come. A deep, peaceful, dreamless sleep.

XXIV

Road Trip

"Wake up, Tal. Dusty's on the phone. Says you were going to buy him breakfast this morning!"

Tal had been so sound asleep he didn't hear Bekka enter his room. He opened his eyes just as she pulled the curtains open. The brightness of broad day light hurt his eyes. "Wha . . . what time . . . ?"

"It's almost eight o'clock. Get up. I got some coffee ready to jump start your heart. What should I tell Dusty?"

Tal jumped out of bed. He hadn't slept this late in a long time. "Tell him I'm on the way. I'll be there in ten. Tell him to wait."

"Okay."

Tal dressed quickly and was in the kitchen in minutes. Bekka handed him a cup of coffee as he rushed by her towards the door. He was in his truck and out of the drive in seconds. The truck stop was only ten minutes away so he barely finished his cup before he found a parking spot, near the door. The morning crowd was beginning to thin as people headed out for the days business. Dusty waved at Tal from a back corner booth.

"Sorry I'm late. I can't believe I overslept. Must've been tired."

Dusty smiled as he gave Tal a handshake. "Yeah, you were up 'til all hours getting your friends out of bed."

"I'm sorry about that. Guess in my excitement I just lost track of time."

The waitress brought more coffee and took their orders.

"Since you're buying, I'm ordering steak and eggs."

"Hey, anything for my best friend." Tal looked at the waitress. "I'll have the same." Then he turned his attention to Dusty. "So, did you have a chance to find anything about Gemima?"

Dusty pulled a folded paper from his shirt pocket and tossed it to Tal. "Found this on the web this morning. Here ya go. Everything 'cept what she's wearing today."

Tal's eyes grew wide. "Really?"

"No, I'm kidding. This info should help you find where she's living now. I found Renner Road Construction in Cottage Grove, Illinois, a small town near Springfield. George died several years ago but the company is still family owned. I don't know who runs it. On their home page I found Darbi Renner Lincoln. Remember her?"

"Yeah, she's the daughter I was talking to the night I had the heart attack."

"There's her address and phone."

"Dusty, you are a genius. How could I ever live without you?"

"'Bout time you realized it."

The waitress interrupted their friendly repartee` with their meals. The two friends talked as they ate. Dusty had to leave as soon as they were done. Tal's tardiness had made him late for a meeting. Tal paid the tab and walked with Dusty to his truck. Just before Dusty got in, Tal offered him a handshake and a big, brotherly bear hug.

"Thanks a million, Dusty. I love you and appreciate everything you do for me. I always have. I just never told you."

Dusty pulled back and looked at Tal with suspicion.

"Who are you and what have you done with my friend?"

Tal smiled. "I've been getting that a lot lately. Gotta get home and pack. I am heading for Illinois, probably tomorrow. I'll tell you all about it when I get back."

Tal started towards home. He hadn't gotten far when he thought of Father Frank. This trip was Father's inspiration. He needed to tell him. Father answered the door.

"Hi, Tal, come on in."

"I can't. Gotta go pack. I just wanted you to know I'm leaving town tomorrow for Illinois. Dusty found an address where Gemima might be. I need you to pray for me."

Father smiled.

"I would be glad to. This is something that needs to be done. I will pray that this pilgrimage will bring you the peace and closure you are seeking. Come see me when you get back. I want to hear all about it. I was going to call you tomorrow and invite you to an info series about the church, if you're interested."

"You bet I will. Shouldn't be gone more than a few days. And yes, I am interested in learning more about the church."

Father gave his friend a blessing and a hug. Then Tal headed for home.

Bekka was in the laundry room starting the washer when she heard a loud crash followed by some loud complaints emanating from the garage end of the house. She ran to see what it was, afraid it might be Tal falling. She found Tal standing in the midst of a pile of rubble that used to be a set of storage shelves against the far wall. Her worry quickly turned to amusement.

"What on earth . . . ? Tal, you okay?"

"It's not funny, Sis!"

Tal kicked at the pile and muttered a few expletives, just for good measure.

"Yeah, I'm okay. I was trying to get my old suitcase down from the top shelf when everything gave way."

He reached down into the pile and pulled out his old bag.

"Here it is."

He brushed the dust off the bag as he kicked aside enough of the pile to step out it.

"Have you talked to Doc Fagin?"

"Yes, he did call back. I told him 'bout your road trip. He said you should be all right if you take it easy and don't forget your medicine."

"Cool! Gotta go pack."

"What about this pile of junk? You're gonna pick it up?" Bekka scowled at him. "Aren't you?"

Tal ignored her and rushed down the hall toward his room, Bekka in hot pursuit.

"Wait a minute! We need to talk about this." Bekka caught his arm in the door way to his bedroom. "Tal, please, listen to me. This won't work. Gemima is a memory. Too many years have gone by. What could you possibly hope to find. You can't relive old . . ."

Tal turned to face his worried sister. She saw his face change. The frustration was gone. He had a look of earnestness, truth and sincerity. He dropped his bag and looked deep into her eyes. He took her by the shoulders to convey his determination. "You need to understand what I'm doing here. I tried to explain it last night. This is not about renewing old relationships. I know it is too late to go back. What's gone is gone. This is about reconciling with the past. I need to tell her how much I loved her back then and how sorry I am that I wasn't able to show it. I need to ask her to forgive me for hurting her. If I could see those eyes once more, kiss her just once more. If I can tell her there is still a spark of love for her, always will be, then, I can come home and live in peace with myself and with you. I will have found closure."

Tal pulled her close and held her for a moment.

"It's important that I do this. I need to do this. Please try to understand. I need you to understand. I'll be careful. Promise."

Bekka took a step back and looked at her brother. She saw a pleading in his eyes. She smiled and caressed his cheek.

"How can I say 'no' to such an earnest plea." Then she shook her finger in his face. "You had better behave. If you come home dead, I'll never speak to you again!"

"Thanks, Sis."

"What about the mess in the garage?"

"I'll pick it up when I get back. Trust me. It ain't going nowhere."

Bekka went back to the garage door and took another look at the pile of junk occupying most of the garage floor. Her need for order urged her to start picking up after him. She took a few steps towards the pile then stopped.

"Nah," she thought to herself, "He's right. It ain't going nowhere. Besides, out of sight, out of mind."

She closed the door behind her and went back to her laundry.

Tal spent the rest of the afternoon sorting and packing. He figured this was a golden opportunity to get rid of some of the old clothes he didn't wear anymore. He ate supper with Bekka and went to bed early. Sleep did not come quickly, despite the weariness he felt. He laid in the dark, staring at a ceiling, mulling over many questions. Would Gemima remember him? Surely she would. They had meant so much to each other. Would Gemima still be angry with him? He had hurt her by leaving without looking back. What would she look like? He was heavier, grayer than he was at seventeen. Would she still have any of the old feelings for him? He just wanted to talk to her, to tell her someone still loved her. What did her voice sound like? What did her hair smell like? And those eyes . . . He so hoped they still sparkled sky blue. Slowly the weariness took over and Tal drifted off to a deep, dreamless sleep.

Consciousness came quickly. Suddenly Tal was wide awake. He glanced towards his patio window. Still dark. He looked at his clock. A quarter to four. His next thought was about the road trip, his pilgrimage to find Gemima. At a quarter to four? Too early. He got up, went to the bathroom to relieve himself and get a drink of water. He got back into bed, determined to go back to sleep until dawn. That was not to be. Finally, at four-thirty, he decided to hit the road. He got up and dressed quickly. He took his bag out to the truck then went to the kitchen for some cold, bottled water. He started back towards the front door when he remembered something he wanted to take with him. He went to his room to find a souvenir that he had saved all these years, a souvenir that had a special meaning to only him and Gemima. He looked in his box of trivia from high school. Not there. He looked in his sock drawer. Found it! He put the souvenir in his pocket and headed back towards the front door. Just as he opened the door he heard a voice behind him.

"Tal, please be careful. I need you back in one piece."

Tal turned to his sister. "I'm sorry I woke you. I tried to be quiet."

"It's okay. I would have heard you anyway because I'm worried about you. I still don't think this is good for you, and I wish . . ."

Tal stopped her in mid-sentence. "I will be back. I'll only be gone a few days. I promise."

Tal gave her a hug and kissed her on the forehead. Bekka was well aware of Tal's determination. And her intuition told her all would be okay.

"All right, go. Go on, get out of here before I let the air out of your tires. Drive safe. No, wait." She ran to her room to retrieve the cell phone she had gotten before Tal's transplant. "Take this with you. Just in case. And may God bless and keep you."

"He does . . . because this is His idea."

Tal got in and started his truck. He flashed his headlights at his sister as he pulled out of the drive. He looked in his rearview mirror. She waved, closed the door and turned out the light.

Tal pulled onto the interstate. He set the speed control for a few miles over the limit, the radio to his favorite oldies station and leaned back to enjoy the ride. It wasn't long before Tal began to see the first faint orange and crimson light spread across the horizon, heralding the coming sunrise. He felt wide awake, alive and eager for what surprises the coming days may bring. He could feel his heart beating strong and true.

"Tomorrow," he thought, "tomorrow would be the day when I finally have the chance to hear her heartbeat one more time."

Tomorrow would be a day of high adventure and he was ready for whatever would come. Or so he thought.

XXV

The Reunion

Tal glanced at his watch as he eased his pick-up onto the Cottage Grove, Illinois exit ramp. It was a quarter past seven.

"Too early to go looking for the house," he thought, "think I'll stop for some breakfast."

He took a right turn off the interstate and pulled into the first café he came too. He took a seat at the counter. The waitress greeted him as he perused the menu.

"G'mornin', Cowboy, what can I get ya'."

He looked up to see a pudgy, middle aged woman with slightly graying hair and a bright, cheery smile.

"I'll have classic country breakfast, with sausage and grits. And fry the eggs hard."

"Grits? What's grits?"

He had forgotten. He was in the north.

"How 'bout hash browns? Biscuits and gravy, too, if you got 'em?"

"You got it. Coffee?"

"You bet!"

The waitress brought Tal's order. It tasted as good as it smelled. He ate slowly, taking his time. There wasn't any rush. He didn't want to go looking for the house too early. He had all day to visit with Gemima. If he could find her. Finally, the waitress brought his check.

"Need anything else, Cowboy?"

"Yeah. You live around here?"

"Twenty some years." She said it with some degree of pride.

"Good. Maybe you can help me. Do you know where I could find Gemima Renner?"

The waitress thought for a moment. "No, I don't think I know her."

"How about Darbi Lincoln?"

"Yeah, I know her. She lives up the road from me, just a few miles from here." The waitress laughed. "'Course in this town, everything is just a few miles from here." She pointed out the window. "Turn left out the parking lot, go across the interstate and through three lights. The first stop sign you come to, take a left. That's Berger Road. She lives about a quarter mile down on the left. If she's home, there'll be an old blue Oldsmobile in the drive. Her husband drives a Chevy pick-up." She glanced at her wrist watch. "He'll be at work by now. He drives for Renner Road Construction."

Tal's pulse quickened. He knew he was in the right place. He gave her a ten dollar bill for a six dollar ticket. "Thanks, honey. Keep the change. You've been a big help."

"Well, I sure do appreciate you, Cowboy. If you get lost, come on back and I'll redirect you."

Tal waved back as he headed out the door.

Tal followed her directions carefully. They were good. He found the house and the old blue Oldsmobile. His pulse quickened even more as he walked up onto the porch. He paused as he reached for the doorbell. He could hear sounds of life coming from the inside. The noise of a child playing, cartoons on the television, a dog barking and, over it all, a vacuum. Tal rung the bell. A young woman answered.

She was a pretty woman with that harried look that mothers of young children usually have. Her house dress was spotted from the chores of housekeeping. She was wiping her hands on her apron. Her dark, almost black, hair was tied back in a ponytail with the strands that had escaped the tie hanging loosely across her face. Even without make-up, she was very pretty. The one thing Tal noticed, the one thing that struck him the most, was her eyes. She was Gemima's daughter. He was sure he was in the right place.

Tal spoke first. "Are you Darbi Renner?"

She brushed the strands of hair from her face. "That's my maiden name. Can I help you?"

"I hope so. My name is Tallet Jinx. I'm looking for a high school classmate. Her name is Gemima Renner. I was hoping you could tell me where I could find her?"

Just then they heard a crash and the painful cry of a young child. Tal saw the sudden panic on Darbi's face.

"Please, please come in and sit down."

Darbi turned and rushed to the back of the house. He entered the front room and looked around. The family photographs were spread across the mantle. In the center was a large picture of Gemima. Her face was rounder, hair a little grayer but her eyes were just as beautiful as he remembered. He sat down on the couch as Darbi returned.

Darbi came back into the room carrying her crying child, doing her best to comfort her. The source of the pain was obvious. The child had a big bump on her forehead.

"This is Joanie, Mister Jinx."

"No, please, call me Tal."

"She tried to help herself to the cookies and she fell."

Darbi settled her girl. She kissed the child and put her down. Joanie wandered off to play as Darbi sat down on the other end of the couch.

"You asked about my mother, Gemima?"

Tal saw her face grow drawn and pale. "Yeah, I sure would like to see . . ."

Darbi interrupted him. "I'm sorry, Tal, but Mom is gone. She . . . she, well, she died . . . , lastFebruary."

Darbi saw an instant, complete change in Tal's demeanor. The brightness of his smile was gone. His shoulders drooped as his eyes began to mist.

"I am so sorry I had to be so blunt but I didn't know how else to put it. It was a shock to all of us."

"How did . . . ."

Tal started to speak but had to stop and clear his throat as he fought back tears. Suddenly he realized that his hope, his dream was gone. He could never have the one thing that meant the most to him, the chance to hear her heartbeat.

"I mean, what happened?"

Darbi looked at the floor then raised her eyes to Tal's.

"Would you like a cup of coffee or something?"

"No, no, I just finished breakfast." He paused again to gather himself and calm the riot of emotions that flooded his mind. "I don't mean to intrude on the privacy of your family but, if you don't mind, I would like to know . . . well, I need to know . . . what happened?"

Darbi could tell by his reaction that her mother had meant something to him. She reached out to touch his arm.

"No, please it is not an intrusion. Joanie was sick and needed medicine. I couldn't get out and my husband was stranded at work. It was a day of heavy snow and the roads were very icy. She brought the medicine here. It happened on her way home. She was rounding the curve just up the street when a gust of wind caused her to lose control. She skidded off the road and hit a utility pole. Our neighbor heard the crash and called for help. Mom suffered massive head trauma. She was alive when the ambulance got her to the hospital. Tests showed she had no brain activity. We took her off of life support about one in the morning. It was so, so heart rending. As sudden as it was though, it was also a gift of life."

Tal looked at the floor and shook his head. He couldn't believe what he was hearing. He remembered the night he was taking her home from their snowy swim in the thermal springs. He remembered her panic when he spun out of a turn.

"What day, I mean what was the date?"

"Oh, that's easy. It was February twenty-ninth." Then she laughed, embarrassed by her comment. "I mean something so traumatic like that is not forgotten. It was just . . . well it seemed so strange that it was leap year day."

Tal was still fighting back the emotions that roiled in his chest. Darbi's serenity, as she told the story, helped him relax. Tal paused to think about what Darbi had said. It struck him as curious.

"You said her death was a gift of life. What do you mean?"

Darbi looked away from Tal. Her emotions were about to flood her eyes. She rose from the couch to fetch some tissues. She sat back down and, looking at the floor so as to avoid his eyes, began slowly.

"As I said, Mom was on life support when she passed. An organ donation coordinator asked the family if we would be willing to give the gift of life. There were people who needed something that nothing in modern medical science could give." She rose again. "Are you sure I can't get you something?"

Tal became aware of his cotton mouth. "Some ice water would be great."

Darbi rushed off to the kitchen. Tal took a tissue from the box and dried his nose and his eyes. Darbi returned with the drinks. She took her seat and paused to gather her thoughts. She wondered if she really wanted to talk about the sacrifice she and her family had made. She took a sip of her soda, looked at Tal and asked the question slowly.

"You say Mom was a classmate of yours. How well did you know her?"

He smiled slowly, weighing his options. He decided to answer the questions honestly with carefully chosen words.

"Well . . ." He paused for time to gather his thoughts. "We really were classmates. We shared a table in art class. And we were sweethearts . . . for a while."

"Sweethearts?"

"Yeah, we went steady for a while and, well . . ."

He remembered the nights behind her father's barn, the front seat of his car after the swim, the talk about marriage. He wasn't sure how much he should tell Gemima's daughter.

"She was someone special to me in my senior year of high school. She was my first real love."

Darbi could see a great deal of sincerity in the mist of Tal's eyes, sincerity that merited her trust.

"Well, as I said, we were asked by an organ donation coordinator if we would be willing to give life. We thought her age would have precluded, that is, diminished the viability of her organs. We were assured of her health. It was a very heartrending decision. In the end, we decided that this would be her legacy. She lived her life to help others. In death, she could still help others and . . ."

Darbi's voice trembled as the pain and anguish of her mother's passing returned in full force. Tallet didn't know what to say. Two strangers sat in the silence of charged emotion. The only thing held in common was the memory of a person they both loved in very different ways.

Finally the silence grew too heavy and Tal asked to be excused.

"May I use your rest room?"

"Please, do." Darbi pointed. "Down the hall. Last door on the left."

Tal went in and locked the door. He relieved himself and went to the sink. He washed his hands and face in cold water hoping that it would calm his emotions. He could feel pain in his chest. He was sure it was only from the emotion of the morning but it reminded him of his promise to Bekka. He remembered he hadn't yet taken his medicine that morning. He thought, "I've only had this heart since February. I need to take care if it." He dried his face then reached into his pocket for his pills. It took a few moments for the details of his conversation with Darbi began to coalesce. Suddenly an odd coincidence flashed across his mind, like a lightening bolt. He turned to the sink and began to talk to the man in the mirror.

"Now wait a minute. Gemima died February twenty-ninth. I received a new heart February twenty-ninth. Could it be that . . . ? Is this just a coincidence or . . . ?"

He took his pills and turned back to the mirror.

"Okay, what do I do here? Do I really believe what I am thinking? Do I really want to know?"

Tal shook his head in disbelief. He opened the door and went back to the living room where Darbi was. He looked at her then began pacing nervously. His behavior began to unnerve her.

"Mr. Jinx, I mean Tallet, are you okay?"

The question began to emerge from deep in his soul. It was a question that needed an answer yet he did not want to ask it. Tal stopped pacing, walked over and sat next to Darbi. He took her hands and looked into her eyes. He began to speak slowly, cautiously, afraid of the words he needed to say.

"Darbi, I need to ask you a very important question. I need an honest answer. Do you know what happened to your mother's . . . , I mean, do you have any idea who may have received Gemima's heart?"

The somber firmness of his question startled her.

"Well, not precisely. I did overhear the doctor say that someone in the Texas Panhandle received her heart within a few days of their impending death. That made me think we did the right thing and . . . ."

Tal could no longer hold it back. All the brute force of all the emotions in his soul came pouring out. He fell forward, buried his face in the folds of her apron and sobbed. Uncontrollably. Darbi was stunned by what she was witnessing. She had seen men cry before. Her brother cried as their mother's casket was closed for the last time. But not like this. His whole body convulsed with every sob. Darbi didn't know what to do.

"Are you okay?"

He could not answer, not even with a head shake. The raw emotion poured out of every pore of his body. Simply trying to breathe was consuming all his strength. Darbi just sat there, her hand on his shoulder, trying to comfort this stranger who was sobbing over the death of her mother. It was several minutes and several tissues before Tal could calm himself enough to speak.

Finally he sat up. He dried his eyes and cleared his throat. He took her hand, looked her in the eyes and simply said, "I am from the Texas Panhandle."

Darbi immediately understood the implication. And it was her turn. The emotion poured out of her in torrents. The sudden realization by these two strangers was that they had much more in common than a memory. They were both alive because of the actions of a woman they loved. Darbi because of her womb, Tallet because of her heart. After what seemed like hours, they both calmed as the emotional flood waned. Finally Darbi looked at Tal and laughed.

"I don't believe it! This is all too surreal! Are you sure?"

Tal pulled open his pearl snap shirt and showed her his scarred chest. Then he laughed too.

"I don't believe it either. But it's true. It happened the morning of February 29th."

Then they both leaned back on the couch and laughed, almost as uncontrollably as they cried. This incredible quirk of fate was as totally unbelievable as it was true. Darbi went from drying tears of sorrow to drying tears of joy. She stopped laughing long enough to speak.

"Tallet Jinx, would you and my mother like some lunch?"

Tal dried his eyes. "We would love it. Besides, the tears need to stop." He turned the box of tissues over. "We are out of wipers."

XXVI

Closure

Darbi went to the fridge as Tal took a seat at the table.

"You like roast beef and cheddar?"

"Yeah, that would be perfect."

Darbi made sandwiches, roast beef for her and Tal, peanut butter and jelly for Joanie. She brought lunch, drinks and condiments to the table. They talked about family as they ate. She told Tal about the passing of her grandparents, George and Martha, how and where she was born. Tal's curiosity drove the next question.

"If you don't mind, I'd like to know about your father."

Darbi took a bite of her sandwich then put it down. She took a sip of her drink and sat back in her chair. Tal saw a sadness come across her face. He was about to ask the question again when Darbi began to speak.

"I never knew my father. His name was Ben Leander. He and Mom met after the family moved here from Texas. They had been married four months when he got drafted. He didn't want to go in the Army so he joined the Navy. Mom was just a few months pregnant when he left."

Tal was stunned. He could not believe the irony of what he was hearing, but he kept it to himself.

"Ben was assigned to a river patrol boat. He was killed in the Mekong River delta during the Tet offensive."

Darbi's voice was almost matter-of-fact in tone. There was, though, some wistfulness in her voice. Tal suspected she wanted to know more than she did about her father.

"Gemima took it hard. She never remarried and decided to keep her maiden name. One night, just before I got married, we had a few too many glasses of wine. I asked her why she never remarried. She told me she had lost two loves. She couldn't bear losing another. I asked her who it was. She shook her head and would say no more about it. I asked a few more times. She wouldn't even acknowledge the question."

Tal reached across the table and touched her hand. He knew who the other love was. Towards the end of lunch, he posed a question. It was one of the questions he had come to ask Gemi, not Darbi. Now, only Darbi would know the answer.

"Did Gemima ever mention me?"

"No, not that I can remember."

Darbi saw Tal's face fall a bit with disappointment. He asked again.

"Did she ever mention Tally-Boy?"

Darbi's face lit up. "Are you Tally-Boy?"

Tal blushed a bit. He knew he needed to explain.

"Gemima and I had pet names for each other. She was My-Gem because she wore a ruby ring I had given her and, well, she was precious to me. My mother called me Tally-Boy when I was a kid. That was her special name for me. Gemi first heard the name when I took her to meet my father. I didn't like it at first because my mother had been dead only a few years at that time, but Gemi said it in such a gentle, disarming way that I had to let it be. Finally, well, let's just say I grew to like it."

Darbi smiled as Tal talked. She indeed remembered the one time she had heard the name, Tally-Boy

"There was one time. My husband, Brad, and I were dating in high school. He was a senior and I was a junior. We were in love and we had talked about marriage. After he graduated, he was planning to join the military. I didn't want him to leave so I thought that maybe if I could make him jealous, he would stay with me. Mom found out about my plan and told me it was a bad idea. She said that if I loved him, I should tell him and trust the rest to God. She told me that if I tried to make him jealous and he took it as being unfaithful, I could lose him forever."

Darbi sat back in her chair and took a drink from her can of soda. Both of them had glistening eyes.

"I asked mom how she knew all this. She told me the story of a boy she knew and loved when she was in school. She said his name was Tally-Boy."

Tal sat back and sighed deeply. He had found peace. He had received what he had come for. He knew she had forgiven him . . . a long time ago. Now he could go home in peace and put whatever regret he may have been carrying, out of his life forever.

Tal thought about the one last thing he needed to tell her. He knew now that there was no reason not to.

"Darbi, the story your mother told you is true. That is what happened to us. Had I known how to love and forgive, we would have been married. But I let Gemi go out of hurt and anger. One reason I came here, to find her today, was that I wanted to tell her how sorry I was that I had hurt her, how much I wanted her to forgive my hardness of heart. I think she knows that, now. When we were alone, I loved to press my ear against her breast and listen to her heartbeat. I came here in hopes of hearing her heartbeat one more time. It's a great gift that I have her heartbeat any time I want to hear it."

"Yes, she knows. And I know her heart has found a wonderful home."

"Darbi, this has been one incredible day. What has happened to us only happens in fairy tales. No one is going to believe this story. You have given me everything I had come for. I wanted so much to see your mother one more time. Now, I have that one piece of her that I had thrown away so long ago. I need to head home but before I go, I would like to visit her grave. Could you take me there?"

Darbi looked at the clock.

"No, I really can't. I have to meet Brad. The cemetery is easy to find, though. Go back towards town. Turn left on Paxton road. Go down about two miles or so and you will see the cemetery on the left. There are three gates. Go in the middle gate then straight back to the last row. Off to the left, you will see a old oak tree. She is buried there."

"One last thing. Can I give you a hug before I go?"

Darbi smiled. "Sure. We have so much in common now."

Tal stepped close to her and embraced her. He held her close and kissed her gently on her lips, her cheek and her neck, pausing each time to relish the moment. Suddenly he felt her body stiffen and pull away. He realized he had over stepped a boundary. He blushed and looked at the floor.

"I . . . I'm . . . so sorry if I offended you. I meant nothing by it except, well, for a moment, I was seventeen and you were Gemi and I, well, I was with her and . . .

Darbi realized how special this man was and how much he truly loved her mother. She reached out and touched his hands.

"No need to apologize. I understand. Drop me a note once in a while and let me know how you and Mom are doing. Will you do that please?"

Tal turned and walked towards the door. Darbi went to the fire place mantle for her mother's photo. Just as Tal reached the door she spoke.

"Tal, wait. I want you to have this. You need it more than I."

He looked at the photo and smiled. His first inclination was to refuse the gift, but he knew she was right. He did need it. He had her heart. Now, he also had her eyes.

"Thanks. I will treasure it. It will go in my bedroom in a special place where it will be the last thing I see each night and the first thing I see each morning."

He turned to leave. Half way down the steps he paused and turned back to her.

"I just had a thought. Darbi Lincoln, do you think that maybe we could adopt each other? I mean, you don't have a Dad and I don't have a daughter. I can love you with a father's heart . . . ." Tal stopped to think about his current condition, then with a smile and with a chuckle, he added, ". . . and a mothers' heart."

Darbi smiled at the idea. "Tallet Jinx, I would like that very much."

Tal walked back up the stairs and embraced her with all the fatherly gentleness and caring he could muster as her kissed her cheek.

"Thanks, Darbi."

"If you are going to be my Dad, you have to write me and come see me!"

"I will. Promise. And please, tell your family I love them all. Give them a huge thank you for their gift of life."

Tal got in his pick-up and drove off. He had one more stop to make.

XXVII

A Final Good Bye

Tal glanced in his rear view mirror as he rounded the curve near Darbi's house. She was still on the porch waving good bye. "She's a sweetheart," he thought, "I will come back, sooner rather than later."

He came to the corner of Paxton road. Just before he turned toward the cemetery, he saw a strip mall with a drug store, just ahead. He went to the store to buy some paper, a pen and some zip top sandwich bags. Back on the road, he found the cemetery just as Darbi described. He knelt down on Gemima's grave and touched her headstone ever so gently as if it were her cheek. The sun was dropping low in the west. The orange and crimson of dusk was beginning to appear on the horizon. He sat on her grave and leaned back against her headstone. He mused at the mystery of death. She was so close to him. Only a few feet away. Yet so far, an eternity away. He reached in the bag and pulled out the paper and pen. He began to write his last love letter.

My dearest My-Gem,

How do you say thank you for so great a gift as life, given to someone who hurt you so?

He paused to gather his thoughts and to wipe his eyes. There was so much he wanted to say but so few words could really express what was in his heart.

You were my first love but I did not know how to love you. As a result, I lost you. All these years I blamed you for ending the story of us when all along it was me. I guess that's the price you pay when you are so young, so selfish, so ignorant of what true love is. I beg of you, wherever you are, please forgive me for hurting you. Please forgive me for leaving you behind. What happened to us was my fault and I regret it.

He stopped and reread what he had written to make sure he had chosen the right words. He looked up and the sky through the ancient oak tree. He saw the first star in the east. He was going to wish upon it but he knew what he would wish for was not possible. He went back to the letter.

It's been so many years, so many miles yet I still remember you as if it were yesterday. What I wanted today was to hear your heartbeat as I did that first time we sat in dark and looked at the stars. I have something better. I have the heart you first love me with. And I can take it with me wherever I go for the rest of my life. I also wanted to look into the eyes that so captivated me once upon a time. I have to settle for second best, a photo. But that's okay. I can take it too, wherever I go.

When my life is over, it is my deepest hope that I may meet you in heaven and return to you your most precious gift of love. In the mean time, pray for me and my family as I pray for you and your family.

With deepest, eternal love,
Your,
Tally-Boy

Tal slid the letter into an envelope and sealed it with tears from his cheek. He put it inside a zip top plastic bag. He closed the bag and leaned it against her headstone. He knelt before the stone and kissed her name. He touched his thumb to the tears on his cheek and made the sign of the cross over her name. He stood, reached in his pocket for a toy, the souvenir he had gone back to retrieve just before he left home. He put it next to the bag with the letter. He stood there for a moment more, reading her headstone one more time. He wanted to be sure he had committed every word to memory. Then, it was time to leave. He returned to his truck and went looking for the interstate. It was dark when he found I-70 west. He looked up through his windshield at the stars. He felt the night air coming through his dashboard vents and found it comforting. He felt completely at peace.

"It was a great day, it will be a good night. I should be home by tomorrow night," he thought. "I need to see everybody. Bekka, the boys, Dusty, Doc Fagin and Fr. Frank, they are not going to believe a word of the story I will tell them."

The truck cab was filled with the roar of his laughter as he tried to imagine the look on their face as he told the story. As his laughter died down, a more somber, serious thought came to him.

"I need to learn more about love. I need to learn how to love like Gemima. I need to pass on the gift she gave me . . . a heart full of love. I think I need God to help me do that. I need Fr. Frank's help to show me the way. Maybe that info series he mentioned would be a good place to start. Yep, him and me, we got a lot to talk about. And I need to make another trip to Cottage Grove as soon as I can. I need to see my adopted family."

* * *

"Come on, Joanie, we don't have much time to do this. We need to meet daddy."

Darbi was making her weekly visit to the cemetery to make sure her mother's grave was clean and neat. She unbuckled her daughter and put her down. Darbi got a rake from the back of her car as Joanie ran ahead to the grave.

"Mommy, why is there a polar bear and a letter on Nana's grave?"

Darbi reached down to retrieve the items. She thought immediately of Tal and wondered why he left the bear with the letter.

"I don't know, sweetie, but they are there for a reason."

She quickly rake the leaves from the grave and straightened the flowers. She returned to the car. She buckled in Little Katy, then got in herself. Before starting the car, she opened the letter and read it.

"Mommy, why are you crying? Are you sad?"

"No, sweetie, I am very happy. Nana's heart has a good home."

"Can I keep the polar bear?"

"No, it was put there by someone special. We need to leave it there. If you want one, I can buy you one the next time we go to the store."

Darbi put the letter and the polar bear into the zip top bag and returned it to Gemima's grave. She put a rock on it, just in case. She knew that it would get windy and she didn't want to go looking for it.

"I hope Tal writes to us and comes back soon. I'm sure he can tell us what the polar bear means. And I bet it's a funny story."

* * *

Tal was on the road about an hour when he saw the sign for a rest area. The emotions of the day were very draining and the weariness was rapidly consuming him. He had hoped to drive straight through to home but, he remembered his promise to Bekka, not to take any risks. "Driving sleepy qualifies", he thought. He took the off ramp and followed the signs around to the truck parking behind the visitor's center. The parking lot was almost deserted and one of the street lights was out providing a quiet, dark corner to park. He turned off the ignition, slipped off his boots and laid across the seat, using his duffle bag as a pillow. He made himself as comfortable as he could on the seat of a pick-up. He looked out of the windshield at the sky. So many stars. They never ceased to amaze him. Just then he saw a meteor. It created a big, orange ball and a streak of sparkling dust. It reminded him of the night he took Gemi to the 'drive-in movie' on the prairie. He remembered her question. "Do you believe in God?" He laughed at himself. The answer is so much different today. He remembered something Fr. Frank had told him about faith's journey. "God chases you until you catch Him." Tal began to think out loud. "God, I have done so little for you, you have done so much for me." Lying in the deep silence of the night, with his cheek pressed against his make shift pillow, he could hear her heart beating in his chest. "Whenever I want, I can hear your heartbeat, Gemi, thanks to God. Gemi, I so wish you knew how much I loved you and how sorry I am for allowing my selfishness to keep us apart. I wished you knew."

Just then another meteor flashed across the sky. For a moment he felt the heartbeat jump . . . and, somehow . . . he was sure. Gemi did know and where ever her spirit was, she was letting him know by reminding him of that special night they shared under the stars.

"Yeah, he whispered, I believe in God. Beginning tomorrow, when I get home, I will start my new life. Got to see go Father Frank. Tomorrow is the day. Tomorr . . . ."

Sleep came quickly, a deep, comforting sleep filled with dreams. He dreamed of angels, the possibilities of all his tomorrows and the joy of Gemi's memory.

The end.